MW00777767

THE BODY AUCTION

Lisa Mathis

Vertū Publishing, 2022

A Component of Vertū Marketing, LLC

Copyright © 2022 by Vertū Publishing

All rights reserved. No part of this publication may be reproduced, distributed, or transmitted in any form or by any means, including photocopying, recording, or other electronic or mechanical methods, without the prior written permission of the publisher, except in the case of brief quotations embodied in critical reviews and certain other noncommercial uses permitted by copyright law. For permission requests, write to the publisher, addressed "Attention: Permissions Coordinator," at the email address below.

VERTŪ PUBLISHING

A Component of Vertū Marketing LLC

Ordering Information:

Quantity sales. Special discounts are available on quantity purchases by corporations, associations, and others. For details, contact the publisher. Orders by U.S. trade bookstores and wholesalers please contact: Tel: (866) 779-0795.

publishing@vertu-marketing.com

Printed in the United States of America

ISBN 979-8-9870674-0-6

Prologue

Orchids.

No…tulips?

Maybe roses?

Yes, roses…definitely roses.

The odor is overwhelming and very sickeningly sweet. Nausea wells inside me, moving through my system in strong waves. I feel my stomach muscles contract. I wait for an involuntary gag, but my body does nothing. I am overcome by a profound feeling of weakness. As I hang somewhere in the abyss between confusion and panic, I feel thousands of tiny pinpricks in my arms and legs. I try to force my body to move, to relieve the agonizing sensation, but nothing happens.

Am I paralyzed? Why can't I move? My mind raced from one terrifying thought to another. I expect to feel my heart race. I expect the familiar pounding of my pulse in my ears, but it never comes. Why? Am I dead? Is this death? My mind screams at my body, *Open your eyes!* Nothing. Not even a flutter. Full blown panic overtakes me as my confusion overpowers my senses. I want to take a deep breath, but I can't. What is happening?

Every cell in my body is on edge, pulsating with fear. I cannot move, cannot open my eyes, but I am acutely aware of every inch of my skin. Why can't I move? My arms are pinned at my side, bent at the elbows, hands folded across my chest. I will myself to wake up, beg my body to respond to my brain. It feels like a horrible nightmare. Is this a night terror? Sleep paralysis? Cold medicine gives me nightmares; did I take cold medicine? No, I'm sure I didn't take any medication.

Finally, I feel my heart begin to race. It feels like a sledgehammer in my chest. It's pounding in my ears. Thank God. But my breathing feels so odd, so slow. I am an educated woman. I know I need to think rationally and calm down. I have been a nurse long enough to know something is wrong with my body. Maybe I've been in a car accident, or I may be dead. No, that's crazy. I'm not dead.

I strain to hear any sound, and a realization sends chills down my spine, the feeling you have when fingernails go down a chalkboard. My husband, Tripp, is crying. He is very near my head. He is sobbing, talking to me, saying how much he loves me, needs me. I can hear others talking and weeping faintly in the background. Sadness and fear overcome me. Slow, sad music plays softly, almost imperceptibly from somewhere above me. This feels so familiar, and I realize this must be a dream I've had before.

But the next noise should have awakened me. I hear my daughter, Aubrey, screaming, crying as I have never heard in all her twenty-one years. She is begging and pleading for me to be awake, to be with her. She begs me to be there for her wedding, to see her first child be born, going on and on about the things I will miss. Then her voice softens, and she starts to thank me for being a great mom, for all the great times we had together, and she tells me how she cannot make it without me. Then I have a horrible realization. I am in a funeral home, in the casket. I am the pale lifeless bag of flesh that people walk around and stare at, weep over, and remember in life.

Being a preacher's daughter, I have attended hundreds of funerals and viewings, so this scene is not strange to me. I picture my family there, tear-streaked faces, tissues twisted in their hands. I imagine large flower arrangements lining the sides of the room. They are for me. I wonder who sent them? Friends, family, my work family? I try to picture what is going on outside of my metal box. Are they going through the line, shaking hands with my husband? I picture my elderly parents weeping, probably sitting in chairs, too stricken by grief to stand. I have such a great family, I realize. As I lie there, I cannot help but to feel guilt knowing that they are heartbroken and that I cannot do anything to help them. Helplessness, sadness, and anguish wash over me. Sudden awareness of the tight box I am in seems to make the situation even worse. I am already claustrophobic, but knowing in that moment that I am crammed in a tiny rectangular box is terrifying.

They think I'm dead. *Am I*? I try to move, try to scream, but nothing happens. My body feels like it is asleep, but all my nerve endings are firing at top speed. As my mind races through the possibilities of how this could have happened, it's too much, and I lose my grasp on consciousness. This repeats over and over for what seems like hours. People come and go as my awareness comes and goes.

Some voices I recognize; some I do not. I hear close friends tell me what they loved about me, how they will miss me. Some people just stand there and cry.

Tripp remains standing near my head, and I hear people tell him words of encouragement over and over. I picture him in his black suit, Carolina blue tie. He is so handsome. I miss him. I am grieving my own loss of family. Sadness weighs heavy on my chest. I don't want to lose my family.

Condolences seem to go on and on. Tripp's voice sounds so weak, so deeply broken and sad. As the voices fade and the music stops, I can hear that fewer and fewer people are coming. The funeral is coming to an end. My eyes still refuse to open. I cannot move any part of my body at all. Then a shroud of silence, and that is the end of the first night that forever changed my life as I knew it.

Chapter 1

My name is Layla Matthews. I am a nurse practitioner and have been for fifteen years. I have a wonderful husband named Tripp and a bright and beautiful daughter in college, Aubrey. We live in a small town in North Carolina, deep in the Bible Belt. Raised by a Baptist minister in a very strict, conservative home, I have a great faith in God, and by all accounts, I live a good life. I know to respect my elders. I don't cuss, don't drink, and I've lived my life by the Ten Commandments. So, as I lay there, trapped in my own body, I questioned everything I had ever heard on Sunday mornings. I questioned everything I had believed my entire life. I was not in heaven, and I didn't think this was hell, but...it may have been.

Streams of thoughts invaded my mind. I latched on to memories of my many years as an intensive care nurse. I never liked giving paralytics to patients on life support. These are intravenous medications that paralyze the body. Doctors prescribe them only for critically ill patients who need special ventilation, when the body needs to be completely still. But the issue with those patients is that you have to be sure they receive certain other medications to adequately sedate them so they are not "awake" and paralyzed. If the patient is not sedated enough, they will be able to hear and feel everything. This is torture for the patient. That night, I knew just how those patients must feel. I thought back to all those patients I had cared for over the years. In my mind's eye, I could feel the cool skin of the person in the bed completely at my mercy. They were helpless and needed me to provide care while they were in their most vulnerable state. They could not move, could not protect themselves. I was all they had at the fine line between life and death. I administered the medications that literally took away the reflexes they came into this world with. The reflex of movement, breathing, swallowing. With that cold, plastic bag of liquid, I took that away. I wondered what happened to those few people who survived.

After all the noise stopped that night and I was alone, I did panic for what seemed like hours. I questioned my faith, God, and all that I knew to be true, fact, and concrete. When I could calm myself, I realized I was not dead. I refused to believe this was it, this was the end. I decided to use my brain and analyze what I knew around me. Something had happened to make people believe I was dead. How was this even possible in this day of modern medicine? I could hear, I could smell, and as time passed, I started to have different sensations in my body. Why couldn't I move? Maybe I was close to death, paralyzed, but not completely dead? Who would pronounce me dead if I was not? I had a pulse. I was breathing, very shallowly but breathing. I had seen many people very close to death over the years, with weak pulses, slow respirations, grey color, sunken eyes. But still not dead.

So, I knew where I was: lying in a casket in a funeral home. Since I had determined this was not a dream and I was not dead, my emotions had been a like the proverbial rollercoaster. One moment I felt relief that I was not dead, but that was quickly replaced with the horror of knowing I was alive and closed in a casket. Terror, the feeling of impending doom, and panic ebbed and flowed. I felt hopeless, helpless, until I wished I could die just to escape. But I am a strong-willed woman, and I knew in my rational mind that panic was my enemy. I concentrated on the fact that there had to be some type of air hose or opening allowing oxygen into the casket. Otherwise, I would have suffocated already. I tried to breathe as deeply as I could, but it wasn't much.

I tried to think back to the last thing I could remember. I tried to focus and calm myself, relaxing my already closed eyes and concentrating on my breathing. Slowly, my mind cleared, and the fog lifted. I had worked for the hospitalist the night before.

Hospitals currently use "hospitalist groups" who handle the admitting and rounding on patients. The prior era of your primary care physician treating you in the hospital has long since gone in most places. The special group of physicians, physician assistants, and nurse practitioners admit and manage inpatient care. I did this sometimes to moonlight. It was good money and easy work. The night had been slow, only five admissions from the ER, but since I had worked the day before seeing patients in the office, I was exhausted. So, as always, I would go to the on-call room to try to sleep a little in between admissions.

I hated that room. It had a dark feeling of sadness and death. The room was in the back of the hospital, the old part. This used to be where the end-of-life patients were placed. It was closed to patients now, but countless people had died down that hallway and probably in the very room where I tried to catch a few minutes of sleep. The pale green walls had years of old, dried bodily fluids on them, permanently stained with the signs of dying and tortured souls. I would always wonder about the last breaths taken in the room, cries of pain, souls damned for hell who closed their eyes to awaken in a pit of eternal torture. For some reason, I never thought of the precious souls entering heaven. Maybe that is why I always felt uneasy in this space. I always heard strange noises and felt on edge when I went there in the middle of the night. But this was the only on-call room the hospital had available to get a little sleep.

But none of that was new, nothing out of the ordinary. I clearly remember stepping into the dreary room. The housekeeping staff, who knew doctors and nurses used the room for naps, had changed the bedding. I could smell the cleaners and Clorox hanging in the air, but the staleness of the air hung thick. I lay on top of the covers as I always did, but that is the last memory I had. I don't even recall closing my eyes.

I would have cried if I could. But there were no sounds, no tears, no nothing. The frigid air inside the box shrouded around me like a dark cloak. My arms were by my side, close, very close. The sides of the box seemed to be pressing in around me, and the panic inside me rose once again, erupting through me like a volcano. The fabric touching my skin was soft and cool, satin. I fell in and out of exhausted sleep, alternating between terror and calm.

Then, finally, I awoke to a new sensation...pain! I welcomed it. I delighted in it! I could *feel* something. My back was throbbing. The coffin was hard, like lying on a cement slab. If only I could have moved, repositioned, but I couldn't, no matter how hard I tried. I guess no one ever worries about the comfort of a coffin. I mean, they are built for the dead. Who cares if they are hard and uncomfortable?

Before I could linger too long on the discomfort of the dead, something outside the casket caught my attention. It was the turning point for me in this nightmare. I heard more voices. Not knowing how much time had passed but being aware that the typical timeline between a viewing and a funeral is about twenty-four hours, my time was running out. From their voices, I could not recognize who had come into the room. One voice was of an older man, deep but almost sounding giddy with excitement.

"This one is perfect! The price will be high and groundbreaking for the operations in this area."

Other men—how many I couldn't tell—agreed with high-pitched, childlike cheers. Their enthusiasm reminded me of grown men when their favorite team wins the game. Then a loud scraping sound, and I felt my coffin move. With this movement, I felt a pull and a stinging sensation near the upper part of my inner thigh. *What is happening?*, I thought. But I was hit with another realization: there was an IV in my body, infusing a medication. It felt as if the IV tubing had become dislodged, and the flow of the venomous fluid started to leak. Suddenly, a surge of cool air covered my flesh. I was still unable to open my eyes, but the faint hint of light bled through my thin eyelids. Once again the antiseptic smell of the funeral home, a mix of flowers and chemicals, infiltrated my nostrils. I had not realized how little air the box allowed in until that moment. One of the men touched my arm to check a radial pulse.

"Wow, she really looks dead! Unbelievable! This process is outstanding," he exclaimed.

The men poked me, touched me, and yet I was still unable to move. My mind reeled as I tried to figure out what could possibly be going on. I felt a pulling sensation at my groin once again. Whoever the men were, I deduced that they were putting medication into the line.

Despite my terror, I couldn't help but also feel slightly relieved. I was not dead, and I had an idea what was happening to me. But something had gone wrong with the process the men thought was so outstanding. I felt a cold liquid drip down my left buttock and thigh. I tried to focus on what they were saying. Two men, laughing and joking. One voice was so familiar, yet they sounded so distant.

Before they moved my coffin back to the original position and closed the lid, I strained to understand what they were saying.

"I want to be certain attendance is up and that our clients are willing to pay top price. Please make all attendees aware that the merchandise is the best quality."

Before I could learn more, they closed the lid, and I could barely make out muffled footsteps moving away. Cold wetness saturated my once-numb buttock. I could feel the liquid; it was miserable and amazing at the same time. Each moment that passed, the sensations in my body increased. A tingle here and a little pain there. My mind was searching and rationalizing what was going on. It was obvious I had been given a drug that would make me appear dead. They wanted me to have only enough muscle function for shallow respirations but not the ability to move any other muscles.

The question I replayed over and over was *why*? Who would do this and why? What kind of sick psychopath could ever even conceive of something like this?

I slept for a while—I don't know how long—when more noises awakened me. Music. The soft, sad music was playing again. But it seemed different. I could hear more voices, noises and sounds of movement around me. More light was permeating into my previously dark box. Like when you wake up in the morning and the sun is coming into the window. It is bright even before you open your eyes. That's how it seemed to me. I felt extremely wet now. The medication had leaked up to my lower back and down to my knee. It reminded me of wearing a wet bathing suit home from the beach, miserable and cold. It was quite clear that the intravenous line had come loose, unhooked, or malfunctioned. Suddenly waves of nausea assaulted me. The smell of those roses was so pungent now. It burned my nose, and it seemed like rose fumes were blowing straight into the casket.

Another form of torture, I assumed. As the nausea worsened, I gagged, and as sick as I felt, excitement surged through me as I noticed my tongue move!

I could hear the pastor talking about my life, offering words of comfort for my grieving family. He offered them the peace of the assurance that I was in heaven. I literally felt like jumping out of my skin. I wanted to cry and scream.

God, help me! I prayed, begged. *I'm not in heaven! I'm right here. Why can't you see that I'm alive? Help me! God, why don't you hear me? Why are you letting this happen to me?*

Despair, anger, and terror twisted inside me with every word that the pastor spoke. His words of comfort for my family were torture for my ears. I had listened to sermons my whole life that provided love and comfort, but at this moment, it felt like his voice and words were mocking me. For the first time, I felt myself start to hyperventilate.

A choir began to sing.

There is a place of quiet rest,

Near to the heart of God,

A place that sin cannot molest,

near to the heart of God.

I made a mental note to discuss with my family the horrible song choices they made for my funeral...when I got out of this nightmare.

Loud cries—I could hear sobbing from someone. My chest hurt and filled with emotion for the person who was so distraught. They didn't know I was right there with them. I wanted to scream, yell, comfort them, but I could not. Even though my tongue could move, I still could not open my lips.

The service was coming to an end. Knowing what came next, after the funeral, the emotion that had become too real to me reared its head again: terror! I would be buried alive soon. I lay there, and my mind raced around the possibilities that lay ahead. Would I just be awake and starve to death? Will that hurt? Will I suffocate when they put me in the ground?

I tried to concentrate on the men who had come into the room last night. The words I couldn't understand must hold some clue about what was happening. Why would anyone murder me by burying me alive? I was scared. I didn't want to be in the pitch dark. When they put me in the ground, would my little air tube be taken out so I would suffocate? I was so scared and lonely at that moment that I felt like God had truly forsaken me. I prayed and cried, and then I felt it. A tear rolled slowly down my cheek. I had a glimmer of new hope.

Thank you, God, I prayed. *Thank you for hearing me*. Focusing all my attention on my body, I tried to move a digit at a time, twitch a muscle. Something. Anything. Finally, after channeling all my energy, my big toe on my left foot moved, my right pinky, the muscle in my left thigh, and my right shoulder. Suddenly, my left leg jumped, hard. Did the casket move? It had to because that was a hard spasm, but no one came. I heard no sounds, no screams that indicated anyone noticed.

I could hear a different preacher saying a long prayer, and over his booming voice, no one heard or saw my momentous accomplishment. My time was running out, and I prayed for something to happen, anything to happen. I felt the same terror start sneaking back into the box with me. I was not going to get out. I was going to die a horrible, painful, miserable death. They were going to bury me alive.

Chapter 2

Like most people, I had always heard that your life flashes before your eyes before you die. In this moment, just knowing that I was soon going to breathe my last, it was more like a ribbon of memories that floated through my mind rather than a quick flash. Life was simple for me as a child. I was in church every time the door was open. Money was tight as my mom drove a bus and my dad worked at a local factory in addition to his preaching. My parents were not educated past high school, and they never really encouraged my brother or me to go to college. Somehow, we had a drive to be educated and both found a way to make it happen.

I had always wanted to be a nurse. I loved to take care of people, from my elderly neighbor to any sick family member. So I knew that nursing school was the only thing for me. I did struggle as I have severe dyslexia, but after fighting for every grade, I graduated as a registered nurse. After working as a nurse for ten years, I then decided to advance and be a nurse practitioner so I could have better hours and a much better salary.

I had met Tripp in high school, but we didn't date until I had moved back home from college. He was the popular one, good looking, very athletic. Everyone in the county knew him. I, however, was the ugly duckling, unpopular and non-existent in high school. He would never have given me a second look. But after college, I had my own money and was not held to the strict devices of my very conservative parents. So I purchased trendy clothes, exercised, got a modern haircut, and taught myself to apply an appropriate amount of makeup to accentuate my best features. I was no longer the ugly duckling when I met Tripp.

We were married within four months after our first date. We were excited to be independent and start our lives, so we wasted no time. I got pregnant with Aubrey the week after our honeymoon, so the gossip in the small town was that we would never last. But we proved them wrong. Of course, we had hard times, fights, and almost ended our marriage many times, but we held on to what mattered the most. Love. We had a strong, deep love that was hard to find. The three of us were as close as any family could get. We had lost a second baby four months into the pregnancy, but we handled the grief well. Tripp never seemed to want to talk about his emotions, but I knew down deep he had longed for this son.

I felt I could tell my husband anything, and as Aubrey grew older, she became my best friend. I took care of myself and was hoping to live a long happy life, play with grandkids, and travel with my husband. I had no plans to die at the age of forty.

To the world we were the perfect American family, and to each other we were also pretty perfect. But on the inside, well, that was a different story.

As the old proverb says, everyone has three faces. The first face everyone sees, like your colleagues and peers at work. This is the one that you work hard on to make people have a good opinion of you. The second face is the face that your close circle sees, like your spouse and family. Others may or may not see the true second face. This face is the one of someone who abuses a wife in private, has a temper, or is bad at managing money. Then the third face is the one we only see in the mirror. The face that has those bad thoughts, sometimes wanting to kill someone, some secret addiction to pornography no one knows about, the serial rapist who has a happy family to the outside world. The problem is, some people are far worse on the inside than people realize until it is too late.

My third face was one of restlessness. I wanted more out of life. Excitement, adventure. I longed to leave the small town where I was born and raised and have an adventure. I wanted to walk away from the fake people who went to church every Sunday but were molesting the little children at camp. I wanted to secretly kill my pervert uncle who molested me as a child. I had an evil side that I kept hidden. Evil thoughts of depravity and secrets.

But I also loved to help those in need, the really sick and dying. I loved to make them better and see them walk away. I think this is why I am in the situation I am in. I am being punished by the only one who knows the true me, who knows my three faces. Good, bad, and ugly. God is punishing me by burying me alive. I will lie in my box and repent for all of the things I have thought about doing and wished I could do. I reflect on my childhood, my family, but mainly the secret side of me. Most of all I have regret. I regret not killing my uncle when no one believed me. I regret not telling everyone at church my suspicions about the pervert deacon. I regret not living more because I was certain that very soon I was going to die!

Chapter 3

Darkness, vibrations. The casket was closed, and I was in the hearse, moving. Despite everything I tried, I could not move my body enough to be noticed. Miserable did not begin to describe how I felt. As the medication effects were wearing off, every nerve ending and muscle seemed to be revolting against me. I felt like hundreds of hornets were in the box, stinging me all at the same time. This dress was too tight; the wet satin was making me feel damp and cold. But what was awaiting me would be even worse than this. I would be buried alive and feel myself die slowly.

Those same thoughts of regret came back to my mind. The same questions of how I would die played over and over in my mind. I prayed I would just fall asleep and wake up at the gates of heaven. I pictured my grandparents waiting for me, my little son I never got to meet. I tried to calm myself as best I could, but it was no use.

The good Lord must have heard my plea because the hearse suddenly made a sharp turn on one of the windy country roads. It was then that I felt a pulling on the skin near my groin, and I knew a miracle had happened. The last piece of tape holding the IV in my body had just come loose. Fluids poured onto my already wet groin like a faucet had been turned on. That was what was good about these types of medications; they had a very short half-life, meaning they wore off quickly. By the time the hearse was parked, my whole body was exploding from the inside out. My nerve endings starting to fire and sent sensations of pain and electricity over every inch of my body. It felt horrible but exhilarating at the same time. As I felt the car come to a stop, I could hear the drivers talking about the ballgame coming on that night. I heard the back door open, and my hard crate of doom slammed against the ground. It was like they had no concept that a human body was inside. I felt the wheels on the gravel shake my body, which sent the little electrical shocks through me even faster. Soft music was already playing as my casket was lifted and placed on the frame that is meant to lower me into the dark hole in the earth. I recognized the voice of a lady from church as she started to sing "It Is Well with My Soul." Pleased at this song choice, I listened, and for a moment, I felt a semblance of peace. But *just* for a moment.

The preacher was giving more words of encouragement to my family. Promising them I was in a better place, that I was at peace. Each moment that passed, more and more sensations seemed to awaken in every cell of my body. I could feel my toenails, but at the same time, the hairs on my head and arms were standing up. Excitement about the pain and feelings in my body made me feel powerful. I knew my time was very limited as the long-winded preacher would be done soon. Adrenaline was pumping in my veins with every single beat of my heart. And with every beat my range of motion increased. I could move my wrist and right hand enough to knock against the coffin, feeble at best against the lining of the casket. I wanted to cry in frustration, knowing no one could hear it. Gathering my will and my strength, I knocked harder, continuously as my body became my own again.

The knocking did it. When Aubrey came up to the casket to lay the traditional last rose, grief overwhelmed her. She threw her body over the top and wept. As bad as I hated to do it, to traumatize her, I had to do something. I knocked as hard and as loudly as I could.

My daughter's scream was ear-piercing. The type of scream that, as the saying goes, could have raised the dead. Even in the coffin, I could hear the shriek echo off the mountains that circled the graveyard. Of course, commotion ensued after this very shocking event. Now I could hear Tripp's voice, trying to comfort his baby girl. He begged and pleaded with her, trying to move her off the top of my coffin.

"Come on, baby. I know this is hard, but you have to let Mom go."

"No, Daddy!" she yelled back with great conviction and force, and I could hear she was trying to break free from his embrace. "I heard something inside! It's Mom! She's in there! Mama is not dead!"

"Aubrey, now that's enough. you are upsetting everyone with this insanity." Tripp was stern this time and sounded weary and as if his patience were running out. "Come back and sit down. Its almost over, and then we can go home."

But I had to admire my hard-headed daughter. She was sure she had heard something, and when the casket shook, I knew she had a death grip on it. I was trying to knock again and again, but with the other hysteria going on outside, no one else heard me.

Finally, Tripp's voice rose above the others. "Everyone needs to just calm down. I am so sorry for this interruption during this already horrible time. Can we all just sit down and get control of ourselves?"

A hush fell over the rumbles of noise, and I heard Tripp whispering once again to Aubrey.

"Baby, I love you. I know your heart is breaking. I know how much you loved your mom. I loved her too, and I will miss her. My heart is breaking also. But she is gone, you didn't hear anything. This has to stop, baby, please."

Refusing to let this chance slip away, knowing that being buried alive was the only alternative, I tried again. One last knock did it.

There was a brief silence. Then all pandemonium broke loose. I could hear yelling and screaming.

"I heard something!"

"Open it up!"

"She's alive!"

"How could this happen?"

Shouts came from every corner, it seemed.

Tripp had heard me. My husband's voice boomed orders to the funeral directors.

"Open this up immediately! My wife is in there! I heard her!" His voice was stern and strong, but I heard it break, and I knew he was crying. I was so elated that I would be rescued. I tried to keep making any noise I could.

"Mr. Matthews, once a coffin is sealed it cannot be reopened. It's impossible that she is alive. I am sorry to say that occasionally the corpse expels air and gasses, and noises can be heard for up to a few days post-mortem. Your wife is not alive, sir." The man's voice was quivering with anxiety.

With no further anxiety in his voice, I heard Tripp yell at what had to be his loudest voice, "You listen to me. If that coffin is not opened in a few minutes, I will get a hammer and crowbar and do it myself! I don't care what you have to do, who you have to call, but you better make it happen!"

I knew my coffin was different. I knew there had to be openings a normal casket did not have. So I wasn't about to give up. My casket had some way of letting oxygen in and had been opened by the demons who had done this to me. This was no normal coffin mainly because the inhabitant was alive! But the funeral directors did not back down. They had no intention of opening the casket.

Living in the South you can count on people carrying guns, driving big trucks, and having big tools. I heard someone offer a crowbar and a chain saw. I heard a voice offer a pry bar and hammer, and that did it.

"NO! NO!" the funeral director was pleading over and over. "You cannot do this! This is illegal. A sealed casket cannot be reopened without a court order!" His high-pitched voice was riddled with panic. But Tripp and many others joining him ignored the pleas. After what seemed like hours but was probably only a few minutes, Tripp's persistence paid off. I heard beating and banging, the casket moved and tilted, then it happened. The lid opened! No words can ever express the relief that flooded my body and soul at that exact moment.

The light was so bright it hurt my eyes, even with them still closed. The heat on my skin was immediate and so warm. I felt like it had been years since I'd felt the warmth of the sun. I felt the presence of Tripp lean over me as he wrapped his strong arms around me and lifted me up out of the box that had held me captive. I don't remember what felt the best at that moment: the fact I was rescued or the feeling of my husband's arms around me.

"I have you, baby. I'm here. I got you!" He was weeping. I felt his chest heaving with sobs. I could smell his cologne. He was wearing my favorite, Polo. Ever since we started dating, I used to bury my face in his neck and inhale his scent. The familiarity warmed my heart and mind.

My chest hurt from the fresh air, the deep breaths I could finally take, but mainly from the relief I felt at that moment. Emotion poured out of my loving husband as he wept. I wept with him. He repeated the same sentences over and over, "I got you, baby. You're safe."

Tears trickled down my face, and I could feel myself shaking from the inside out. Tripp must have felt it, too, as he seemed to hold me tighter. I longed to see his face, see my daughter, my family, but I still couldn't open my eyes. I felt Aubrey pulling at me, touching me.

"Mama! I heard you. I knew you were in there. I love you!" That's all she could manage to get out between her sobs.

Thank you, God, I silently prayed. *Praise God for sparing me from this torturous death*. My nightmare was over at last! Or at least that's what I thought.

Chapter 4

Being at the same job and working at the same hospital for fifteen years gave me the blessing of having a large group of friends, many of whom attended my funeral. Some were in shock; some passed out. My parents stood in utter terror. Really, in this day and age, how many people do you see literally rise from the dead?

Paramedics and police arrived, and the scene quickly became crazier than you can imagine. Tripp lifted me out of the box and laid me on the ground. I was too weak to walk. The muscles in the body are meant to be moved and exercised daily, and I had been lying perfectly still for days. I have always been amazed how fast muscles atrophy when people don't use them. I could do nothing for myself. The paramedics treated me like I was a piece of glass.

"Mrs. Matthews, can you hear me? If so, nod your head."

It took effort, but I was able to nod. I was able to squeeze their hands at their request and slightly move in response to their instructions.

"Let's give her some oxygen and start an IV."

I could hear the orders from the paramedics to each other. I could still hear the scrambling, sirens, and what sounded like arguing from around me. But when I was finally in the ambulance—Tripp and Aubrey on one side and the paramedics on the other—the door closed, the noise was blocked out, and I felt safe, finally, safe.

Finally in the ER, doctors gingerly dissolved the glue that had been used to close my lips and then, after more tedious work, my eyes. The lights were unbearable since I had been in the dark for so long. But seeing my family, hearing them, and touching them was the best feeling in the world. Of course, Tripp and Aubrey were there, my parents and brother and close cousins.

It seemed that they were still in utter shock. Each repeated over and over, "How is this possible? How is she alive? Who did this to you?"

These questions were not a shock, but I became weary of hearing them over and over. The nurses tried to weave in and out of the maze of my family. I felt bad for them, but I did not have the energy to intervene. My family wanted answers, and they threw question after question at me. I had no answers, no idea how this happened, and no energy to try to figure it out.

Tripp was the first to seem somewhat irritated at me, his assault of questions had a sting to them. "How did this happen? Where were you? What do you remember? My God, you have no idea what we have been through!"

This stinging comment hurt me deeply. What *he* had been through? Seriously? I just closed my eyes and listened to the barrage of the same thing over and over. I did have sympathy for them but more for myself. After all, I was the one almost buried alive.

My rescue came when Dr. Ricardo, the physician in charge, had finally had enough of the interrogation and the crowd.

"Okay, everyone," he commanded, "we need you to clear out so we have room to work."

I heard mumbles of irritation from the onlookers.

"Please, everyone," the doctor insisted. "Step out to the waiting room, except the husband and daughter."

Reluctantly, the rest of the crowd stepped out, tearful and restless. The doctor asked a nurse to show them to the waiting room and followed them into the hallway to make sure they made it to the lobby. I was alone with Tripp and Aubrey. For the first few moments, we just held one another and cried. Emotions ran over all of us—mine relief and theirs relief but of a different kind.

Finally, Dr. Ricardo returned and asked for a few moments alone with me. Javier was a friend to me. I had worked with him for many years. A brilliant physician, caring and funny. We both had crazy personalities. We laughed and joked and both had a warped sense of humor; that was important in medicine. We could both trash talk with the best. So when we had the same schedule, we always liked to talk and hang out. He was about ten years older than me, with dark hair and in great physical condition. He knew he was attractive and loved to flirt with all the young, cute nurses. But he really was a great and brilliant physician. He had been at the funeral that day, getting a coworker to cover while he was gone. He had not left my side once he was able to reach me. The events of the funeral had been so intense he was helping attend to people who had passed out and hyperventilated.

He examined me, and this was the first time I could assess the damage for myself. I could feel how emaciated I was, and I had a large hematoma down my left thigh, starting at my groin. Holding my hand up, I could not believe how pasty it looked, white as chalk, and I was sure my face was just as pale. My muscles looked wasted and my skin was thin and frail. My extremities felt like Jell-O. The doctor noted odd bruising all over my body and asked if I knew how I had gotten them. I did not. He ordered labs, took hair samples, and sent me for multiple CT scans.

News of this magnitude spread like wildfire. Soon, news vans, reporters, and police swarmed the small, rural hospital. On the little TV in my room, I watched as reporters raised many questions, made outlandish assumptions, and were quick to place blame wherever it would stick. I lay there in the bed, weak, clueless, happy to be out of my box. No satin sheets for the rest of my life, I decided, and I did not care to ever smell the putrid aroma of a rose again. A plethora of visitors came by, limited to only immediate family and closest friends. We shed tears of joy over and over, and I could only shrug at the same questions:

"How could this happen?"

"Who did this to you, Layla?"

"Are you going to sue the funeral home?"

It felt like the same record was playing over and over. By the time visiting hours ended, I was exhausted. Tripp and Aubrey slept with me at night, in my hospital bed, lights on, cotton sheets. Aubrey posted updates on my condition on Facebook and Instagram, and most importantly, she begged, "At Mom's request, *no* roses!"

Three days passed before the real investigation began. The police and FBI had been trying to gather what information they could, but the key piece of the puzzle was me, and I just could not wrap my mind around what had happened. I would awaken and feel like this had all been a very weird dream.

A police detective named Jimmy Whiteside came to see me daily. He was Southern and charming, not pushy, but clearly, he wanted answers. Answers I could not give. Over and over, we replayed that night.

"Mrs. Matthews, can you tell me your last memory of that night?"

"Going into the on-call room to lie down."

"About what time was that?"

"I'm not sure. Maybe ten o'clock?"

He jotted in his notebook. "Do you remember taking care of any interesting patients, seeing any odd visitors?"

"No. A baby with a fever. A man with chest pains. A possible appendicitis. Normal stuff."

"Can you tell me everything about when you woke up and became aware that you were in a coffin?"

Step by step, I went over what I felt, things heard, and what events happened up until the lid opened.

"Did you see anyone here at the hospital who seemed odd to you? Suspicious?"

My head was starting to hurt. I wanted to forget this whole ordeal, but he was making me relive it. "I wasn't looking for anyone."

"Professionally, how would you think something like this could ever happen?"

That was enough for me. "I literally have no idea!" I snapped. "I cannot conceive why or how this would ever happen."

Tears started to flow, not like when I cried with my family. This was different. The sobs came from deep within my soul. The hospital bed shook, and my body convulsed with grief and fear. I tried to will my mind to remember something to help, but I could not. This made me cry harder.

According to Tripp, I had texted him that I was leaving that morning as I always did but never made it home. The drive home was only twenty-five or thirty minutes at the most.

Police found my car off an embankment. They informed my family that I had fallen asleep at the wheel and died at the scene of massive internal injuries. I was pronounced dead at the scene, and I was never taken to the ER—straight to the funeral home. But what was so strange is that I could not remember getting into my car at all. The last thing I could recall was going back to the call room to lie down. I didn't remember even texting my husband.

Day after day, I became stronger. Paralytics are not used often due to the severe muscle damage they can cause, and I could see why. Learning to walk all over again at the age of forty was rough, to say the least. My legs had lost a lot of muscle tone. They were thin and pale, and just to stand was a huge effort. I felt like a child learning how to ride a bike. This is why I hated using paralytics on my patients. After only just a few hours, muscles start to break down. Within forty-eight hours, the muscles literally start to atrophy. Twelve hours being paralyzed is devastating to muscle memory and strength.

Fellow nurses, doctors, and friends came by my hospital room often. Aubrey stayed by my side at all times. After two weeks, Tripp went back to his job working as a sales rep for a computer software company. All that was left was for me to regain my strength so I could go home.

My test results were normal, except I had been intentionally sedated and made to look dead, and the reason was still a mystery. One odd thing did become apparent. At some point during this ordeal, I had undergone a liver biopsy, a heart catheterization, and a kidney biopsy. This explained the odd bruising on my body.

Detective Whiteside kept me up to date on the investigation. Federal authorities immediately closed the funeral home, and the FBI was looking for answers. While it was clear this was not just a case of mistakes at a funeral home, investigators felt like the funeral home held those answers.

One day, all of that changed with one voice.

Due to the muscle weakness in my legs, I had to do physical therapy daily. Some great friends worked in that department and always went above and beyond to help me. They pushed me to my limits and encouraged me. Some of the highlights of my day were to get up and try to recover, walk, and get stronger. But the fatigue was overwhelming. My muscles would shake and tremor in revolt.

Sleep was hard for me; the nightmares were horrible. I felt as if I were in a dark cave. I would try to scream, but no noises came. I tried to feel around in the dark but felt only a tight box. The darkness was terrifying. No light at all permeated the tiny, confined space. I felt as if small insects or snakes were crawling on me, but I could not move my hands or arms to remove them. The dreams were so vivid and seemed to change and evolve to horrors I could not imagine. Aubrey slept with me, but I still awoke in terror.

Of course, they had the psychiatrist come see me. I was given antidepressants and anti-anxiety pills, but I refused to take them. I was never a fan of taking medications before, and now I was adamantly against it. Losing consciousness or losing control was something I never wanted to experience again. I was determined to deal with it my way, on my own.

This specific day, I was in the hall right outside my room working on climbing steps when I heard *his* voice. I froze. Urine leaked from my bladder before I had any warning to control it. The severe trembling came next. Sweat poured from my forehead and ran down my face.

"Are you okay, Layla?" Sara, the physical therapist asked. "What's wrong?"

I could not answer. I could hear her voice, but it sounded like she was in a tunnel far away. I just stood there.

Aubrey's panicked voice called, "Mom! What's the matter? Sara, what's wrong with her?"

Someone was wiping my legs with a paper towel.

"She's all right, Aubrey," Sara reassured, easing me into a wheelchair. "She must have just overworked herself. Her bladder muscles are weakened too."

But Aubrey knew—she knows me better than anyone, and she knew something else was wrong. I could see it in her eyes.

Dr. Ricardo had remained my attending physician and came by daily even when he was off. He happened to be on the fifth floor that day and came over when he heard the commotion. As he assisted Sara with getting me back to my room, I looked around at the faces. I felt like everyone was staring at me, whispering about me. New nurses who didn't know me well acted embarrassed for me. Nurses who had worked with me had expressions of concern and pity on their faces. As Sara wheeled me around the corner of the desk, I could see into the small dictation room where physicians dictated notes and consults. That was where I saw him, and I knew whose voice I had heard that night in my box of death.

Dr. Michael Pierce had been with the hospitalist program for only about six months. He was a young doctor, and I immediately found him cocky and rude. He thought he was brilliant, but he was an idiot. He was certain he was God's gift to the young, pretty nurses, and he did manage to seduce a few of them. He was the type of new physician all seasoned nurses hated working with—condescending, never taking a recommendation even if the nurse was correct. He would let a patient die before he would admit he was wrong. He had MD by his name, and in his tiny brain, that made him a *god.*

I had a few issues with him over some patient care, but I was older and experienced and not intimidated at all. The last confrontation I could recall was over a patient who had shortness of breath. He completely misdiagnosed her and treated her for pneumonia. Then he proceeded to yell at me when I explained it was not pneumonia but more likely congestive heart failure. He had to apologize when he removed fluids and she was instantly better. But on this day, clinging to the arms of the wheelchair as Dr. Ricardo and Sara took me back to my room, Dr. Pierce terrified me because I knew that voice. I knew that was the voice I had heard and recognized as I lay suffocating in the casket.

Like a flash, I remembered something: I had seen him the night I was working. "Why are you here so late?" I had asked him. "You are typically gone by now."

"Just catching up on some dictations." He did not look at me, and his answer was short and curt, but this was nothing new for him. His personality was anything but bubbly. I really didn't give it another thought.

Dr. Ricardo walked beside me, Sara pushing my chair from behind, and they both noticed the tension surge once again throughout my body. Fear ripped to my very core. That was the last thing I remembered before I passed out.

Aubrey had called Tripp, and he had immediately come from work and was at my bedside when I woke up. My handsome husband looked exhausted, and this ordeal seemed to have aged him ten years. Typically, he was well groomed, every hair in place, mustache and beard trimmed to perfection. But not now, his hair needed a trim, his face was pale and unshaven. He had a constant look of worry and stress on his furrowed brow. He was nodding, rubbing at his forehead, as Dr. Ricardo spoke.

"I'm sure this was just anxiety and exhaustion. Once she has some rest, it will pass."

"No," Aubrey insisted. "Something happened. I saw something change in her."

"I did, too, Dr. Ricardo," Sara offered. "Her body tensed like something horrible was about to happen to her.

Detective Whiteside had made his daily visit right after I had passed out, but Aubrey let him know that something just wasn't right. He was also by my bed when I woke up. When my head felt clearer, I asked everyone to step out of the room but him.

"Remember when I was explaining to you about that night in the coffin," I began, "the voices I heard?"

He nodded."I recognized one but could not figure out who until I heard it again today. It was Dr. Pierce. That was the voice that I heard. That was who was trying to kill me! I did see him that night when I was working, but I never thought it was strange until now."

After taking notes, the detective finally spoke, “I’ll get back to you ASAP. I need to look into some details of your story.” And then he rushed out of the room. I was insulted and confused. Was I insane? Did he think I was imagining things or experiencing side effects from the trauma? I closed my eyes and let the exhaustion carry me away.

Tight, suffocating, pitch darkness. Something is stabbing me, cutting my flesh in little pieces. The feeling of tiny teeth chewing my fingers and toes. I feel certain that my bones are exposed at this point. I want to scream but my chest is so confined I cannot get enough air into my lungs to force a noise, any noise, out.

I woke up in a panic. I feared that sleep would never be the same for me again.

Chapter 5

That very week, I was moved down to the first-floor skilled unit for more rehab. I didn't hear from Detective Whiteside for two days, which, under the circumstances, made me anxious, if it were possible to be more anxious than I was already. I did notice some differences, subtle as they were. I had fewer visitors, a guard was posted outside my door all the time, and I was told to keep anything I heard and saw to myself and tell no one else. I remember feeling sick every time I considered the detective's directive, "Trust no one." My *normal* life before my "death" felt like a dream, almost like I'd never even existed before waking up in a surreal, alternate universe.

The day the detective returned, I was anxious to hear what developments had taken place.

"The last time I was here," the detective explained, "I left in a hurry because I remembered something odd about the accident report." He opened his notebook and scanned the pages until he found what he was looking for. "A physician was the first on the scene. He pronounced you dead, informed the first responders, and called the coroner. When the paramedics arrived, this doctor refused to let them near you. They put this in the police report, and no one looked into it even though it was quite odd and doesn't follow proper protocol." He flipped through his notes. "I questioned the paramedic who was at the scene, and he had been very upset and did not agree with how it was handled. But he said by then, the police were there, and he felt it was okay to bypass the hospital. After all," the detective cleared his throat and read directly from his notes, "'She was already dead, so what good would it do?'"

I felt my blood run cold.

"And guess who the physician was?" the detective asked, lowering his voice. "The one and only Dr. Pierce. At the scene, he had used the name of another physician, but when we showed a picture to the paramedics and first responders, they verified who it was."

I wasn't crazy. It had been his voice that night, and he was there at my crash scene. Questions were pouring from me. I was like a four-year-old who pesters her mother with question after question.

"Why did he do this? What's going on? Are you going to arrest him? Am I safe?"

But Detective Whiteside just sat there and shook his head. He did not know what was going on, but he wanted to wait before making any moves.

"You are perfectly safe," he assured me. "No one can hurt you here. But," he repeated his warning, "you must trust no one." He cautioned me not to tell anyone of these developments, not even Dr. Ricardo.

My thoughts were flying. I asked myself, *Is he insane?* Did he think my coworkers and friends had anything to do with this? I lay there furious, hurt, and confused.

That night, while Aubrey slept in her bed pulled up beside mine, I saw my cellphone light up. I quietly peeked at it and saw a new post on Snapchat. It was from Sara, which was odd, especially in the middle of the night, so, of course, I opened it.

The thing about a "snap" is that when it disappears, it is gone for good, but what I saw in those ten seconds sent a chill to my bones. She said, "You are not safe here. Get out. Hurry!" Then, as quickly as it had come, it was gone. It seemed that each day brought a bizarre turn on this absurd, twisted road. As I lay there in shock, I looked over at my daughter. She was so innocent and sweet, keeping vigil in a hospital room, having no idea what was going on. Was she in danger too? I had the strong parental urge to grab her and run far from this place and never look back. I wanted to protect my family from whatever horror was coming to them and me. Now I added Sara to the list of people I feared for.

Sara Davis was a young physical therapist who was passionate about her job. She kept her dark, thick hair cut short in a modern cut. Her pouty lips were round and full and always painted a shade that matched whatever color her scrubs were for the day. If anyone could be fashionable in scrubs it was Sara. Hers were typically tighter than normal scrubs and hugged her perfectly shaped body. She exercised daily, and her beautiful curves proved that. She was married to Tony Davis, a respiratory therapist who also worked at the hospital. They had not been married long, and when they worked the same shift, they would sometimes steal an intimate moment in the stairwell, which seemed to keep their romantic fire burning even on the clock. No one knew about these liaisons but her close friends because, of course, Sara and her husband would be fired. But I loved her and thought it was romantic and sweet. She always made me laugh, and I never saw her sad or acting harshly with her patients, no matter how difficult they could be. She was always laughing and joking, one of those people who never had a serious moment.

The morning after that bizarre Snapchat, Aubrey ran home to shower, so I asked my nurse to have Sara help me out of bed. I was hoping to be alone with Sara and ask her what the snap message meant, what had disturbed her so much that she sent that urgent message to me.

Sara walked into my hospital room, pale and anxious. I had never seen her this way. She wouldn't say anything in front of my nurse and quickly began making preparations for me to take a shower. I was embarrassed. Did I smell? Lying in a hospital bed doesn't allow you to be the freshest, but I did try to sponge off daily. After her persistence, she told the nursing assistant that she would help me shower and do my exercises, and she watched as the confused girl slinked out of the room. Then Sara helped me out of the bed, practically carried me into the bathroom, and turned on the shower and the sink full blast before yanking my hospital gown off and almost shoving me into the shower.

Then I knew what she was doing—trying to make sure no one could hear what she had to tell me. Who was she so worried would hear? She acted so paranoid, and I could not understand why. I could feel the tension and nervous energy radiating from her.

"Layla," she said, her voice low and urgent, "I was in the stairwell with Tony when the door on the upper level opened. Tony was able to slip out quietly, but I was stuck hiding behind some boxes." I knew this was not a big deal. Sara and her husband liked the excitement of almost getting caught. It happened all the time, but this time Sara heard something.

"It was a man I did not recognize talking to Dr. Pierce," Sara explained. Her grip on my arm tightened. "The strange man was furious, and he kept asking over and over how a mistake of this magnitude had happened. I could feel the tension between them. The scorn in the man's voice. Dr. Pierce explained that 'the line must have become loose.'" She looked at me as if I should understand the meaning behind those words. "He said that 'she did not get enough of the medication to keep her sedated.' They were talking about how, when it finally became dislodged from the vein, 'she' was able to move. I knew they were talking about you, Layla. They were really arguing, and I was getting scared!"

While Sara was talking, I became dizzy. I could not imagine in my rational mind why anyone would ever do this to me. Why would a physician, someone who had sworn an oath to provide care and save lives, do this to anyone? Why would they do it to me?

She grabbed both my arms now, steadying me, and whispered intently, "The man threatened Dr. Pierce. The man was reassured when Dr. Pierce told him that he had been reviewing your chart and the medical team overseeing your care was worried that you had severe PTSD." She leaned closer, her eyes wide with fear. "Dr. Pierce said he is planning to 'take care of you' and make it look like you overdosed. They couldn't be sure what you had heard or could remember, so they have to get rid of you." She choked on the last words, and her eyes filled with tears.

The hot water from the shower was beating down on my naked, frail body, but I shivered. Sara tried to feed me all the information she could remember. Her voice quivered with fear and anxiety, which was very unlike her. I could feel that she was terrified.

"That's all I can tell you now," she said. "We've been in here too long. Let's get you dried off."

Sara turned off the water and held me steady while I dried off with a stiff, white towel. Noticing I was shivering, she quickly helped me redress and again expressed her concern for me.

"Listen," I whispered, my eyes on the closed door to my room, "don't tell anyone what you heard. I am worried about your safety too."

She agreed and left me alone and wondering what to do next. I tried to gather my thoughts and get a plan together. I had to look completely normal to the nurses, and I had no idea whom I could trust at this point. Requesting a laptop was the top of my priority list. But not a hospital-issued one, so I had Aubrey bring hers to me. I started researching Dr. Pierce, quickly discovering that the hospital clearly did not screen physicians closely enough. Pierce was virtually unknown until five years ago. I found no records of him anywhere. No awards, no publications, not even evidence that he graduated from medical school—very odd, I thought.

Then Detective Whiteside arrived. I needed to tell him what had happened, but I couldn't very well take him into the shower with me. I requested a wheelchair and asked to go outside. It had been so long since I had been out in the open air.

When the detective pushed the wheelchair out the doors, the warm breeze hit my face, and it felt so good. The sun was so bright and felt amazing on my skin. The air was so refreshing. I had no idea how good it would feel. I felt almost normal, free in some ways. The world was out there, big and beautiful. I wanted to get up and run, run home to my familiar house. My plain, modest home with its pool and flowers that I loved and cared for so much. I wanted to forget this nightmare ever happened to me. But instead, I waited until we reached the cement benches in the courtyard of the hospital. He sat on one of them, and then I explained everything to him.

Leaning over with great intensity on his face, he said, "I have already found out that this man is not who he says he is. We have discovered that he has used many aliases all over the US and Europe. Tell me more about how you heard this information."

I replayed once again the account from Sara and the revelations during their romantic interlude in the stairway.

While Whiteside and I sat and discussed the current situation, a tall man walked up and sat down. He was handsome, with dark hair and eyes, and his expression was serious and almost sad. I was horrified when the detective kept talking so openly.

Whiteside seemed to just notice this man on the bench next to him. The men exchanged barely noticeable nods, and Whiteside said, “Johnson this is Layla Matthews. Mrs. Matthews, this is Agent Steven Johnson with the FBI.”

The agent extended his hand for me to shake, and I could hear Whiteside’s voice still speaking, but I was suddenly nervous and self-conscious. He made me nervous and aware that I probably looked horrible. Since my rescue, I had not cared what I looked like. I was depressed and overwhelmed and in too much pain to worry about my appearance. But in his presence, I was embarrassed to look disheveled. I was suddenly aware that I had no makeup on, had not had a recent hair appointment, and was swimming in the oversized jumpsuit the hospital required for rehab patients.

I don’t know why I cared so much, but suddenly I could not control my thoughts. I wanted to reach out and touch his biceps, run my hand over the sculpted muscles that were pressing against the front of his shirt. His dark eyes watched me, but I had no idea what he was thinking. I had to shake my head to keep from imagining myself alone with him while he revealed his secrets.

"Mrs. Matthews, are you alright?" Detective Whiteside's voice brought me back. "Do you need to go back inside? You looked flushed."

"No, no, I am fine," I said too quickly, pressing my palms to my burning cheeks and forcing myself not to look at the FBI agent. His knee was mere inches from mine, and I felt like a little bolt of heat radiated from him to me. Then I felt a bolt of shame. I shouldn't be ogling another man after everything Tripp had been through emotionally since my near-death experience.

Snapping out of this I tried to focus on the details in front of me. Agent Johnson did not interject for a while, and the detective continued.

"We will be placing undercover agents within the healthcare team to help protect you. Just try to stay calm, and I will always be available to you. Do not refuse medications or question things. Just try to cooperate as much as possible."

I just nodded my head and tried to understand the plan.

Finally Agent Johnson spoke. "You do not need to *try* to stay calm. It is imperative that you maintain a weak, mild demeanor until we have time to place our agents and get to the root of this. You cannot act panicked or suspicious of anyone. Please remember this is an active investigation that has multiple moving parts. I need you to be the strong woman I have heard about and pull yourself together." He gave me what could only be described as a condescending pat on the arm.

Furious was not the word to describe how I felt. How dare this man I didn't even know come in here and lecture me? I suddenly felt foolish for indulging in momentary fantasies about this man. I had every right to feel sorry for myself. I'd almost been buried alive. I could still barely move my extremities. I could not sleep. And I did not need his attitude.

"I am well aware of the seriousness of this investigation," I said through tight teeth, "so please do not speak to me that way. Please do not belittle the trauma I've been through, Agent Johnson. I am trying my best to do whatever is asked of me."

The agent exhibited no compassion for the horrible ordeal I had gone through and didn't even seem to acknowledge my indignation. "Mrs. Matthews," Agent Johnson said as if I hadn't spoken, "is there anything more you can tell me about your last night at work? Any details you remember?"

Having been ask that same question over and over I had officially had enough.

I looked at Whiteside. "I think you're right, Detective. I do need to go back to my room if you don't mind."

Johnson followed us into the hospital, and as we got onto the elevator, Dr. Ricardo got in with us.

"Hey Layla, how are you feeling today?"

"Fine, thank you. I feel stronger than a few days ago."

"Who is this with you? I don't think we have met," the doctor said, looking toward the agent with suspicious eyes.

A big toothy smile covered the agent's face as he reached his hand out for a shake. "I am Steven Johnson, her favorite cousin. I just came in from Kentucky. I have been worried sick and wanted to come check on her myself."

I was shocked at his response and how there was not even a moment of hesitation. Why, I wondered, had he felt the need to lie to Dr. Ricardo? But then the words of the detective echoed in my mind: *You are to trust no one!*

The doors opened, and after a quick goodbye to Dr. Ricardo, I exited the elevator with the agent and the detective.

The events over the next few weeks seemed like they happened in a whirlwind. Tripp told me that the detective and Agent Johnson had met with him and Aubrey and updated them, divulging the details I had been told to keep secret. A computer specialist from the FBI worked on tracking the activity in my electronic medical record and could see how often Dr. Pierce accessed it.

Early one morning, my appointed psychiatrist, Dr. Narran, came to see me. He was friendly but wasn't pleased that I had previously refused the medications he wanted me to take. However, the agents had asked me to not refuse any medications or treatments. Soon, Haldol, Ativan, and Cymbalta were added to my med list. Anti-anxiety medications and antidepressants were going to help me sleep and help my PTSD.

In the medical world, we call someone who has not used certain drugs and has not built up a tolerance to them "drug-naïve." That was me. I knew a lot about medications, but I had taken very few beyond over-the-counter pain pills or cold medicine. Being drug-naïve, I never could have taken these psychotropic medications, especially not all three of them, and not been in a drugged stupor. So when the nurse brought them to me on schedule, either Aubrey or Tripp would make some small distraction to give me a chance to hide them somewhere in my bed or chair. I hated the fact that my family was involved in this, but the more information we obtained, the more disturbing the case became. The fact that physicians working in this hospital were so involved kept me and my family focused on getting to the bottom of what was happening.

The plan was to let Dr. Pierce make his move. From the previous altercation heard by Sara in the stairwell, he wanted to tie up loose ends and make sure I was out of the picture. Having no idea why I was a target and why he wanted me dead gave me the drive I needed to stay focused. In addition to my regular PT sessions with Sara, I worked extra on my own in my room. I got stronger and more determined every day. My depression and anxiety turned to anger and rage.

The first encounter with Agent Johnson had been strained at best, but as the weeks passed, I started to feel more comfortable around him. He was a serious man, who revealed to me that had served in Desert Storm Special Forces. Due to his incredible experience, he'd been invited to join the FBI. He had skills that few others had and contacts that the FBI didn't even know about. Special forces are trained in a variety of situations, but rapport-building is the one that the agent seemed to work in his favor the most. His ability to communicate with others, build trust, and gather intel seemed to be impeccable.

The only people who knew what was happening with my case were the detective, Agent Johnson, Sara, and my husband and daughter. At first, the fear overpowered me, Sara, and my family. But soon, we wanted answers and worked secretly with the FBI. We had no idea whom we could trust, so we told no one else about our plans to trap Dr. Pierce. When the nurses did their assessments, I faked weakness, lay still in the bed, and appeared depressed. I think I should have been an actress; my performance was quite exceptional.

Aubrey played it up also. She even cried one day when I refused to get out of bed for the nurse and ran from the room dramatically. I almost laughed at her emotional display. But it worked like a charm. They charted day after day how lethargic, depressed, and unwilling to participate I was. Sara also made sure she documented how weak I was, how I could not stand up without two people to assist. I felt terrible for Dr. Ricardo. He tried day after day to reason with me. He tried every technique he could to motivate me, but nothing worked. I wanted to tell him the truth, but Agent Johnson quickly reminded me that we did not know all the players in the sick, twisted game.

It seemed as if we were at a standstill. I wanted to get this over with and have answers so I could go home and get on with my life, but the detectives worked slowly and calculated carefully. They knew much more information than we did, and I was getting restless and impatient. Those four walls and bed were starting to drive me insane.

One morning, I knew by the look on Agent Johnson's face that something had changed. In addition to his usual seriousness, his expression looked strained, and he barely spoke at all until he had rolled me outside to talk. He was unusually impatient with me while I put on my act of struggling to get out of bed, and I knew he had something important to share.

His news was disturbing. Dr. Pierce was accessing my records much more frequently. Johnson and Whiteside felt we were running out of time. Since they knew the who, the goal was to find out the why. Why had they faked my death? Why did they keep me alive? And why me?

"There's something else," he said, his eyes flitting right and left to ensure no one was near. At the uncharacteristic concern in his eyes, I felt alarm rising in my chest. "Your medication regimen was adjusted early this morning."

I frowned. I had been carefully depositing my anti-depressants and sedatives in the toilet each day, and the nurses seemed satisfied that the medication was working.

"Adjusted how?" I asked.

He let out a long breath before saying, "Dr. Pierce has ordered an IV sedative for you at bedtime."

My mouth went dry. I could fake taking the pills, but what could I do about an IV medication? In a flash, I was back in the coffin and could almost feel the cold IV medication dripping down my groin. IV medication works very quickly, and, again, being drug-naïve, it would be very difficult for me to handle.

Agent Johnson saw my worry and his expression softened. “Don’t worry, Layla. I have everything under control. I just wanted you to be aware of what’s going on.”

As he rolled me back to my room, we saw Dr. Ricardo and Dr. Pierce in the hallway. Like nothing out of the ordinary, Dr. Ricardo stopped us and tried to have a conversation. I tried not to have a full-blown panic attack and was proud of myself when I was able to speak and be as normal as possible. I focused my gaze on Dr. Ricardo as I spoke and ignored the peering eyes of Dr. Peirce. What kind of sick maniac lurked behind those black orbs? In his starched, white lab coat, Littman stethoscope around his neck, Mont Blanc pen in his pocket, Pierce looked like an ordinary physician. But his accessories were no different than a Halloween costume to me because I knew he was no healer. This was a monster, and for some unknown reason, this monster had picked me as his victim.

That night, my worst fear came true. There was nothing I could do about the Valium that the nurse put into my IV line. I tried to refuse, but my protests were quickly dismissed. I slept like a rock all night and half the rest of the day. I was scared that I may not wake up, but thank God, I did. Though, that brain fog and the lethargic feeling lasted for hours.

That afternoon, Dr. Ricardo stopped in my room as he made rounds.

"How are we feeling today?" His smile was warm as always.

"I feel so groggy and out of it."

"Mm-hmm," he said, taking my wrist between his fingers to check my pulse. "That's to be expected with the Valium."

"But why was the Valium added?" I asked.

His eyes became soft and fatherly, and he released my wrist and gently patted my hand. "I am concerned about your nightmares. You know how dangerous they can be, especially in your weak condition. If you should try to get up out of the bed, you may fall and seriously hurt yourself."

I stared at him. Whiteside had been correct when he told me to trust no one. I was sure I had not told anyone about the horrible dreams that haunted me, so why would he assume that? I was indeed having nightmares but had not complained about them even to Tripp or the nurses. Had the night shift nurses witnessed me dreaming or being restless in my sleep? No, I was sure they would have mentioned it.

Puzzled, I responded, "They have gotten much better since I have been taking the Cymbalta."

He nodded and patted my hand again. "We're going to see if the Valium can take care of those nightmares," he said simply, then turned and left the room. I had considered Javier Ricardo my friend. He was so handsome and charismatic. He had a personality that made me enjoy just working with him. Honestly, had I been single, I would have been interested in him romantically, despite his age as he was about ten years my senior.

But just because he knew about my nightmares didn't mean he was involved in the plot to kill me. The nurses must have reported my lack of sleep to him, I decided, but I resolved to be even more cautious.

Chapter 6

Due to hospitals' poor treatment of nurses, exhausting patient loads, and poor benefits, many experienced nurses retire early or simply resign, and turnover is typically high. So that night, I was not surprised to have a new RN taking care of me. She was a travel nurse the hospital brought on from an agency to work for a temporary period. She was in her thirties, with dirty-blond hair that I suspected was enhanced by a chemical concoction because she had a Native American look. Her eyes had a dark color, and her skin was a beautiful, smooth olive tone. As she adjusted the tape on my IV, I saw a small tattoo on her arm that appeared to be a tribal-type marking. She had a small diamond nose ring that enhanced her beauty. Her nose was another indicator of her possible heritage as it was the aquiline nose, hook nose, which is typical of Native Americans. She had very unique features indeed. It seemed she wanted to look different but somehow still hold on to her heritage, and her blond-toned hair seemed a little rebellious.

Some may not have found her attractive as her features were quite strong, but her personality was even harsher. Nurses coming on shift typically try to be cheerful, introduce themselves, and put their patients at ease. Not this nurse. She was focused on her task at hand and made no attempts at small talk.

"Do you need anything, Mrs. Matthews?" she asked, but before I could answer, she added, "If you do, please don't hesitate to use your call bell." No smile, no warm bedside manner, nothing.

I had continued to work with Sara daily and was amazed at how much stronger I was becoming. I could walk up steps, lift weights, and was in better shape than I had ever been, all things considered. If I hadn't been such a convincing actress, I felt sure I would have been discharged home by now.

One day when Sara took me back to my room after therapy, my new nurse, Kayleigh, was waiting there.

"You must be the travel nurse," Sara said. She held out her hand. "I'm Sara. I do Layla's PT. She's really starting to make some progress."

Kayleigh's lips remained tight, and she did not return the handshake. "You can go now," she said to Sara.

Taken aback, Sara's smile grew tight. "Okay." She dropped her hand. "I will. I'm just going to help her back into her bed."

I was shocked as Kayleigh stepped between Sara and my wheelchair. "You can go now. I'll take care of Mrs. Matthews."

The women stood staring at each other for a moment. Then Sara looked down at me, her cheeks red, and said, "Okay, luv. I'll see you tomorrow." With a parting glare at the nurse, Sara left the room and closed the door behind her, leaving me alone with Kayleigh.

I was thinking maybe Kayleigh was working with Dr. Pierce, and later that evening, Aubrey and I were trying to figure out how to get a message to the agent when Kayleigh came in. I started to shake. I was sure this was it, and she was going to overdose me, and I tried not to hyperventilate. She had the syringe in her hand, and she picked up my IV tube. But instead of putting the needle into the port, she placed it right beside the port, squirting the medication onto the sheets. I heard Aubrey gasp. My mouth fell open, and when I looked up at Kayleigh, she winked, still without smiling.

She leaned close and whispered, "Kayleigh Harris, FBI." She pulled off her rubber gloves with a snap. "I trained as a nurse before joining the bureau." With a gentle hand on my shoulder, she said, "I'm here to keep you safe."

I almost cried with relief.

Night after night, Kayleigh came to my room and repeated her unique administration of my sedative. Since she worked nights and there were few nurses on this shift, she would sneak me down the stairs and let me walk outside or go to the PT room to work out. I was smaller and leaner than I had ever been, and since I had no junk food, I continued to get in better shape and keep my weight down.

We all knew my time was running out and Pierce was going to act soon. His behavior was erratic, and Whiteside told me they had caught him on camera in a heated argument while on his cellphone.

I loved getting to know Kayleigh. She was funny, smart, and very supportive. She helped me overcome my fear, never judging but offering no pity. Instead, she made me realize I was strong enough to deal with the nightmare I was in.

Then, one night, it all paid off. Since my new nurse was there five nights a week, Tripp and Aubrey went home those nights because they knew I was safe. Kayleigh would take me to the PT room, and she would often look around the hospital while I worked out. She observed how the night shift worked, who was there, who could access certain parts of the hospital. Then she would come back and get me. We did the same night after night. Often, Sara would stay late to keep me company and help me with my exercises. But one night, this all changed.

Chapter 7

The night started like any other. I had my FBI nurse, Sara was on second shift, and Tripp and Aubrey had left. I loved these nights because it was a nice break. Kayleigh came in and started fussing around my room, finally coming to the bed to adjust my pillows and check my IV lines.

"I just saw Dr. Pierce arrive for a night shift," she whispered.

This was his first night shift since the night I had "died." I hoped he was just covering, but I had a weird feeling something was wrong.

As usual, she pretended to inject my nighttime sedative. "Sit tight," she said before leaving the room.

A little later, Sara texted that she was going to grab a snack around eleven p.m., and she would be down to get me. So I curled up in the bed and pretended to be sleeping in case any of the other staff came in to check on me.

By 11:30 p.m., no Sara. Kayleigh took me down to the PT room and about drove me crazy pacing the floor while I exercised.

"I really need to get out of here and find out what Pierce is up to," she finally said. "Where is that physical therapist?"

I punched some buttons to start the treadmill on a slow walk. "Sara is a talker," I said. "She's probably gossiping somewhere and lost track of time. Go ahead and go. I'll be fine. No one knows I'm here, and Sara will be here any moment."

Reluctantly, Kayleigh agreed and left me exercising in the dim room.

I guess I lost track of time because, after working on the treadmill and using the rowing machine, I could not believe it was midnight. Where was Sara? This was not like her at all. *What should I do?* I could go up to my room alone, but the other nurses may suspect something if they caught me wandering the halls. After all, I was supposed to be heavily sedated.

Finally, Kayleigh came in. She was all FBI now, and my nurse was gone.

She hurried me into my wheelchair and made sure all the machines were off before heading toward the door.

"What's going on?" I asked, flustered by her sudden movements.

She paused for a moment, checking the hallway. I almost thought she wasn't going to answer, but apparently satisfied that no one was going to burst in, she said, "I was just informed that Sara was diagnosed with an acute appendicitis and was taken to the OR."

"No, that's impossible," I insisted. "She literally just texted me a few hours ago and was fine. If she was sick, she would have told me!"

"Apparently," Kayleigh explained, "she had been in pain when she came into work. She appeared ill and complained to one of the ER physicians. She was quickly evaluated and diagnosed as a surgical emergency and arrangements were made. The OR was available, and she was taken."

I knew hospital procedure, and I knew who worked at night and how long it took a surgeon on call to get there. Something was terribly wrong.

I dug my cellphone from the pocket of my robe and quickly reached out to Sara's husband, Tony.

"What is going on?" I asked as soon as he picked up. "I just heard Sara was sick."

Tony's voiced was strained and full of anxiety. "I have no idea, Layla. She was fine when she left home. Some physician I have never even heard of called me and said Sara was very sick and needed emergency surgery. I ask to speak to her, and he told me that she couldn't talk. She must not have had access to her phone because I tried to text and call her over and over. I am freaking out, Layla! What is going on? You know this is not normal procedure."

My mind was racing along with my heart. The dizziness came, and nausea and sweats came soon after. Kayleigh was in the corner on the phone with Agent Johnson. She had requested that he have the FBI pull up the electronic files and see what was going on internally. But this would take a little time. None of this was making any sense to me.

Having worked at the hospital for so long, I knew the back stairwells, supply rooms, and secret places most people didn't know existed because they were no longer used after the most recent renovations. The new physical therapy department was right under the operating room suites. I had to know who was doing surgery and make sure Pierce had no part in this emergent situation. It was hard to wrap my brain around what was transpiring.

Kayleigh finished her call and came over to me. “So I have been thinking,” I began before she could speak. “I know you will not like this idea but just hear me out. The new OR is connected to a lot of the old, unused areas of the hospital. I know the areas that are closed off. I think we should try to get into one of the OR holding rooms and see what’s going on. We can make sure this appendix issue is legit. I have to know that she is okay and who the surgeons are.”

“Absolutely not!” she said, folding her arms across her chest. “You are not allowed to even think of something like this. She probably just has a bad appendix, and because she works here, they gave her professional courtesy by rushing her surgery. She will be fine. We cannot risk blowing our cover! I am getting you back to your room now.”

“I am fine, and you know that. Remember my weakness and frailty is a façade. You of all people know how far I have come. We would only be walking to take a look, not running a marathon! Sara is my friend, not just my coworker, not just my therapist. I cannot explain it, but I will not be able to rest or sleep until I know she is okay. I have a very odd feeling something is terribly off about this. And you know I am right!”

With eyes glaring at me as sharp as daggers, Kayleigh reluctantly agreed to take a “quick look.”

We moved quietly and slowly along the dark, dusty corridor. An old hallway that I remembered had been sealed off years ago with several slabs of sheetrock. It took some time, but we made a small enough hole to crawl into. After a few minutes, we had reached one of the outside walls into the operating room. The only way we could see into the OR was through a small vent in the corner. But luckily, due to the stainless steel and flooring, the voices from inside the OR carried well. Kayleigh's frustration with me was palpable. The quick look and small walk had turned into slightly more. But we proceeded.

I did not recognize the man dressed as the surgeon. My heart began to pound. I thought I knew all the surgeons. In a large hospital, maybe not, but in a small rural area like this one, everyone knew the surgeons. But this man was a stranger. I recognized the anesthesiologist and the scrub nurse, and then as beads of sweat broke out on my forehead, I saw Dr. Pierce. The moment I recognized him, I started to shake.

Kayleigh must have felt my trembling because she gave me a sharp look, and I took deep breaths to calm myself. I apologized to her with my eyes. But there are no circumstances in which a hospitalist would *ever* be in the OR, and Kayleigh and I both knew this. A hospitalist is not a surgeon and does not perform procedures in the OR.

But who we saw was not the most terrifying; it was what we heard. The men were talking about me.

"We should not even be here!" the strange surgeon said, his tone sharp and venomous. "You," he said, directing his anger at Dr. Pierce, "have put all of us and this operation at risk. Taking a new specimen and cleaning up the mess you made is costing us time and money."

For the first time, Dr. Pierce looked scared. Sweat beaded on his forehead.

"I have apologized over and over," he insisted. "This one will bring a better price than Matthews anyway. Please trust me when I say we can fix this. We are fixing this!"

Sara was not having surgery. They were doing a heart catheterization, then a liver biopsy. I saw a central line in her left groin, and then I knew they were doing to Sara what they had done to me. The staging was different, but I could only guess that the plan was the same. What in God's name were these men up to?

They worked together in a very synchronized dance. Each member had a job to do and was focused on the task at hand. They discussed future arrangements. It was like Sara was not a human on the table but a piece of produce. The surgeon who had belittled Pierce did most of the talking.

"The dates for the next month are the same," he said as he worked. "We cannot change anything now due to the clients arriving. After tonight, our numbers are back up to the promised amounts. We have twenty-five possible candidates and thirty high-end brokers coming in." His hands paused, and he looked around at the other men in the room. "We must always keep our word, gentlemen. We can't make any further mistakes. Are we all in agreement?"

Mumbles of yes and nods rippled among the men. Pierce held his eyes low and appeared to be pouting, like a toddler or a puppy that has been scolded.

I had not looked over at Kayleigh in a while, but when I did, I could tell she was taking mental notes of all of this, and with her training in the FBI, she was already contemplating a plan. She put one finger to her lips and pulled me back down the hallway. We didn't speak until our secret door was closed and we had made our way back to my room. I was mentally and physically exhausted.

"What are we going to do?" I pleaded, feeling the panic welling up into my chest.

"Well, you're not going to do anything," Kayleigh responded in a stern whisper.

"Shouldn't the FBI, CIA, police, whoever else burst in there and stop this immediately? This place should be shut down now!"

She shushed me with a quick shake of my shoulders, "Keep your voice down! Go to bed and please try to get some sleep. It is my job to handle this, and I promise I will."

"But *Sara*!" I practically shouted. "Someone has to help her now, right now!"

"I swear," she hissed through her teeth, "if you don't lower your voice and be quiet, I will sedate you myself, but for real this time. I said to trust me."

I finally gave in to her demands and went to bed. Exhaustion must have taken over because I did not awaken until the next morning. My dreams were filled with Sara and how much I loved her and how much our friendship meant to me. When I woke up, tears were pouring from my eyes. I just wanted to see my friend and make sure she was okay.

Chapter 8

I could hear crying, and lots of it, from the hallway. The door to my room opened, and Aubrey came in, looking confused.

"What's going on?" she asked.

I did not have time to tell her about the events of the night before my day-shift nurse came in. Her eyes were swollen, mascara in dark lines smudged down her face, and tears continued to flow as she crossed the room to my bed and began to take my vitals.

"What's the matter?" I asked, feeling fear and dread at her answer.

"One of our own," the nurse said with a sniff. "A sweet physical therapist passed away last night. She was a favorite of all the nurses. We heard from our charge nurse that she had a ruptured appendix and did not survive the surgery."

"Sara?" Aubrey asked, starting to cry. They had also become close, having gotten to know each other during my recovery. As soon as the nurse left my room, I quickly gave Aubrey a rundown of the previous night's events. I tried to assure her that I was certain Kayleigh had this under control and Sara was fine. But somewhere, deep in the pit of my stomach, I knew this was not the case.

As the truth sank in, I just sat there in shock. What the hell had happened? Where was Kayleigh? She promised everything would be okay. What happened to the FBI? Then the tremors started again. Since being paralyzed and locked in a dark casket, my body had revolted against me and responded to stress in a new way. Uncontrollable tremors, elevated blood pressure, and rapid heart rate was how it started. These turned into panic attacks, and I had no control over them, and that is what really pissed me off. My nurse returned right in the nick of time to witness this ugly event.

"Oh no!" my nurse said, her eyes wide. "I'm so sorry, Layla. I shouldn't have brought my emotions into your room."

"No, it's okay," I tried to say, but I was having trouble catching my breath. Aubrey ran to my side and rubbed my back.

"Let me get you something to help you relax, only a mild sedative," the nurse suggested.

"No, no, I don't want anything," I insisted. "I don't want to sleep the day away. If I need it, I will call for you, I promise." She finally relented and left.

Hysterical is probably the best word to describe me for the rest of that day. No one could calm me down, but I did have enough mindset not to blow our cover by saying too much or losing control, which would force them to sedate me. I finally got Aubrey to go to the car and call Agent Johnson and get him to the hospital. When he finally sauntered in, I was livid.

"What in the hell is going on?" I demanded. "Where is Sara? Why has this hospital not been closed down? Why isn't there a SWAT team here arresting these criminals?" I shot questions at him like a gun. My voice was loud and irrational.

He stood there staring at me, and when I had finally exhausted myself, he spoke. Calm, cool, and carefully, he said, "We have eyes on Sara. She is not dead, and she has not been removed from the hospital. We want to see what the next move is. Obviously, as you are aware, Layla, there are many other lives at stake here. We want to see who did this to you and Sara. This may be our best chance. They have no idea we have surveillance on them. At this point, we have a huge advantage."

For the first time, I saw a semblance of compassion in his expression.

"Look, Layla, I know this is a lot to handle. You have been through so much, and I know it is hard to sit here and feel as if we are doing nothing to help. But we are doing everything we can. We have eyes everywhere. Please try to calm down and believe me."

All I could think of was my friend and how she probably felt—how I had felt. But then the agent made a valid point.

"You have repeated to me over and over what happened to you. The horror you experienced was when you were paralyzed, correct? Well, the only reason you were aware of what was happening to you was the malfunction of your IV line. I feel as if this will be a mistake they will never let happen again. So at least Sara should be sedated. She is not having to endure the torture you did."

In some weird way, this did give me some comfort. At least she wasn't in pain or aware of what was happening. At least she wasn't feeling the same terror I had felt. I repeated the agent's words in my mind, trying to reassure myself.

When Kayleigh came in for her shift that evening, relief swept over me. Aubrey wanted to stay, but I finally got her to go home. After the commotion of shift change was over, we finally got to catch up.

"They were discussing a huge operation," Kayleigh said. "Something is scheduled in two nights. Multiple people are coming in for whatever business venture is going down. They referred to some people by name, all seemed to be women, but I cannot be sure." She looked over her shoulder at the closed door to my room and picked up my chart to pretend to read it. "The main surgeon," she continued, her eyes on the chart, "the one you didn't recognize, seemed to be in charge and was furious that you were discovered. This is why they took Sara, to take your place. The question is," she closed the chart and took my wrist in her hand as if checking my pulse, "what for? We have constant surveillance on Sara." Her hand lingered on my wrist for a moment after she was finished counting my heart rate. It was a comforting gesture. "I know this is very difficult for you."

Tears filled my eyes. "Yes, it is," I said. "This is my fault. Sara may die because I am alive. I will never forgive myself if anything happens to her." Warm tears slowly trickled down my cheeks. I felt like my heart was breaking.

"I know, Layla, but this isn't your fault," Kayleigh said. "We have an agent watching Sara, and I am on the next shift to watch her. She is in the morgue, alive and being guarded. But remember, they have no idea we are watching them. We continue to have the upper hand. When anyone tries to move her body, we will be able to follow and see what's going on. We have agents all around the parameter on standby for immediate action when needed."

Still, I felt uneasy and scared. Even when she reassured me, I had a nagging feeling that this would not end well. Once again, my sixth sense was firing at 180 percent. I just knew something horrible was about to happen.

Chapter 9

Kayleigh was a travel nurse, so she did have other patients and assignments within the hospital. We had been lucky up until this point with her assignments. Even though she was with the FBI, to maintain her cover, she was always at risk of being floated to another floor if they were short staffed. She had always been on the rehab floor and had me as one of her patients. None of the other nurses wanted to take care of me; they felt awkward since I had been their supervisor, so they gladly handed me over to Kayleigh.

But this night was different: there had been a huge influenza outbreak over the past few weeks, and the hospital was packed, with the ER census being exceptionally high. The nursing supervisor had pulled Kayleigh to the ER to help. This was horrible—who would keep an eye on Sara? This was the first sign of concern I had seen on her face, when she rushed into my room to update me of the staffing changes.

"I have no idea how to stop this from happening," she explained. "I have tried to call headquarters and get this rectified, but it has to go through hospital administration for obvious reasons, and the supervisor is the older lady named Janet."

I knew who she meant. Janet was the nighttime supervisor, an older lady who had been a RN for at least thirty years. She had become bitter and had little patience with anyone, staff and patients alike. She was overweight and had horrible knee pain, and this made her quite difficult to deal with at times. Janet was not the kind to give anyone a special favor.

"I made an excuse to get back up here to warn you," Kayleigh said, "but Janet's timing me. She took my phone out of my hand when I was trying to call Johnson. I swear," she shook her head in disbelief, "when this case is over, I am gonna arrest her for something!"

I laughed in spite of the situation.

"I'll try to get in touch with the agent and update him," Kayleigh assured, checking her watch, "and tell him to get me out of that ER!"

She turned and was gone in the same rush with which she had arrived, leaving me speechless and having no idea what to do next. Kayleigh had no choice as she could not refuse her assignment or she could be sent home, and that could not happen.

Okay, stay calm, I repeated to myself over and over. I had to do something. As I sat, mind spinning, my door opened and my new night shift nurse sauntered in, looking quite disheveled. Her uniform was wrinkled, hair looked as if it had not been washed in a few days. Some type of crumbs were sprinkled across her large breasts, and as she swiped them away, the loose skin of her arm waved at me.

Her name was Wanda. I was ecstatic to see her. I knew this type of nurse. She would be in my room the bare minimum, try to put all of her other tasks on another nurse, and doze like a sloth at the desk. Exactly what I needed tonight. I acted lethargic and pretended to be falling asleep, and it worked well because she made a fast exit. I gave her enough time to be at the desk lost in a good bag of cookies or eyes closed in slumber, and I made my way quietly from my room.

The morgue was on the other side of the hospital, so I tried to look as normal as I could. I had my rehab jogging suit and sneakers on, and I walked calmly, trying to appear as if I were out on a stroll. I could feel nurses and staff glancing at me, but luckily not many were out making rounds, so no one stopped me or inquired what I was doing. My façade of weakness and need for physical therapy would be gone after tonight. But right now, my only priority was Sara and making sure she was okay.

I am no FBI agent, but I have watched enough movies to know that I could not just burst into the room and have a look. I decided once again to use the old back halls to my advantage. I went out an emergency exit door and into a restricted area. This, once again, led me to an unused hallway and a forgotten entrance into the morgue. No one would see me come or go, and I felt sure that I could watch what was happening without being noticed. I wondered how Kayleigh had planned on doing this, and I was proud of myself for concocting such a smart plan.

Good Lord, I hate spiders. You would have thought a hospital would not have so many, but I guess an old, closed-off area did. I had to bite my tongue to not scream a few dozen times as I encountered webs and crawling spiders of all sizes.

After what seemed like hours, I finally found the way to a small panel. If memory served me correctly, it should have taken me directly to the morgue. When I pulled the panel back, I saw that the area was small and that I would have to crawl for about fifty feet to get to the part of the morgue where Sara was. But what if my memory was wrong? It was dark in there, closed in, and I hadn't been in total darkness since "the night." What if I had a panic attack in there? The only light I had was my cellphone, and I hadn't charged it, so I knew it would not last long. My heart started to race, and I didn't know what to do.

I have always hated scenes in horror movies when the woman screams, runs, and trips. The monster gets her and kills her. She could have a gun or knife, and the killer would get it out of her weak, little, female hand. I always thought I would be able to run faster or just turn and kick the monster's butt. But let me assure you, when someone is facing real monsters, it is very different.

What happened next I guess I owe to Agent Johnson, who told me once that I was a strong woman and commanded me to act like it, because I did get control of myself, and I got down on my hands and knees and crawled into that tight, dark space. Looking back, I still can't believe I did it. The space was longer than I had thought, but as I moved along, I started to hear voices and knew I was in the right area.

Deciding to go forward was the best decision of my life because I eventually reached the end of the crawl space and could see into the morgue. My view of the room was limited. I was lying flat in a large air vent across from the stretcher where Sara lay. It was like looking through a small window. Looking through the grate of the vent was difficult, but I was able to turn my head to the side and had a better view. Sara had the IV line in her groin. She was naked, bruised, and deadly still. I could see the rise and fall of her chest, but her breathing was very shallow. She was pale and appeared mildly cyanotic. To the untrained eye, she looked dead. I could feel the panic start to stir within me, but I quickly composed myself. My friend needed me. I had to save her no matter what.

I tried to take in everything I could see from my vantage point. These were the same four men from the OR. I recognized their voices despite it being hard to make out their faces from my vantage point. Pierce was there as well as the man who had been doing the procedures.

"All of the testing came out perfect," the surgeon reported, reading from a patient chart. "The heart, lungs, and kidneys are in great condition, which is not shocking as she is the perfect specimen." As the surgeon went over the results, he lifted Sara's arm, checked her IV site, and seemed to examine her.

Another man walked over and gingerly poked Sara's left breast. "They may not be interested in her internal organs, however."

A low laugh and snort erupted from another one of the men. They took turns looking her over, commenting on her excellent body. I knew Sara exercised daily and was in amazing physical condition. I could not help but think these men got a much better deal with her than if they had kept me because I was forty, not in great shape, and my breasts were far from perky.

The examination continued, the men looking into her mouth, squinting at her teeth, palpating her abdomen. Then they moved down to her vagina and inspected it. I was shaking and didn't even realize it. My beautiful friend was being violated and probed by these psychotic men, but why? I could only pray that her IV was infusing correctly and she could not feel or hear anything. Tears filled my eyes, and anger boiled up within my core. If I had had a gun in that ugly blue jogging suit, I swore those psychopaths would have been dead.

Time seemed to go slowly. My back was killing me, my right leg had fallen asleep long ago, but shifting was out of the question. I was afraid they might hear me. But when the surgeon received a phone call, the momentum in the room seemed to change. They quickly covered Sara up with a sheet and moved her with a sliding board to a different stretcher, double- and triple-checking to make sure that none of her lines had been removed or loosened.

She would not be going to the funeral home; she had donated her body to science, so her husband had already said his goodbye, and the memorial service would be without her body. When I had spoken to Tony after the news of Sara's death, he had informed me of her wishes. She always joked that she refused to have people come around and stare at her dead body and say, "Oh, she looks so good!" I was impressed that Sara's husband had respected her wishes.

The cart to move her was large and bulky, not like a normal stretcher. The larger stretchers like this were used when a complex patient had to be transported with special equipment. The large shelf underneath could hold an EKG monitor, a defibrillator, and any other emergency equipment needed. I assumed they used this type of cart to hide the IV pump and meds they were using to keep her sedated. My mind raced—what was I going to do? I looked at my phone. Of course, no signal in here, and I had 16 percent battery left. I needed to get in touch with Kayleigh or someone immediately. But time was running out; it seemed like they were getting ready to move Sara any minute.

"Let's go grab a cup of coffee for the road." I could hear the excitement in Dr Pierce's voice. "Everything is fine in here, and we are all set for transport. Let's also make sure we have enough medications for the trip." He looked at his watch. "Meet back here in five minutes."

I had about a three-minute break when there was no one in the room, so I reacted without really thinking. As soon as the door clicked shut, I pushed the vent cover open at the bottom and was able to squeeze out, the hinged cover closing behind me. I dragged myself across the floor and climbed under the bottom of Sara's cart. Luckily, I fit, and if they didn't pick up the large plastic drape that was standard for covering up a corpse, the men would not see me. It was fortunate that I was still very thin and was able to squeeze onto the shelf.

My plan worked like a charm. I lay under the cart undetected when they came back in. It seemed like only a few moments when I heard the door open and the click of their shoes on the tile floor. They rolled Sara and me out to some type of van and rolled the cart in. The IV pump was right beside my head. I could see what they were infusing.

One bag was Pancuronium. This is a neuromuscular blocker, a paralytic agent. But there was also another bag, Versed. This is also a drug used with anesthesia, and it causes amnesia. Relief washed over me. At least Sara would not remember anything that was happening to her.

The ride seemed to take forever, so I knew I had a very small window to tell someone what was happening. I texted Kayleigh.

Sorry! Don't B mad, had to act fast. Found S. They are moving her. Hid under transport bed. Safe 4 now. Find me. Plz hurry!

Anger probably does not begin to describe what I imagined Kayleigh's reaction would be. She would be furious at me for doing this without her and putting myself in danger. But I clearly had no other choice.

The ride seemed smooth, like we were on an interstate. I could hear traffic passing, and the driver kept switching the stations on the radio. My mind raced. *What in the world is going on? How is this happening right under the noses of the authorities and the hospital?*

Quickly, I sent one more message to my family. Since I had so much to say, I sent a voice message. I knew this would kill my battery, but I had to try. Hoping the noise of the traffic, the radio, and the infusion pump would drown my whispers, I spoke as fast as I could.

"Tripp and Aubrey, I am sorry. I know you have both been through hell the last few weeks. I hope you understand why I had to try to help Sara. I could not bear to think about this happening to another person.

There is no way of knowing if I will survive whatever is facing Sara and me, but I wanted to tell you both how much I love you.

"Tripp, you are an amazing husband. I love you so much. You have been a great husband, father, and my best friend. I was so worried that when Aubrey left for college, we would grow apart. But we have only gotten closer, and for that, I am so grateful. You are truly my soulmate and the love of my life."

I was sobbing by then, but I kept going, keeping my voice as low as I could.

"Aubrey, baby, I am sorry for all of this. You are the best daughter a mother could ever ask for. I am so proud of you. The young woman you have become will make some man a wonderful wife and mother. Please stay strong. Don't let fear overcome what you know is right. That's what I am doing now. I hope and pray to see you both soon, but if I don't, please remember that we will meet again in heaven! I love you both."

I wiped my tears away and hit send. After a few minutes, I checked my phone. The battery was dead.

Chapter 10

Finally, something went right for me. We arrived at what appeared to be some type of warehouse, but I only had a very limited view. The bumpy ride from the van to the entrance on the bottom of the hard metal frame of the cart assaulted my already sore joints and bones. Sara and I were rolled into what appeared to be a holding room. I was absolutely exhausted and could barely hold my eyes open, but I had to dig deep within myself to find the strength to persevere. No one spoke as we were transported into the cold building, and the atmosphere seemed serious.

The man whom I knew only as the surgeon quickly checked over Sara, inspecting her IV and covering her back up.

"Let's go check on the arrangements and be certain everything is in place to proceed," he said. "We need no further incidents."

A few voices muttered in agreement, and they left the small room. I needed to get out from my hiding place while I had an opportunity. So carefully and very quietly, I crept out from under the stretcher. A quick look at my surroundings revealed I was in a drab little room. There was a small couch and what seemed to be a small closet in the corner of the room. I peered under the couch and considered it as a hiding place but decided on the closet. It had the normal cleaning paraphernalia, but I would be able to stand up and hopefully go unnoticed. I stepped inside and pulled the door together, leaving it open just enough for me to peer out.

Once my eyes adjusted to the bright ceiling lights, I could see we were in what looked like a sitting room. This did not have the appearance of a hospital or medical setting. The smell had the undertone of cleaning supplies but with an odd floral hint. I could see the small couch that was brightly colored and walls overfilled with artwork. I could not fathom what type of building we were in. It resembled what you would see in an art gallery, possibly, or a waiting room at a business where the consumer would sit and await the viewing of whatever they were planning on purchasing. I could hear noise from the adjoining room, voices and soft music playing. It was classical music, laughter, and cheerful sounds. My ears strained to understand the conversation, but it was too faint to make out words.

The door to the waiting room opened, and two women came in with small bags. They walked with their heads hanging low, eyes toward the ground. One was heavy-set with a gray bun pulled tightly back. She wore what resembled a hotel housekeeping uniform. Her hands were brown and careworn, like tanned, worn leather. They were obviously hands of someone who had worked hard at manual labor. Her face was full of deep lines and years of hard living. Her double chin moved independent of her head and reminded me of a turkey. The second lady did not appear quite as old but was not well kept. Her hair showed the remnants of a black chemical concoction that had been applied in the past, probably in her own bathroom; however, the gray roots were starting to invade.

They did not speak as they uncovered Sara's body, once again exposing her frailness and vulnerability. Through the small opening in the storage closet, I watched as one woman brushed Sara's beautiful hair, taking time to pull it around to frame her face and shape it nicely. Then she washed her face with a cloth and applied a light coat of makeup. She even applied pale pink lip gloss. The other woman washed Sara's body. She applied lotion to her skin and concealer where there were bruises. She shaved Sara's legs, and she cut and painted her fingernails.

To my disgust, great attention was given to the grooming of her genital area. The women waxed and cleaned her with some type of antiseptic soap. They were extremely careful around the IV site so as to not dislodge it. The younger woman inserted a Foley catheter to remove the urine from Sara's bladder, and then she administered an enema to clean out Sara's bowels. This gave me the impression that the women had some type of medical training since not everyone would know how to perform these procedures.

Neither one spoke; they moved methodically and with purpose, obviously having done this many times before. This process lasted for at least a couple of hours. My feet, legs, and back were throbbing from standing so still in the closet. My bladder throbbed, past the point of just needing to urinate, and spasms were now radiating from my lower abdomen to my back. But I could not move. I could not risk being heard.

When the women had completed their gruesome tasks, they stood back and surveyed Sara.

"Nice work," the older one said.

"You did a beautiful job on her makeup," said the younger.

Without another word, they gathered their supplies and left the room.

I was finally able to reposition myself. When I did this, I saw something that made my heart fill with joy: a phone charger. Someone had left a charger plugged into the wall beside the couch. I was silently thankful for a society that is glued to devices and the desire to keep them alive. Slowly and quietly, I moved from my small hiding place, my back and joints rejoicing at the change in position, and ran over to the charger. I plugged my phone in and prayed that Kayleigh and Johnson would still be trying to track my location. I slid the phone under the couch and resumed my hiding place in the closet.

Plugging in my phone was a great idea—they could track me—but it was also what gave me away. I was back in my little safe haven, peering out of the little crack in the door, when I heard heavy footsteps. I knew immediately the men were returning.

"It is almost time," the surgeon was saying as they entered the room. They stood around Sara's bed, getting a fresh look at her, nodding in approval. "We have everything ready," he continued, "and she looks to be a more profitable specimen."

The three other men nodded and mumbled their opinions. They had all changed into suits, and the room now hung with the scent of expensive cologne.

Suddenly a scowl transformed the surgeon's already evil face as his eyes slowly moved around the room. I tried to disappear into the shadows of the closet. My heart raced as I saw his eyes land on the phone charger, its wire disappearing under the couch. He again surveyed the small room, but his eyes did not stop at the closet. I had only a moment of relief. But that dissolved quickly as he stepped over to the couch, bent over the little white cord, and picked up my phone. He held it softly in his hand, but as I watched his fingers slowly curl around it, he suddenly whirled around and practically sprinted across the small room, yanking the closet door open. Before I even had a moment to react, he had grabbed my shoulders, jerked me out of the closet, and slammed me against the floor so hard I couldn't catch my breath.

When Dr. Pierce came in, I knew I had made a terrible mistake. He laughed so hard he couldn't speak. The other three men just stood there staring and in shock.

Finally, after regaining his composure, Pierce said, "Thank you so much, Layla! You have literally fixed the problem you created. I have been in this game a long time, in multiple countries, and you single handedly almost ruined me. But since you have returned to me so generously, you will practically double my money."

He was so elated with my presence that he did not seem concerned at all about my being discovered. "Gentlemen," he declared, "this is something to celebrate! We have just added another valuable product to today's agenda."

His enthusiasm seemed to be contagious, as the smirks were spreading in the room.

I struggled to an upright position, still sitting awkwardly in the floor. I finally found the courage to speak. "But why, why would you do this?"

"Oh, my dear, you see, I am a man who loves the finer things in life. Travel, homes, cars, art...women."

The other men chuckled and exchanged salacious glances.

"Do you know how much money an internal medicine physician makes, Layla?" Dr. Pierce asked, leaning over her. "Not enough, not even close. So I am a physician and have this little business on the side. I work for about six months in the US or Europe and then enjoy life the rest of the year. It worked like a charm until you came along. You see, we have a great team of physicians, nurses, and others who help us to find the proper..." He looked toward the ceiling and tapped his chin, searching for the appropriate word, "specimens. Identifying healthy young women. We diagnose and treat them, but sadly enough, they supposedly die from complications of some sort. We have used a variety of these complications over the years." He smiled, self-satisfied. "We make them appear dead with just the right amount of sedation, and the family has closure. The funeral home attendants are paid a small fee to turn their heads, and after the funeral services, the family has said goodbye, and we retrieve the merchandise. The product is then sold at auction. Oh Layla, you should be honored, really, that we chose you!"

As he was speaking, one of the other men left the room and returned with two more men, whom I did not recognize. One of them pulled a gurney behind him. The room seemed to be closing in.

Thrilled to see me and quick to work, they lunged at me, grabbed me by the arms, and dragged me across the room to the gurney. I fought with all my draining strength as they strapped me down. Then I watched with horror as Dr. Pierce slid the needle of an IV into my arm.

"Stop this! Please stop!" My voice betrayed my terror. "The FBI is coming," I warned, not at all sure it was true. "They will find me! Please don't do this!" I screamed and begged with all of my soul. Then I made eye contact with Dr Pierce as I pulled at my arm restraints. "You will never get away with this," I hissed. "You took an oath! How could you murder innocent people? You are a sick psychopath, and you will burn in hell for this!"

Then I felt the warmth of the medication travel into my vein. The calm euphoria replaced my terror and fear. They had not given me a paralytic, just a mild sedative. I could hear and feel but could not put up a fight.

As the same two ladies entered the room once again, I knew what was coming next. "Prepare her, and hurry!" Pierce snapped sharply at them. He left the room with the other men. As I lay on a gurney beside Sara, the two women started the same ritual I had witnessed earlier.

Body wash was smoothed all over me, and they scrubbed me gently with a loofah sponge. I was freezing. Then the women shaved my entire body and, like they had done to Sara, applied makeup to my face. The ladies, who never spoke a word, made fast work of preparing my body. They applied very aromatic lotions to my entire body. I wanted to beg, cry, ask them for help, but I could not.

The women turned me onto my side. I felt the pain and discomfort as they inserted a cold, rigid tube into my rectum to evacuate my bowels. Tears of shame and embarrassment rolled from my eyes, and the older woman tutted impatiently and repaired my makeup. Next they inserted a Foley catheter into my body to empty my bladder as they had done to Sara. I had performed these same procedures on patients over the years and never had any idea how it made them feel. The difference is, I was gentle. These ladies seemed to have no compassion, no remorse for these horrible things they were doing to me.

Throughout the procedures, I would fall into a twilight sleep and awaken when they would move me or do something painful. Trying to keep my eyes open was next to impossible. I wanted to see these women, to get them to help us. But they functioned like robots with no emotional response to their nefarious task at hand.

The men came back after I was sufficiently prepared and did the inspection I had witnessed on Sara earlier. All I could do was pray that Agent Johnson or Kayleigh would burst into the room and rescue me, but this did not happen.

Pierce held a medical folder and was flipping through its papers. "We can use her recent labs and screening. Her heart cath, liver biopsy, and renal function were all excellent, and even though they aren't as recent as we prefer, they will be acceptable."

Dr. Pierce stepped close, took my knees in his cold hands, and spread open my legs so the men could inspect my genitals while another was commenting on my breasts.

"She has a nice body," he said, touching my chest and stomach. "Youthful is valuable. I am sure she will be considered by both types of clienteles."

Even though I didn't know what this comment meant, the horror of my situation sank in. I could only pray for death. I closed my eyes and tried to think of something else, focus on something else, but nothing could take me from the terror I was in. Being examined in this manner, helpless and sedated, I prayed as hard as I could for unconsciousness.

Finally, when the process was finished, Sara and I were left naked on our side-by-side gurneys. She was chemically restrained, but I had on wrist restraints. The tall anesthesiologist had started an IV drip that was taking me in and out of consciousness for what seemed like hours. Eventually, one of the men returned and rolled me down a long hallway. The ceiling lights were so bright I couldn't keep my eyes open. No one bothered to cover me, and I shivered in the cold. But I didn't care.

I wanted death to come and come swiftly. I thought about my two sets of grandparents waiting for me in heaven, and I was not afraid to die. I just did not want to fight any longer. I wanted this nightmare to be over. Of course, I was sad for my family left behind. Would Tripp remarry? I hoped so. He deserved to be happy. I prayed for my beautiful daughter to find a great man and have a wonderful life. I didn't want to miss her wedding or meeting my grandchildren, but I was resigned that I would not escape what was happening.

My gurney stopped at a large, open room. I tried to look around and see what was surrounding me. When I finally got my bleary eyes to focus, I could not believe what I was seeing. This had to be some type of dream.

As my eyes cleared so did my mind. I remembered the comments Pierce had made about his business on the side, his specimens, his clientele. Suddenly all of the unknowns became apparent to me.

In my profession, we are trained to be alert for any signs that our patients are victims of human trafficking. I was well versed in the statistics. I had been to a variety of seminars, and the flashes of slide shows, data, and photos of black-market trading flashed into my memory.

Human trafficking is a $32 billion annual industry. It is estimated that eight hundred thousand women and children are trafficked each year across international borders. The women are used as sexual slaves or forced into prostitution. Then you have the issue of organ trafficking. The demand for organs is very high. It is estimated that there are over one hundred twenty-three thousand men, women, and children awaiting organs right now. An alarming number of hospitals and funeral homes worldwide engage in illegal organ trafficking. An average healthy person could save or improve up to eight lives if they could donate everything. Apparently, these greedy psychopaths had taken these two industries and created an open market, so to speak.

I was rolled into a large room and placed in a position at the back. Gurney after gurney was rolled in. The first few were directly beside me. I could see that they were young, fit, and sedated women. I could hear more commotion as multiple men rolled bodies in the room.

"Let's put the white ones over there, then all other ethnicities on this side. We really need to try to get some Latinos!"

"Where do you want this one?"

"What is the count now?"

"I think we're up to nineteen. One more, right?"

Voices were surrounding me, even though my eyes were in a haze of sedation. I could hear multiple men discussing the business at hand as I managed to force my heavy lids to raise and move my head from side to side.

The room was elaborate with large vases of vibrant roses everywhere. There appeared to be flowers placed on every surface, and the pungent smell was burning my nose. Exquisite chandeliers hung from the ceiling, and seductive music lulled in the background. Young men in tuxedos carried trays of hors d'oeuvres and crystal glasses of champagne. Leather chairs lined the walls where well-dressed men and women of all ages sat. They drank and ate and laughed like they were at a party.

I wondered where Sara was. Was she placed close to me? Still sedated? I could hear laugher, clinking of glasses, and the murmur of conversations around me. *Where is Kayleigh? If I could only get my IV loose, maybe I could get up and run. No that's crazy. I am surrounded by people wanting to kill me.* I could not escape. I could only hope someone was coming to rescue us. I could not help but wonder what comes next. How will this process work?

Eventually, the man I recognized as the surgeon addressed the audience.

"Welcome everyone! Please take your seats."

The room hushed.

Chapter 11

"We are so glad to have you all here," the surgeon gushed to the crowd, "and I am certain you will find exactly what you are looking for." His voice was almost giddy with excitement. "This will prove to be one of the best auctions of the year. For those of you who are new to the process, let me give a brief explanation of how this will go. What makes our product so spectacular is that our specimens are alive. They cannot be tracked or be investigated. We have taken care of those loose ends, so to speak."

There was polite clapping and mild laughter.

"Of course," the surgeon continued, "you will have time to examine all of the product for yourselves. All attendees are confidential, and all purchases are handled with the greatest of discretion. All services we offer are carried out by board certified physicians."

Nausea was sweeping over me. I could not even fathom something like this happening. The fact that the whole operation was so brilliant and apparently worked so well was the most disturbing factor.

"I will start from the front of the room and go over all data with you," said the surgeon. "I know you are excited about viewing the product for yourself. However, this will save some time for you. We have provided you with a spread sheet. I suggest you take notes and mark off the ones you are not interested in. I will make our recommendations for the use of each specimen. Some of the specimens will be better for organ procurement, and others are excellent for childbearing or...entertainment. You ultimately get to decide for yourselves."

I seemed to doze off and on as the doctor toured his clients among the women on gurneys. I would hear him discuss one person and wake to him standing beside another. His voice was calmer now, almost soothing, making it hard for me to focus. At times I could hear some mild rustling of papers, other times low cheers, like the clients were more enthused about the person he had just presented. I tried to focus and will myself to be more alert. I wanted to find where Sara was.

"This is a twenty-four-year-old Asian female. All testing excellent. No past pregnancies. Height 160 centimeters, weight fifty kilograms. Would be excellent for organ transplant or other uses."

This went on for quite some time.

Finally he reached me. Pierce was with him.

"This subject will appear a little more alert when you evaluate her. Just a little medication issue and of no concern."

Through the blurry slits of my eyes, I could see him standing over me. "This is an excellent specimen for organ procurement," he stated. "All test results are excellent, and the specimen is in great physical condition. We will be able to take multiple bids on heart, lungs, liver, and kidneys." His tone became stern. "This specimen is only available for organ procurement, no exceptions."

I should have probably been shocked at this, but of course Pierce and the others could not let me live. I was too risky, so this had to be the end of me. He looked down at me, and for a second, we made eye contact, and he gave me a smug smile. I wanted to kill this man. I wanted to choke the life out of him with my own hands. I have never hated anyone and wanted to kill them until that exact moment.

He was selling our organs or our bodies at an auction. The buyers were here either to procure an organ for a loved one or themselves or to purchase one of us for sexual slavery. Why did someone not figure this out? Dozens of missing women, and no one figured this out? How did the FBI miss this? Because it was brilliant, that's why.

Next was a time for the buyers to have a closer look. They all walked around the beds, looked at us, touched us, and discussed us like we were cattle at a farm. The buyers were of all ethnicities, young and old. What was the most shocking was the number of female clients.

Waiters in tuxedos walked around offering more juicy morsels of delicate finger foods. My stomach rumbled, and I couldn't remember the last time I had eaten. I also could not help but wonder how much these caterers were being paid to work in this obscene situation. How did someone not report this, tell the authorities? I guess money can buy anything, and there are a lot of crazy people out there willing to do anything for the right price.

An older woman and man came over to my stretcher. I could smell her sweet perfume, and she held a champagne flute in her perfectly manicured hand, which was adorned with a large diamond ring. It seemed to be hanging over my face, and I could not help but focus on the shiny, impressive rock.

The man studied the printout in his hand. "She's the right blood type," he said. "And her heart is in good condition too."

"What about the lungs?" the woman said. "For pulmonary hypertension, he'll need lungs too." She choked and put her glittering hand over her eyes. "He's only twenty-two!" she sobbed. "How does this happen to someone so young?" I realized she was talking about someone she loved. Her son? A grandson?

The man put a hand on her shoulder, then turned back to the printout. "Lungs seem fine too," he said, clearing his throat.

"Help me…" I tried to speak, plead, to beg them for help, but I could not get my words to come out. *I'm here! Please don't let them kill us! I have a family too!* But these words never articulated. Only my lips could move. It was no use. The man made a notation on his paper and led his wife to another victim.

This process continued for possibly a couple of hours. I was not sure of my time perception. Eventually, Pierce came to the microphone and directed the customers to return to their seats.

"I hope you have had time to review our outstanding selection," he said, and there was gentle applause.

Since I was not paralyzed and could move, I tried to wiggle loose from my restraints. I was hopeful maybe as people were returning to their seats, someone would have compassion for me, help me, but the medication had me so drowsy I could not make any progress loosening the straps that held me down. Still drifting in and out of consciousness, I heard the auction start.

"As you can see," Pierce explained, "the products are numbered. We will start in order and take bids. For specimen number one, we will start the bidding at fifty thousand dollars."

I could not see the persons bidding since they were back in their seats, but the auctioneer of death raised the price up and up until the bids stopped. Pierce went down the row in order. Some of the women received multiple bids.

I was startled from a brief sleep when a sharp female voice shouted, "I only need this one's kidney, so I am willing to split the cost with someone else. Anyone?"

"I need this one's lungs." A deep voice boomed from the back of the room.

Number three went for much more than number one because they sold her off into pieces. A chill went down my spine.

Sleep...Loud voices...

"I want this one as my wife," a man announced. "She is the only specimen of my nationality, and cost is of no object to me!" The forceful voice had a thick accent that I could not place.

"But her blood type is what we need for our son's transplant!" a frantic voice argued. "No one else here matches. I must have her!"

"Then outbid me," the other man challenged.

The argument went back and forth until I was enveloped in my haze once again, floating on a cloud of liquid that dripped into my veins.

Even in my drugged stupor, I was amazed at the money being offered. Waking up intermittently, I would hear figures shouted out that seemed to be more substantial. These sick, deranged men had taken two very illegal enterprises and were making millions by putting them into one huge body auction.

Time seemed to drag on and on until the auctioneer of death stood over me. I started to panic. I felt my heart speed up; beads of sweat started popping out on my forehead. The auctioneer must have noticed because all it took was a wave of his hand for me to get a nice dose of Valium added to my IV. The last thing I remembered was the bid for my heart and lungs and a comment that my liver biopsy had revealed mild hepatic steatosis, or fatty liver. That really pissed me off. I knew I should have laid off the ice cream and cookies. Those darned drug reps always bought us lunches. I mean, I can't help my liver is a little "fatty"!

When I awoke, I came to the realization that my life was ending. I was going to be taken to an OR, where a surgeon would remove my organs while I was still alive. In the large room, some women had already been removed, but it seemed like those of us for organ procurement were still there. I had no idea where Sara was. I could not see if she was one of the women left with me. I didn't even care to try to look any longer. I knew my end was near and was resigned to it, glad I'd sent that last text to my family. I closed my eyes and accepted my end.

I didn't know how long we had been alone in the room when I heard a door open. Suddenly, I felt a jolt of energy. Then the pain and pull of the IV being ripped out of my arm made me look, and to my surprise, Kayleigh was kneeling beside me.

"I gave you some Romazicon to reverse the Valium," she said, working fast to undo my restraints.

Sitting up rapidly was a bad idea. My head went in circles, and nausea overcame me.

"Whoa there! You got to take this slow." Kayleigh wrapped her arms around me and helped me to steady myself. "Do you think you feel like helping me?" Her expression was stern. I nodded, my head becoming clearer by the minute.

"Good. Start unhooking the other women."

Kayleigh was calm and focused on the task, all the time explaining.

"We were able to track your phone and locate you. Unfortunately," she paused to check the pulse on one pale, still woman, "many of the suspects had left before we arrived. We have taken into custody the ones that were still here." She stopped and looked at me, shaking her head in disbelief. "We had no idea what was going on here until we arrived and figured this out." Kayleigh quickly resumed her work of removing IVs and unstrapping the unconscious women. "The 'buyers' are returning tomorrow night to settle with payments and details. The buyers who purchased for personal use were able to pay and leave with their merchandise. However, those who bought products that are to be harvested for organs will have to return."

Kayleigh's words shocked me. I was among those whose organs were to be harvested. Still weak from the sedative, I felt the room swirl and gripped the side of the gurney until the feeling passed.

She kept talking, working her way around the room much faster than I could move.

"The surgical procedures will be performed while the customers wait, and the customers will be given special coolers with the organs inside. They pay in full at that time."

It was, of course, not convenient for the buyers to return and extremely dangerous. But the harvesting was the tricky part, and they had a limited time to use the organs before they were no longer viable. Taking in the details while Kayleigh explained was a relief. For the first time in weeks, I had a glimmer of hope that this ordeal would be over for good.

It wasn't long before more FBI agents, ambulances, and paramedics arrived and helped the lethargic women out. The women could not walk and needed to be carried. At that point, I realized I was still only wrapped in the blanket Kayleigh had provided me. This was made even more embarrassing when Agent Johnson walked in. He came up beside me as I was helping one of the last women to her feet and asked how I was, concern on his face. Despite the blanket, I was visibly shaking. When Agent Johnson took off his jacket and placed it over my shoulders, I felt even more humiliated. My skin flushed despite the coolness of the room when his fingers brushed my bare shoulder. I immediately wanted out of this room, but as I turned, my eyes met Sara's. She was being assisted by a paramedic. I had been so focused I had not noticed she was across the room from me. Tears started to fall as we met and embraced, I was so relieved, so happy she was alive.

Soon, we were all safe inside FBI vans and taken to a hospital nearby. I was crying and didn't even realize it until Kayleigh grabbed my hand.

"What happened to the other women?" I asked. "Do you know where they were taken?"

Hanging her head Kayleigh responded. "Some had already been removed prior to our arrival. I am so sorry, we had no idea and got here has fast as we could."

Sara was okay. She was still drowsy and confused, and she started to cry, shake, and panic. I knew exactly how she felt. My heart broke for her. I got up from my stretcher and positioned myself close to her. Lying practically on top of her, I held her, warmed her, rubbed her hair, comforted her.

The only sound in the van was sobbing, the weeping because we were rescued and glad to be alive but also for those women who had not been rescued in time. Despite the anesthetics, some of the women said they had heard some pieces of conversations and were aware of what was happening to them. I knew that after this experience and the terror and sexual assault we had all endured, therapy would be a new staple in our lives. Traumas like this must be dealt with, talked about and with a professional. I hoped we all would get the help we needed.

Taken to a different hospital in a nearby town, we were all admitted to separate rooms. Nurses scurried to administer IV fluids to help flush the drugs out of our bodies. The women were dehydrated and very weak. I assumed the others who had been given paralytic drugs would need rehab and physical therapy just like I had needed. I, however, was fine after getting fluids and some food.

Seeing Tripp and Aubrey run through the doors made everything better. I could see relief on their faces but something different in Tripp's eyes. Was it anger? There was an undertone of something that resembled irritation and disappointment. I deserved that. After all, I did this to them a second time, and this time was my fault.

Hours passed, and Kayleigh sent me no updates on what was happening. Sara's husband knocked on my hospital room door, and he couldn't even speak. He just cried and hugged me for the longest time. No words were needed. He finally did choke out, "Thank you!"

We had no updates overnight. The hospital was a constant flood of FBI agents and police hurrying up and down the halls, in and out of rooms. Even though the lights were all on, I felt darkness all around me. I feared sleep, closing my eyes. What if I was dreaming and this was not real? If I accidently dozed off, I would awaken with fear, but Tripp held my right hand and Aubrey my left. This helped ground me and remind me that the rescue was not a dream. I could hear their voices asking the doctors questions, always coming back to, "When? How long until she is able to answer our questions?"

Tripp informed me that the hospital had closed the ER to all other traffic and diverted emergencies to another ER close by. The government's handpicked physicians replaced the ER physicians. No one could be trusted, and this was a very delicate matter, Agent Johnson told us.

All through the night, the screams of relief came in waves as the authorities positively identified the women and reunited sisters, spouses, and other family members with their loved ones. I imagined how it must have felt, getting a call in the middle of the night that my loved one, who I thought was dead, was actually alive. These families had witnessed their loved ones be buried and had mourned them. I could not imagine how they felt at that moment when the one they had thought was lost had returned to them.

These women had been taken from all over. Some of their families would not arrive for twelve or more hours. Emotions ran wild that night. Screams of panic, relief, terror, sadness could be heard throughout the night. These physicians and nurses may have been transferred here from a military facility, but in all my years, I have never experienced more compassion and caring from a medical staff. When they examined me for sexual assault, according to protocol, and questioned me about what had happened, they tried to be as gentle and respectful as they could. Kayleigh was always close to Sara or me, going between our rooms, checking on us.

Sometime early the next morning, I finally fell asleep and slept for what seemed like days.

The next forty-eight hours were a barrage of questions, especially for me. Since I was the only survivor who had been somewhat lucid and able to see and hear what exactly was taking place, the authorities needed all the details I could provide. The various agencies spent the day planning the stakeout. Kayleigh kept me up to date as much as possible. The guards at the building had either been arrested or shot, which left the building empty until the masterminds returned to prepare for the transactions to take place. I was on edge all day, waiting and wondering what would happen. Would the FBI catch them? Would they escape to a new place and start the process over? I just could not comprehend that this practice of evil body trading would continue another day.

I tried to see Sara a couple of times, but she was either sleeping or with the therapists. They had assigned therapists to come by and talk to each of us and see how we were holding up.

Aubrey, once again, was a rock. She never left my side. Tripp was in and out, trying to help with food and support and checking in at work. He continued to seem distant, leaving the room often for work calls. I understood as he was our only source of income at this point, so he was trying to juggle making sure I was okay and getting a paycheck. I started to notice Kayleigh hadn't been in for a few hours. When one of the government nurses came in to check on me, I asked where Kayleigh had gone.

"She has left the building," the nurse said as she adjusted my IV and made notes in my chart.

"But where did she go?" I asked.

She smiled. "That's confidential, ma'am. Try to get some rest." She left the room, closing the door behind her.

Irritated by this, I sat up on the side of the bed, my mind running wild. Her leaving was odd to me. Then it hit me: she was at the stakeout.

When the detectives came by later in the afternoon, I had the opportunity to ask questions. Both Detective Whiteside and Detective Johnson were very patient with me.

"You have to get Pierce!" I said. "What are you going to do? How are you going to find the other women?"

They simply reassured me that everything was going to be okay.

"Trust us." Over and over repeating the same thing.

Chapter 12

Nausea, panic, and many emotions flooded me. The information from the agents was sparse, but Kayleigh was an open book. I am certain she was probably violating protocol by telling me what was going on. But for some reason she felt she owed it to me. I assumed since I risked my life to save Sara and had led them to this operation, she figured I deserved some information. She swore me to secrecy and explained what was going to take place.

"We're going to have female agents act as decoys. Ideally, we would have had enough time to gather agents who resembled the women for sale, but that's impossible at this point. Also, the doctors might have other preparations for the women, and we couldn't risk that for our agents."

"Preparations?" I asked, knowing I probably didn't want to know the answer.

"For surgery. Anesthesia, surgical cuts..." Her voice drifted off, and I suspected she realized she was saying too much. "Anyway, the doctors discover the switch, and it would be over before the sale went down. Then we would miss the chance for catching the buyers."

As much as I wanted Pierce to get what was coming to him, I wanted those sick buyers to be punished also. "So what's the plan?" I asked. "I mean, how are you going to pull it off?"

She looked at her watch. “We have about three hours before the operation goes down, and every second matters. We’re setting up a road construction crew to make sure no one arrives unannounced.”

I could see the uncertainty in her eyes. This plan had not been well thought out and had an enormous potential for going wrong. One thing the agencies all want is control, and they did not have it.

Kayleigh checked her watch again. “I have to be on my gurney in less than an hour.” And she left the room.

I caught my breath. The fact that Kayleigh was a decoy disturbed me. She had become my friend. I loved her and was afraid for her. She had given me hope when I had none and encouragement when I needed it, and she had no problem pushing me to heal my mind as well as my body. I owed her a debt I could never repay, and now she was trusting me with confidential information, risking her career. But what could I do? My mind raced. I had to help somehow.

I tossed off the sheet, got out of bed, and began pacing around the room. I felt fine. I wasn’t weak from the drugs like the other women. I felt almost normal. After much thought, when my panic subsided, I had an idea, but the problem would be how to get everyone to go along with it. Also, I had no way of knowing who I could trust at this point.

The first person I explained my plan to was a female detective named Asia who worked undercover as my nurse. I and some of the other victims had been notified which staff were agents, I assume to make us feel safe and so we would know where to go if we needed help. Asia was young, cheerful, and hilarious. She made us all laugh so much, and it helped to get our minds off the horrible situation we were in. Just guessing her age, I would not say over twenty-five.

When Asia arrived to my room, she had that amazing smile on her face, but it quickly turned into a serious scowl when I began to explain my plan. Getting her to listen was the hard part; she was quite a talker.

"Look, I know you will not like this idea," I started, "but please let me explain. I was the body placed nearest to the door at the auction. I would have been the first anybody saw as they walked in the room. If the FBI could stall long enough and the buyers and sellers arrive at the same time, they would not take the time to check all of the products. But they would certainly notice if the first woman they see is not one of theirs."

Asia squinted at me. "Okay wait. Do you actually think you have anything to do with or to offer an FBI investigation? You should not even know these details! This conversation is over!" Asia turned to leave.

"Wait, please, wait! Please just hear me out. Seeing me lying there just like they left me may give them the sense of security to proceed and not check everyone. It may be the break they need."

Asia was still shaking her head.

"I am fine," I insisted. "I have made it this far, and I have to see this thing through. Please, let me help!" I was begging with everything I had left within me. For some reason I had a sick feeling that the end was not coming. I had that feeling nagging in the pit of my stomach that they were missing something. But of course I could not explain a feeling to her.

"This is a ridiculous idea," she said. "You are not an FBI agent. You are a victim. I know you feel like you need to help, but that's just not the case."

I stepped toward her, feeling the urgency growing in me. "Tell me I am wrong," I challenged Asia. "You know the chances are high that they will at least inspect a few of us. How successful will this operation be if they notice I'm not there as soon as they walk in the door!"

I felt like she wasn't hearing me. She was shaking her head no the entire time I was speaking.

"I hate this idea," she said. "This is not protocol. We do not allow civilians to assist in investigations, especially a victim. But," she sighed and rubbed her hand over her mouth. "I admit, your point is correct."

I exhaled, knowing I was winning her over to my idea. "Look, I really am fine. Heck, I've been taken by these people twice now. I am practically a pro!" I giggled to lighten the mood. She was not amused. "Please, can you just ask? I'm not an agent, you're right. But I do have something to offer this investigation."

She stared at me, her lips thin and tight. Finally, she said, "Okay. I'll ask. I'll call the detectives on the case and run it by them." She pointed a finger at me. "No promises."

Aubrey came in carrying bags of fast food. Asia ended the conversation and left. In my mind, I debated on whether to tell Aubrey my proposal, but I was afraid of what she would say. I had put my poor husband and daughter through hell. I knew it wasn't my fault, but how could I ask her to worry more?

"Mom?" Her voice brought me back.

"What, baby?"

"What's going on?" There was no missing the suspicion in her voice.

"What do you mean? Nothing is going on."

"I swear to God, Mom, if you are in danger again—" Her voice broke off and tears filled her eyes. "Tell me what is going on!" she demanded.

So I told her my plan to infiltrate the body auction ring, leaving out as much as I could to keep her from worrying. If looks could kill, I would have died after the first two sentences. But after I explained in detail, she reluctantly understood.

"Let me be there," she begged, taking my hand. I could feel her fingers trembling as she squeezed. "I want to be close to you. Even if I can just wait in the FBI van."

"No, absolutely not."

She let go of my hand and stood up straight. "Then I'm just going to tell Dad." She pulled her cellphone from her back pocket.

"Okay, okay," I said, straining to reach for the phone before she could dial. "I'll talk to Asia and see what we can arrange."

After a few minutes, Asia came back with an update.

"Can we talk alone?" she asked, looking meaningfully at my daughter. I assured her it was okay to talk in front of Aubrey. Reluctantly, she said, "I have no idea how or why, but they agreed."

She was obviously very anxious giving me this news. It was clear she did not agree with the decision, but I was thrilled, excited, and terrified.

"Your *only* role," Asia continued, "is to lie on the stretcher just like they left you. You will not be armed. All other stretchers are filled with agents. When things start happening, you are to drop flat onto the floor and take cover. Do you understand? No exceptions. No heroic actions."

"Okay, I understand. I will lie there not moving."

She nodded, still not looking pleased.

"I have one request," I dared, and she rolled her eyes.

"I can't wait to hear it."

"Can my daughter be somewhere near by? In the FBI van maybe? And I am sure my husband will want to be close with her."

The agent was shaking her head and stepping toward the door.

"I know it's a lot to ask," I begged, "but they have been through so much. Of course, I don't want them close enough to be in danger."

She exhaled loudly, her hand on the door handle. "I'll see what I can do."

Chapter 13

How in God's name did I end up back on this stretcher, naked and cold? I must have lost my mind. But I found comfort knowing that Kayleigh and multiple other women were lying beside me in the room, and they were armed. This place was surrounded by FBI agents, and the roadblock seemed to be doing its job. The buyers and sellers would arrive together. The caveat to all of this was that in order to arrest the buyers, the deals had to be complete or in process, or they could just lie and make up another reason for being there. They had to be caught in the act. This was where I was afraid things would fall apart. For what seemed like hours, we lay there, quiet and trying not to move. I admit I was excited. I hate to say that because this was a sick and horrible situation. I guess it was the adrenaline and the rush to get the bad guys.

When I heard the door open, I tried to keep my breathing slow and shallow. It was Pierce who entered the room first. I could hear the footsteps of others, but I couldn't tell how many.

"I am so sorry I was delayed," Pierce said. "There was some kind of construction blocking the road."

Others commented that they had also encountered the flagman, who stopped them for an unreasonable amount of time before waving them past the work vehicles.

Pierce said, "I think we have everyone here. Shall we start?"

There were a few muffled, “Yes, let’s get started.” Then I could hear the door shut and lock and the soft sounds of speaking in the adjoining room. I assumed that the customers were arriving or perhaps the surgical team.

Just as I had predicted, since my stretcher was first in line, Pierce stopped at my gurney. I breathed slowly—counting to four, holding my breath, releasing for four counts—to slow my heart rate. Pierce took my pulse and inspected the IV bag. The FBI medical staff had made the IVs and the liquid inside look very real, taping them to our inner thighs without inserting a needle.

“She is calm and sedate,” Pierce announced. “She will not give us any other issues, and soon I will be done with this pest!” His laugh gave me a chill down my spine.

“Should we check the others?” someone suggested, and I tensed.

“We don’t have time,” Pierce said. “The road construction really put us behind. Let’s get the operating area prepped.”

The plan was working. The exchange of money was about to take place. I could feel my bed being rolled out into the large room where the original auction had taken place. The lights were dim, but no music played. It was all business.

No one had discovered that these were not the original women they had auctioned off the day before. But the facade didn’t last long.

“Welcome back everyone!” Pierce said. “We apologize for the inconvenience of making a return trip, but the product is handled differently with organ procurement. We will examine each product with you, review the pricing agreed upon, and confirm the organ or organs needed. We will then take your payment. Once this is authorized and confirmed, we will give you further instructions from our surgical team. I know you will be more than satisfied with purchases you have made. I sincerely hope you will spread the word about this amazing auction and the service we provide. We will be releasing the next auction date and location in the next couple of months."

Pierce spoke with such enthusiasm it made me want to vomit. The room fell quiet. I could hear a man's shoes tap as he crossed the floor toward one of the beds for a buyer to review his purchase. My heart thumped. This was the moment.

Pierce spoke casually to the other buyers while they waited, ever the salesman.

The next thing I heard was, "What the hell? This is not what I purchased! What kind of sham is this?"

After this, things happened at the speed of light. Pierce yelled out a stream of profanities. At this point, I opened my eyes and looked around at the chaos. Agents came from nowhere and stormed the room. People tried to run, but the doors were already blocked. The agents jumped off the beds and had guns drawn before I could even sit up. They must have hidden guns somewhere on the stretchers that would not be seen. I was truly amazed at the speed and efficiency of the half-nude female agents. Buyers ran around like scared children as they realized the auction had been infiltrated by the FBI.

Drop flat onto the floor and take cover, I remembered Agent Asia instructing me. *Do you understand? No exceptions.*

"I had to do it!" a woman sobbed. "My daughter is dying! She needs a heart! I'm so sorry! Please understand." An agent pushed her down to the floor and handcuffed her.

"Save it lady," said the agent. "The woman you just tried to buy and murder is someone's daughter too."

I sat dazed on my gurney, and I could hear the justifications coming from multiple people now overcome with the fear of what they were facing. The employees of the auction did not speak but tried to run or fight. They were no match for the FBI. They were cuffed and lined up against the walls, on one side stood the buyers, and on the other the sellers. Everything went smoothly and seemed to happen very quickly.

My only thought was Pierce. My eyes flitted around the room. Where was he? Was he already cuffed? I scanned the walls and tried to find him.

I guess I was in shock at the chaos taking place around me. I snapped out of it when I heard my name. Kayleigh was calling to me. I turned to look at her, and I saw the panic on her face.

Suddenly from behind me, an arm wrapped around my neck. The feeling of cold metal pressed at my temple. I assume only a gun would feel that way. Agents turned their guns toward my direction but could not shoot.

"You are going to let me go! Or this troublesome bitch dies right now! I swear, I will blow her head off!" I recognized the voice of the anesthesiologist. He must not have been where the FBI had projected because when he grabbed me, everyone was shocked.

It was possibly due to the events of the last few weeks, but I swear, I wasn't panicking. Poor Kayleigh looked terrified, and Agent Johnson also looked surprised at this unexpected turn of events. I could feel the cold, hard end of the gun pressed against my temple. I could feel his chest against my back, and his breathing was hard and fast. His breath had a sweet, sickening smell to it. His pulse was racing, he appeared more nervous than I was.

No one moved.

"Don't make me repeat myself!" the anesthesiologist barked, clearly agitated. "I will kill her and everyone else I can shoot! Let me and my partners go right now! I have no problem killing anyone. You should know this by now."

Agent Johnson holstered his weapon and stepped forward slowly, showing his hands. "Can we talk about this? Before you make a terrible mistake?"

The anesthesiologist's grip on my neck tightened. "I'll make a deal with you," he said, trying to sound calm. "You can keep the buyers, but we must be released." He was so nervous his voice was shaking. "We must be released. You can keep the buyers." He repeated.

I was listening to the ramblings of a lunatic. The agents were taking him seriously because they slowly started repositioning themselves.

"Okay," Agent Johnson took another step closer. "Let's talk about this. No one else has to die." With a smooth motion of his hand toward the opposite wall, he said, "My agents will start taking the buyers out now if that is okay. Then," continued Johnson, "we can discuss your and your partners' terms."

"Don't try to trick me. I am a brilliant man, and I will not be tricked!"

"No one is trying to trick you," Johnson assured him. "Remember it was your idea to let us keep the buyers in custody."

With an anxious nod, the anesthesiologist agreed, and several agents slowly started moving the buyers out the door.

"Okay, good! That's a positive decision." The agent's voice was calm and calculated. "Let's decide what the next step is."

The doctor's eyes seemed to be in constant motion, surveying the scene around him. The other physicians were frozen in place against the wall. I could see a hint of relief on their faces as if they felt this bargaining might work and they would escape the FBI.

"I want our vans parked up front," the anesthesiologist demanded. "All agents need to put down their weapons and come into this room so we can see them. We just need a clear path out."

Agent Johnson smiled, tilting his head slightly to one side. "You know we will not lay down our guns, but as you can see," he raised his hands a little higher, "mine is down. You will need to give us a moment to get all things in place for you."

I was amazed at how the circumstances had changed so quickly. As I looked around, the female agents were in their thongs and topless, due to the staging needed. Then I noticed a man in surgical scrubs, probably one of the surgeons who had come to harvest the organs, sneaking up behind Kayleigh. I gasped and opened my mouth to warn her, but the man behind me slapped his hand over my mouth and growled into my ear, "Shut your mouth or you die." Everyone's attention was on the anesthesiologist who held the gun to my head, and no one noticed the man slipping into the room.

With my eyes, I frantically tried to warn Kayleigh.

"I know there are more agents here!" the doctor behind me shouted. "I am not stupid. I am a physician!"

I could see Kayleigh breathing hard, and I could sense she was getting nervous. But I couldn't make her understand that she was in danger. I guess I had forgotten that her training kept her aware of her surroundings. With one backward snap of her head, she head-butted the man behind her as hard as she could. I heard a large crack, and blood poured from his nose. He screamed a loud, girlish scream and grabbed his bleeding snout. Just like a well-played-out plan, when the anesthesiologist looked in shock, the other agents took that moment to attack. They lunged toward the anesthesiologist, who released me and let me fall back on to the gurney.

Once again, my brain couldn't keep up with the events that happened so quickly. I so wished I could see things in slow motion like in a movie. That way, I could see who did what.

At some point, Pierce returned to the room. Or maybe he had been hiding there all along. I saw Agent Johnson fighting with Pierce for control of a gun. They went back and forth until a horrible sound erupted. The gun went off, and in my mind, everything stopped and became very quiet. I heard a gasp and a low moan, and I followed the sound to see one of the agents who had been playing a part in this sick play. She was young and beautiful, with long, blond locks of hair cascading down her back. Her skin was as white as the roses in the vase near her. A small, crimson line of blood grew thicker as it ran from her right upper chest down her bare breasts, and she crumbled to the floor. I screamed out. I wanted everyone to stop and help her, but the chaos resumed.

I assumed the agents in the FBI vans outside had heard the shot because, in seconds, more agents arrived, shots were fired, screams rang out, and then I had a feeling I had never had. In my mid-back, a hot fiery feeling radiated through my upper body. It felt like a branding iron had been stuck between my shoulders. I stood there, looking ridiculous, I suppose, and everyone looked at me with mouths gaping open. *What the heck were they staring at?* I was tired and ready to go home. This day had been exhausting, and I was dizzy at this point. Kayleigh ran to me and took my shoulders in her strong hands.

"Lie down, Layla. You'll be okay."

I frowned. “I don’t need to lie down.” But my voice sounded strange in my own ears. “I’m so tired, Kayleigh.”

“Get that medic in here!” Kayleigh called over her shoulder.

“What—” I couldn’t get the words out to ask what was going on.

Kayleigh’s face was close to mine now, her eyes wide with concern. “You’ll be fine. Help is coming. You’ve been shot. Now lie down, please,” she begged.

Her words didn’t make sense to me until she added, “But don’t worry. I got the bastard.”

Just before I blacked out, I saw Dr. Pierce lying on the floor in a puddle of blood.

Chapter 14

I could not remember anything after I passed out on the bed. Multiple sellers were either injured or dead. Three agents died, and I came very close once again. After a long, extensive surgery, doctors removed the bullet, and miraculously, it had missed every major organ. Not wanting to spend a moment longer than necessary in the hospital, I asked to be released within a few days.

Kayleigh came to visit me often and filled me in on the aftermath of the sting.

One good thing was that Pierce had kept a thorough log of the buyers, their bids, and other details. The FBI and international agencies tracked them down, and they were all arrested and charged, but many of them had unloaded their "merchandise" when they learned about the raid. My heart was heavy to learn that those women were never found.

Kayleigh proudly explained that her bullet had struck that demon Pierce, but he did not die. However, I was certain he would have chosen death. He was shot in the spine, which resulted in him becoming quadriplegic. He became a total care patient. He cannot so much as lift his own finger to care for himself. Kept alive by a ventilator, fed by tubes, bathed, and taken care of by strangers, he was placed in a state institution, and I called that *karma*! I hated to admit it, but I hoped he suffered every single day.

Even six months later, home and fully recovered, I was hesitant to return to work. The time just had not come when I felt I could handle it. Kayleigh kept in touch often, and Sara was back at work. She recovered quickly and was back to her normal self though I could see a darkness under her perky exterior. However, she surprised us all when she announced that she was expecting a baby! The new baby had given her a new focus and something to be excited and happy about. She told me confidentially that she's almost certain the baby was conceived in the stairwell between the second and third floor!

Tripp also had a surprise for me when he announced that he had taken a new position at his job that would require him to travel a lot. I couldn't help feeling surprised and disappointed. After all this, I had hoped Tripp would want us to spend more time together, not travel around the country for work. He must have seen my reaction.

"It was a great opportunity," he explained almost defensively. "We can certainly use the money to help Aubrey pay off her student loans."

"And my medical bills?"

He shrugged a little. "That too. But I'm thinking of our future." He exhaled, and I thought he would touch me or kiss me. But he just said, "I want us to have a good life."

Before the events happened, Aubrey was undecided about her career, but now she had decided to apply to the FBI. She had already completed her four-year bachelor's degree from Appalachian State University, and with the new friends she met during my ordeal and strong recommendations from Kayleigh and Agent Johnson, she got into the academy. It scared me, but I had never seen her happier or more energetic.

I knew I needed to go back to work, but I got that sick panic feeling at the thought of walking into the hospital. Smelling that antiseptic odor, hearing the noises in a hospital setting—all of it scared me to death. I still could not shake that something was not right. That others had gotten away who shouldn't have, that someone was still out there to continue the gruesome business. My therapist explained to me that my paranoia stemmed from post-traumatic stress disorder, but I was not convinced that was my diagnosis. In the back of my mind always were those women who were not saved. Where were they? Were they dead? Were they alive and being used as a sexual commodity? Sometimes when Kayleigh, Sara, and I went to dinner together, we talked about them, said a prayer for them, and wept for them.

Tripp was home the weekend I finally decided to go back to work. I had tried to be "normal" more often and not act like a crazy person. Don't get me wrong, my husband was always understanding, but I had not been able to be intimate since this all started. We had always had a very active sex life. A man's way of expressing love is often different from a woman's, and he felt the way to show his love and affection for me was through sexual intimacy. I needed him to help me around the house, tell me I'm pretty, and do little things like that to feel loved. He does not really understand those subtleties.

Prior to this, we had a great sex life for a married couple in their forties. Aubrey being at college had rekindled a spark, and we could experiment more. But after lying naked while strange men studied and probed me, I had a lot of panic and fear issues and just could not be intimate. I wanted to get back to that. I decided we had to get back to normal.

So, before Tripp got home, I took a long bubble bath. I took great effort in making my body as perfect as possible, and I placed candles all over the house. I put a note on the door that had him follow a candlelit path up the stairs and down the hall to the bedroom, where I had on some very skimpy lingerie. Our favorite songs played on my "lovemaking" playlist. The mood was set, and I could see when he reached the bedroom that he was excited. His face was lit up, smiling wide as a Cheshire cat. My heart melted with love for him, that sweet face and smile. At that moment, I didn't remember why I had held out so long. I wanted him. I needed him. His arms needed to be around me, holding me tight and keeping me safe.

That night was like no other in our twenty years of marriage. He needed me as much as I needed him. He made urgent and passionate love to me, and he made me feel sexy, loved, and safe all in one night.

After hours, we realized we were starving and needed some food. Without bothering to put any clothes on, we went to the kitchen at about two a.m. and made some omelets. We laughed and talked and had the best time we'd had in years. It was like the horror had never happened. The events were forgotten for this night. I was happier than I can express in words.

Eventually, when we had been fully satisfied in every way and were exhausted, we went to bed. For a while, I just laid my head on his chest, and we held each other. The only thing that was mentioned about the events of the previous year was when he kissed my abdomen and gently touched the small scar.

"That's from my liver biopsy," I said.

He kissed it again. Then he looked up at me, smiled, and said, "I think you have a great liver, baby, and I know it's not fatty."

We both laughed and fell asleep holding each other. Safe and happy were feelings I had not had the luxury to have in many months, and right before a blanket of deep sleep covered me, I thanked God for letting us survive.

The next morning in the shower, I sang and was so happy. My mind replayed the previous evening. It had been so wonderful. As I bathed my still thin body, I happened to see the small puncture wound on my right upper abdomen. I could almost feel Tripp's gentle kisses. Laughing to myself about Tripp's comment regarding my "fat liver," the strangest thing happened. Before my brain processed what was happening, my body reacted.

The first thing was my hands. They started to tremble so hard I dropped my loofah sponge onto the shower floor. Then, despite being in the hot shower and sweat pouring from my forehead, I felt a chill that went to my bones. Waves of nausea caused me to dry heave, and then I realized, in utter terror, that Tripp had no way of knowing about my medical report or my fatty liver. As far as I knew, no one had ever discussed it in front of him.

No, *no*, I had to be mistaken. I was in and out of sleep and on anti-anxiety meds at that time. He must have heard it or read it somewhere. This was my husband of almost twenty-one years, my best friend, and the father of my daughter. What was wrong with me? Was I insane? Yes, that was it. My poor brain had been through too much stress. I shook the thought from my head and concentrated on the day ahead, scrubbing my body until my skin was red.

Like a robot, I got dressed and pushed those horrible thoughts into the furthest recess of my brain. I wanted to look nice for my first day back. The day would be full of stares, gossip, and speculation. I wanted to appear put together, sane, and, for my patients' sake, mentally capable of providing care. I put on a cute short dress and Antonio Melani wedges and took my lab coat off its hanger. The symbol of what I do, who I am. I had not worn it for so long, and it felt strange to me. Was I ready to go back? Could I face the questions, the looks of pity and wonder? Yes, I could. I had to. I had to get my life back.

I called Aubrey on my way to work and told her I loved her, set my blue Mini Cooper on cruise, and turned my radio up loud.

Trying to talk myself out of the thoughts I was having, trying to sing along with the radio, praying, nothing worked. All I kept thinking about was Tripp. His smile, his smell, his laugh, the little jokes we shared, the hard times in our marriage.

Then I remembered the beautiful necklace he brought home for me one day, the one I fussed about because I knew we couldn't afford it. And what about that dinnertime phone call he had to take outside? Was there more than one? Wasn't there a time when I looked in my rearview mirror as I drove to work and Tripp was still home, and I was sure I had seen a strange car pull into our driveway? Was Tripp part of a human trafficking ring? Did my husband help with my own abduction? Did he know what was going to happen? I could not wrap my mind around it. I turned up the radio because I had to believe I was imagining it all.

I don't know how I made it to work. But I did. I had to move on, so I put the dark, ominous cloud in the back of my mind to revisit later.

Chapter 15

Walking into the hospital wasn't as bad as I thought it would be. I was greeted with warm smiles, lots of hugs. I must have heard, "You look amazing!" over fifty times. I had always gotten along well with the critical care unit nurses because that was where I had worked as an RN. These were my friends, my peers, and the best nurses in the hospital. Many of them had been there over twenty years. It is weird to say that many had attended my funeral. I had not seen them since that day, and some of them started to tear up as I walked in, but I quickly told them I was fine.

It did take me a while to get back into the routine of things. With the new government regulations, electronic medical records changed often. I needed an update and had to spend a lot of my morning in the IT department. Being proud of myself for maintaining my smile and controlling my nausea, I walked down the stairs to the basement to the CCU.

Going down the corridor gave me some serious flashbacks to the night Sara was taken. I ducked into the ladies' locker room, took some deep breaths, and controlled myself.

It's going to be okay, I told myself. *It's over. It's all over.*

Tears streamed down my face, my makeup ran, and I stood in front of the mirror trying to repair the damage. The longer it took, the more irritated I became at myself. I had to look good, normal, and not emotional. After about thirty minutes of deep breathing and prayer and more makeup touchups, I headed out to see my patients.

A fifty-five-year-old female in CCU-15 had been admitted to the critical care unit during the night after a drug overdose. She was already waking up and trying to pull her tubes out. I examined her, met with the family, and updated her chart. Okay, I was fine, able to focus—what's the old saying? Like riding a bike? I went down my list of patients, and despite being slower than I used to be, I was doing fine.

My last patient of my shift was a sixty-year-old man admitted with pneumonia. He had been a heavy smoker and was declining rapidly and soon needed life support. Dr. Enrique, the pulmonologist I was working with that week, was one who had only been with the practice for about two years. He was sweet, caring, and enthusiastic. He had sent flowers and messages to me almost weekly during my recovery. I had missed him, and when he grabbed me, hugged me, and gave me his customary kiss on the cheek, I felt like everything was back to normal.

It was when I walked into CCU-3 to see this pneumonia patient that I had my first flashback. I did what I normally did: went over to the ventilator to check the settings. This machine gave the patient a certain amount of oxygen, pressures to open his lungs, essentially breathing for him because he was too sick to breathe on his own. When pneumonia becomes worse, the setting must be adjusted. When a patient has improved enough, we wean the settings and eventually can take the tube out.

Next, I examined the patient by listening to his lungs and heart, and looking for swelling in his hands, ankles or feet, or any other abnormal findings. The last thing I did was to check the patient's IV drips. When the patient is this critically ill, he may need multiple IV medications for the maintenance of his blood pressure and always meds for sedation. It is not comfortable to be on life support, so almost all patients need sedation. Some drips just make a patient sleep. However, some are specifically for pain.

And, of course, some medications paralyze the body. This is meant to keep a patient from fighting against the machines. These drugs are not used often due to the side effects. But Dr. Enrique seemed to use them more often than the other pulmonologists. We had expressed our concern in the past, but in some cases, the use was appropriate to give the patient the best chance of survival.

When I reached up and read the label on the patient's IV bag, I froze, standing there with the bag in my hand.

The CCU nurse taking care of the patient that day was a good friend of mine, Heather Hall. She was a short, attractive nurse. She had long, straight hair, always pulled back. Her voice was loud and often seemed as if she were yelling. Many times, she offended people by her tone and her frequent sarcasm. However, she was a great nurse. She knew her job and did it well. Her ICU experience made her confident and sometimes opinionated about what she felt was best for her patients' care. She and I had always gotten along well.

Keeping up with the news and knowing some details, she understood what was happening when I froze. The drip in the man's IV was a paralytic. In an instant, I was back in that coffin. I could smell the roses, feel the satin, cool and soft on my skin. Heat ran up my spine as the sweat began to drop from my forehead. I felt my heart rate speed up, and I started to hyperventilate.

Heather was at my side in an instant. She pried my hand from the IV bag and gently led me to a chair in the corner of the room.

"Breathe, Layla. You're fine," she soothed as she banged through the drawers and cabinets for a bag for me to breathe into. Finding nothing, she knelt in front of me.

"Layla, listen to me," she said in her slightly too-loud voice. "Close your eyes. Let's go to the beach."

I could feel her hands cupping gently over my mouth and nose. "Can you feel the sun on your skin?" Heather crooned. "Hear the water lapping on the shore?"

I focused on her words, forced my mind to imagine what she described.

"Here's a cool margarita for you," she said with a lilt. "So sweet and cool. Now just relax. Everything is fine. Breathe in and breathe out."

My body slowly calmed, and after a few minutes, I opened my eyes. Heather removed her hands from my face. "Okay?" she asked.

I nodded.

"Okay," she said with a nod. She stood and went to the sink. Unwrapping the plastic from a paper cup, she poured some water from the tap and brought it to me.

"You're good," she assured. She rubbed my back while I drank. "You wanna talk?"

I shook my head. "Can I just sit here for a minute?"

"Sure thing." Heather completed my check of the sick man's IV bag and left the room soundlessly.

Realizing I had a flashback was quite upsetting for me. How could I move past this and get on with my life if I never knew when it would come flooding back? If I smelled a rose, would I flash back? Could I go to the funeral home if a loved one died? My mind was racing with panic, worry, and the feeling that my mind and body were betraying me. Next time, I promised myself, I would control it much more effectively.

After about an hour, I felt better and decided to go see patients on the floor. I prayed the entire time on the elevator that nothing would trigger another attack. Again, I tried to act normal, confident. I could not let everyone see my fear and pity me. I ignored the stares and put on an act of self-control and confidence. Whenever I passed Heather, she would raise her eyebrows questioningly, and I would smile and nod that I was fine. She didn't make a scene, and I was grateful to know she hadn't told anyone about my panic attack.

The rest of the day went smoothly without any further episodes. As I finished up with dictations, anxiety started building because I knew I had to go home and face yet another question, this one involving my husband of twenty years.

Chapter 16

Tripp was a handsome man. He was not tall, only slightly taller than I was. His hair was deep brown with some gray sprinkled in, and his hairline was just starting to recede. His face was round, and when he smiled, small dimples appeared. His smile seemed to affect his whole face, and it always melted my heart. He had a laugh that made me so happy, and in the past few months, I had not heard much of it at all.

I arrived home before he did, which was becoming normal because of his new job responsibilities. I typically got home a good two hours after he did, but his new work had taken him out of town. I prepared a salad and watched the news. I hated watching the news. It was so depressing. Either someone had shot another person or there was yet another political scandal brewing. I could never know what was truth and what was fiction. Finally, I turned the TV off.

I sat in the quiet living room and thought about how to handle my suspicions about Tripp. Not saying anything would only make me miserable, and I could not hide my emotions well at all. If I accused him, I risked losing him, especially if I was wrong. But if I was right, my life was in danger.

After much thought and prayer, I made up my mind what to do.

It was after dark when Tripp got home. I made him a sandwich, and we made small talk, with me giving him the highlights of my first day back at the hospital and him telling me about his workday.

After he had eaten and taken his place in his leather recliner, I just came right out and started the conversation.

"Baby, I don't want to hurt or upset you," I said gently. "You know how very much I love you. But I cannot keep holding something inside. I have a hard question to ask."

He looked concerned. "Go ahead, babe, ask me anything."

"The other night was amazing." I felt a little flush just thinking about it, and he reached out and took my hand. "I have missed you," I continued, "but you said something that bothered me. You made that comment about my fatty liver. How did you know that? I never told you that. I have to be honest, I am kind of freaked out about it."

I tried not to sound like this was an accusation but more like I was just curious.

His eyes were wide, mouth hung open, and I could see his mind racing. As this happened, I felt my own heart rate jump to a fast rhythm. I could tell he could not answer without a lot of thought. This was concerning to me—what was there to think about? Unless my original fear was true and he had been involved the whole time.

He stood up and rubbed his hands over his face. "I must have overheard it somewhere. Good Lord, Layla, do you have any idea what hell I was in? I was updated by agents over and over. Someone probably told me." He stopped pacing and looked at me, his eyes squinting. "What are you thinking? You think I had something to do with this? Because of an offhand remark about your liver? If you do, tell me now!"

His voice was angry but nervous. I could see his hands trembling and his face was contorted in a way that seemed odd to me. Was it hurt? Anguish? Or guilt?

"No! No, baby!" I quickly assured him and tried to laugh at my own foolishness. "I don't think that. I'm so sorry! I just had to ask. I know you went through a horrible trauma also. Please forgive me and forget I asked."

I felt devastation, rage, and the breaking of my heart.

Tripp seemed convinced that I had believed his ridiculous story as he settled back into the recliner and started to scroll the sports channels. His red face paled, and he seemed calmer. After a few minutes, I apologized once again and gave him a kiss.

"I am going to take a hot bath, babe. Do you need a drink before I go?"

He shook his head no, his eyes still on the TV, so I excused myself to go take a bubble bath and read. He knows nothing makes me happier or more relaxed than a hot bubble bath and a good suspense novel. I had to be alone, think, and clear my head.

As I ran my tub, I texted Kayleigh and let her know I needed to talk to her alone as soon as she could. She was in Arizona working undercover at a large hospital. We talked or texted at least three or four times a week, so I knew she was out of the state. That didn't matter. I had to talk to someone. I had to get another opinion. Was I paranoid or just crazy? If Tripp was truly involved in human trafficking, I could not let him know that I was suspicious.

I reclined back into the soothing water and took deep breaths to try to calm myself. Why would my beloved husband do this? He seemed to love me. I thought we were happy. I mean, I knew this past year had been hell, but that wasn't directly my fault.

It had to be the money—maybe they were offering him a lot of cash for him to "sell" me. He had always wanted to live at the beach, a tropical paradise. I had refused because I liked the mountains and would not move so far from my family. But surely he would not go to such lengths just for some sand and surf?

I had tried to keep up with what was still going on with my case. Kayleigh informed me that the FBI was still searching for the other buyers who had escaped. Kayleigh had made it her personal mission to look for the missing women on the side, but it was close to impossible to track women who were supposedly dead and buried. Using the process of elimination, Kayleigh was tracking women whom Dr. Pierce had declared dead in all the hospitals where he had been employed, and the process was a virtual nightmare.

Naturally, when the details of what had happened in our little North Carolina town went public, hundreds of families had inquired about their loved ones. Many families had bodies exhumed to be sure their loved ones were truly buried there. It was emotional torture for so many people. Aubrey, in her spare time at the FBI academy, used the resources available at the training facility to try to find the other men involved who had gotten away.

I was not the only one who felt like Dr. Pierce was not the head of this business. We all felt this was a small arm of a much larger operation. Things that Sara, Kayleigh, and I had heard made us feel like this was a huge, worldwide business. They had discussed more auctions, different locations, and global travel. But investigators had nowhere to start. They had no survivors in custody to question. And Pierce could not give any information in his state of health. Of course, I understood that the investigators knew much more than they were telling me, but I didn't really dig for details either. I had overheard details of meetings that were held from my best source, Kayleigh, but the newest findings were kept secret. I could feel the secretive stares of the FBI agents covering as medical staff and see them close out their emails when I would approach their desks.

So many little clues convinced me that I was being kept in the dark, and I was okay with that. I had been trying to put this all behind me and get some semblance of normalcy until this uncertainty with Tripp came up. Now I wanted to know. I wanted to get to the bottom of everything, but a huge part of me wanted to forget it ever happened. I wished I could get a case of amnesia and forget it. Go back to normalcy, whatever that was. Family dinners, trips, game nights, and watching TV together. I was done with spending every waking moment thinking about the hell we had survived.

Chapter 17

A few days later, I could finally update Kayleigh about my conversation with Tripp and my suspicions about his involvement with the trafficking scheme. I could not tell her with Tripp home, so with the time difference, it was difficult to talk to her. Attempting to explain what had happened without putting my opinion in the mix was difficult.

"Okay, tell me if I am going crazy. Did you say anything to Tripp about my liver biopsy results?"

"No, why would I?"

"Well, the other night, he mentioned that he thinks I have a great liver and it's not fatty." I paused, but Kayleigh didn't say anything, so I continued. "I don't know how he would know that. Heck, I don't know if many of the FBI agents knew that detail from my test results. So now I am being paranoid, I think. But then when I asked him about it, he seemed...off. Don't ask me how, but he was odd!"

I heard her breathing, and finally she said, "Layla, I have no idea how he could have known that. I do not recall anyone talking about your test results in front of him, but let's be real. It was a crazy time. I guess he could have overheard it. Tell you what," she said. "Let me call Detective Johnson and update him and get his input, just to be safe."

It had been months since I had heard Agent Johnson's name. The last time I saw him was when I was still in the hospital after I was shot. He had stopped by and told me goodbye one last time before leaving for his next assignment. Guilt aroused inside of me when Kayleigh mentioned his name, and I remembered those few moments when I allowed myself to have inappropriate thoughts about the agent. Now here I was practically accusing my dear husband of being part of the most horrible criminal ring I could imagine. What was wrong with me?

Kayleigh called back quickly.

"Hey, I am flying to Charlotte as soon as I can. We need to meet and talk." Her tone was urgent. I could feel tension radiating into the phone.

"Why? What's wrong? What are you not telling me? Something is up for you to leave your assignment!" A chill ran through me, I knew she would not leave the case she was on unless things were bad.

"I can't talk about this over the phone," Kayleigh said. "Just stay calm, act normal, and don't say anything to anyone, not even Aubrey. I'll update you when I arrive. I have a few loose ends to tie up here, and I'll leave ASAP." That's all she would say. The line went dead.

Not sure how to act normal, especially when it came to Aubrey, I attempted to carry on with my life as best I could.

Going to work got easier as the days passed. The nurses didn't stare and whisper as often, and no panic attacks hit unexpectedly. At home, Tripp and I ate dinner, made small talk, and carried on with a somewhat stable life. We fell back into the ordinary routine of watching our favorite Netflix series, and things seemed normal. Looming in the recess of my mind was the possibility that my husband had tried to sell me to human traffickers.

After a few days, Kayleigh still had not arrived. I was concerned because I had expected her to come quickly, based on the urgency in her tone. But one afternoon at work, I got a simple text from her.

Landed. Dinner? 7 p.m. Nikko's.

Tripp didn't seem suspicious when I let him know I was meeting Kayleigh for dinner that night. She and I had gotten together so many times in the past few months, it wasn't out of the norm. I tried to act casual as I kissed him goodbye.

The restaurant where we met was a small sushi bar that was one of my favorites. The atmosphere was awesome—dim lights and trendy décor. The best part was the booths located in the back, which were very private. Kayleigh and I could talk and not worry about anyone overhearing us. After ordering drinks and appetizers, I was anxious to get into the details of what she had discovered.

As soon as the server walked away, Kayleigh leaned in.

"Johnson and his team looked at Tripp's personal and work computers, and they could not find any record of Tripp being in contact with Dr. Pierce."

"Thank you!" I said, sitting back and taking a long drink from my iced tea. "I don't know what made me so certain." I put my hands to my temples and rolled my eyes at my own foolishness. “Maybe the meds or something?”

“Wait,” she said, motioning me to lean in again. “One thing that concerned us was that when Tripp traveled so much, he seemed to always find a public computer to use. Any idea why he would do this?”

I shook my head no and listened intently.

“For example,” she continued, “at the hotel, he would go to the lobby and use the guest computers. Very odd because he always had his own personal laptop to use.”

I frowned and opened my mouth to protest, but the server appeared, a too-skinny girl with long, black braids, and placed steaming appetizers of tuna tataki and coconut shrimp on the table between us.

“Are you ready to order?” she asked.

I glanced at my open menu and absently selected a veggie roll.

Kayleigh studied the menu, tapping her finger on her chin before saying, “I’ll have the eel roll with extra wasabi and an order of shrimp fried rice.” She snapped the menu shut and handed it to the girl with a smile, then plucked a shrimp from the platter and popped it into her mouth. When the server was out of earshot, Kayleigh’s face became serious again.

“Because of the hotel servers,” she said, “it was almost impossible to know what or whom he had contacted. Johnson’s team is trying to look at hotel surveillance videos and the times Tripp logged in. This will be time consuming, but we are going to try. It seems as if he is doing something he purposely does not want traced or found." Kayleigh's expression was puzzled and concerned. She ate another shrimp. "These are amazing. Try one."

But my appetite was gone. Nothing was making sense.

Seeing my concern, Kayleigh softened her expression. "I can assure you, Layla, that I did not discuss the details of your testing in front of Tripp, and it is highly unlikely that any other agents did either. We did keep him informed of your status but no details." She held up her hands as if surrendering. "We have no idea who to trust at this point, and we have tried to be discrete." With a little flush, she added, "I have given you more information than I should have throughout this whole ordeal."

Kayleigh chewed, and I thought. There were probably countless reasons why Tripp would use a guest computer. It didn't mean he was involved in anything illegal. Soon our dinners came, but I could barely choke down a few bites. Once again, I had that panic feeling, but over the last few weeks, I had been able to get control of that monster that hid within me. I quickly controlled it now, pressing my hand to my chest and breathing slowly. Kayleigh put down her chopsticks and reached across the table to touch my arm.

"I'm sorry, Layla! I didn't mean to upset you."

I didn't know what to say. I looked down at the mounds of untouched food on the table.

"Look," Kayleigh said, "we can take Tripp in and question him, but to be honest, we don't have much to go on. Questioning him now will let him know that he is being investigated."

"Which could end my marriage," I interjected.

She raised her shoulders. "That's definitely a risk. Or you can just continue with your life until we uncover more details about whether Tripp is involved in this, and if so, how much. The choice is yours if you want to raise the suspicion with the bureau."

I knew the agency wanted to try to catch other participants, and questioning my husband may be the way in. That is, if Tripp were part of the operation. A small glimmer of hope was in my soul. But I needed to know. When I finally got the courage to ask Kayleigh, I immediately regretted it.

"Does the FBI think Tripp is involved in human trafficking? Do they think he was part of my abduction? Or," I laughed a little, "is this just a misunderstanding on my part?"

She looked down; her eyes were tired and sad. Fatigue was apparent on her face and in her posture. She had not slept well in many nights, and the stress of her job was leaving fine lines of aging across her face like a tiny roadmap. I felt bad for asking her, and I knew the answer before her eyes met mine.

"At this point," she said carefully, "we aren't really sure who is involved and who is not."

A nagging burn deep in the pit of my stomach reminded me that the FBI had its own secrets. Even though she was my friend, she was still an agent, and I needed to remember that.

I was numb as I drove home that night. Daylight saving time had ended, and by seven thirty, it was black outside. I hated when the time changed, but fall was still one of my favorite times of the year. I loved the crisp feeling in the air and the beautiful colors of the leaves changing. What would I look forward to this year? The holidays would be here soon, and what would they be like? Sadness was weighing me down, and I felt like I could barely hold up my shoulders and my head long enough to get myself home. I just wanted to cry and forget this was happening.

I had thought this nightmare was over. I was moving on. Kayleigh wanted me to carry on with life as normal. She reminded me of my acting skills while in the hospital and wanted me to do this again. I was to act happy, recovered, and as if Tripp and I were happily married. This meant at work, at home, and in the bedroom.

The thought of him touching me made me nauseous. If he wanted to kill me, to sell me, how was I supposed to fake that love for him? She had clearly overestimated me and my strength. I truly felt like this would break me.

Chapter 18

Days became weeks, and the passage of time seemed to muffle the suspicions and doubts that loomed in my mind. Tripp seemed excited for the season, and he was attentive and loving. He even tried to be romantic at times. For the most part, life went back to normal. I went to work. I kept a routine. I could almost pretend the worst year of my life had been nothing more than a bad dream. On good days, I could laugh and actually mean it.

My coworkers, back on the job now that the FBI agents had gone, seemed content to forget the whole thing too. They craved normalcy as much as I did. We sat together and talked about our crazy patients, gossiping about who on the staff was having an affair and who was difficult to work with, and sharing in the strain when things were hectic. It was the normal hospital routine, and I loved it. I was thirsty for friendships, long talks, laughter, and a satisfying hard day at work. People take for granted a slow-paced life, repetitive days, and the boring nights of just sitting at home.

Then, when I least expected it, the dreams would come. The ones that would seem so real I would awaken in utter terror, sweating and shaking and swearing I could smell roses and feel satin sheets on my back. Those nights ended with a hot bath and soothing music. But they seemed to get further apart, which was great.

Sara had a gorgeous pregnant figure. She looked like she stepped off the cover of a maternity magazine. She had the kind of glow that made other pregnant ladies green with envy. You know, typical women like I was, waddling around with swollen ankles, gaining too much weight, and ending up with melasma or really bad gas. Sara was "Instagram" pregnant. Anyone standing behind her could not even tell she was expecting, and it almost appeared she had a ball hidden under her shirt, she was so perfectly round.

Kayleigh kept in touch when she traveled for work, and when she was in town, we spent as much time together as we could. As far as I knew, Tripp was still under investigation, and at first, I tried to look and play the FBI agent myself. I went through his phone, looked in his truck, but never found anything. Not that I knew what I was looking for.

Over time, I felt like I had made a huge mistake in thinking he was involved in the human trafficking ring anyway. I pushed the past and my suspicions in the back of my mind. I refused to let this paranoia consume me and ruin my life.

The holidays came and seemed more special this year. Aubrey was home, and a light sheet of snow covered everything on Christmas Eve. My heart was full of joy and love for my family. The Christmas Eve service at church was wonderful. I loved the smell of the fresh evergreen trees, the glow of the lights, and the singing of familiar hymns. Kayleigh and I had given Sara a holiday-themed baby shower at my house, and the only time we thought of the past was at that gathering. We remembered the agents and friends Kayleigh had lost. We remembered the women who were gone too soon. But we were so thankful that we were here, celebrating a new little baby.

"Hey," Kayleigh said when the other women had left and we were cleaning up after the shower. "I have something I want to tell you."

"I'm all ears!" I dried my hands on a dish towel and started gathering leftover finger sandwiches into plastic containers.

"I'm seeing someone." Her cheeks were red, and she wore a shy smile I had never seen on her before.

"Kayleigh! That's wonderful!" I crossed the room and hugged her. "I am so happy for you! Who's the lucky guy? Do I know him?"

"Actually, you do," she said, turning her back and plunging her hands into the soapy dishwater. "It's Javier Ricardo. Javy."

My mouth dropped open. "Dr. Ricardo? You're dating Dr. Ricardo?" I started to laugh, remembering that I had had a monster crush on Javy when I first started working at the hospital. "He's a catch!" I teased.

"Here's the thing," she said, keeping her back to me. "He thinks I'm a nurse. Well, I am a nurse, but he doesn't know..."

"That you're an FBI agent."

"Right." Now she turned around, her hands dripping soapy water onto her shoes and the floor. "We got to know each other while I was investigating who on the staff might have been involved with Dr. Pierce. We didn't find any evidence that Javy was in any way part of the trafficking, and...," she laughed a little, "he just seems like such a decent guy."

"He is," I agreed.

"Anyway," she said, her face growing stern again, "I'm still undercover at the regional hospital in Winston-Salem, so you have to promise not to let it slip to him that I'm an agent."

I locked my lips with an invisible key, and she smiled and turned back to the dishes. She seemed relieved to have shared her news with me and began chatting about how much she and Dr. Ricardo had in common and how much they enjoyed each other's company. I felt a great peace knowing that she, too, had moved on and found some happiness.

I was pushed further and further into my land of forgetting, and the gift Tripp gave me for Christmas made this happen even faster. On Christmas morning, he surprised me with a box that was beautifully wrapped in metallic green paper. A large red bow was elaborately tied on the top. I knew he had not wrapped this and was intrigued by what could be inside. When I opened the box, I found a white envelope. Inside the envelope was a brochure and tickets to an all-inclusive, five-star resort in the Dominican Republic. The sight made me scream in delight, and I threw my arms around his neck. I had always wanted to go to the Dominican Republic, and he had made a dream come true for us. My heart raced with anticipation as I thumbed through the brochure with pictures of lush, green foliage, gorgeous pools, and fancy restaurants.

"When do we leave?" I picked up one of the tickets and read the information. "January first?" I looked at his grinning face. "But I have to—"

"No worries," he said, holding his palms toward me. "I have already conferred with your supervisor at work, and she agrees that a vacation is just what you need."

I couldn't believe it. He had planned this wonderful getaway for us and had even arranged for me to have the time off work. New Year's Day couldn't come fast enough.

The rest of the holiday was filled with family gatherings, nieces and nephews, gifts, laughter, and an overall wonderful Christmas.

That night, when Aubrey had gone back to her apartment, I gathered some of my new lotions and bubble bath and took a long bath in candlelight. I was so happy. The past seemed like a foggy memory that had faded long decades ago. I wanted to be happy and safe, and I finally was. The future seemed so bright. I could not dwell in the past. I had to move on and take my life back. This is what I was doing, and I was proud of myself.

I lay in the jacuzzi with the soft candlelight dancing around me and the scent of lavender filling the air. *A Pentatonix Christmas* played on the speakers, and at that moment, I was in my own little paradise.

I thought about Kayleigh's news that she had started dating Dr. Ricardo. She seemed relaxed and happy. This was the first time I had seen this side of her. Her relationship with Javier Ricardo gave me even more to look forward to. Tripp and I had been invited to a large New Year's Eve party at Dr. Ricardo's house.

He lived in a beautiful area in Lake Norman that was well known for its elaborate homes and lakefront properties. Mainly physicians and attorneys lived here. Tripp really did not want to go, but I finally persuaded him to go for a little while. With the promise of some good vodka and excellent food, he was more accepting of the idea. Our flight to the resort in the Dominican Republic was not until noon the next day from Charlotte, so we would have plenty of time to finish packing.

I must admit I was nervous and a little scared about going to this party. I had been to work but no social events. Dr. Ricardo was well-liked and popular within the community, so I knew there would be many physicians whom I had not seen since the events that had rocked our small North Carolina town. Hospital management and nurses who were lucky enough to be in Dr. Ricardo's social circle would be attending. I wanted to look amazing and prove to everyone, especially myself, that I was a strong woman who had survived.

Aubrey loaned me a short, off-the-shoulder, Sherri Hill dress with black and red jewels adorning the entire bodice. I had been able to keep off the weight I had lost during my recovery, and to help stay in shape and control any hint of panic attacks, I had continued to exercise daily. My sweet daughter fixed my hair in an elegant updo, and the gorgeous diamond earrings Tripp had given me on our last anniversary sparkled and danced when the lights hit them.

I looked at myself in the mirror and was pleased. I looked darn good for a woman my age. Tripp looked sexy as well, and when he saw me, he just stared. Pride and desire danced in his eyes, and my inner core warmed at his expression.

He crossed the room and put his arms around me, pressing his lips to my ear.

"You know," he said, his hands smoothing up and down the sides of my dress, "We could forget this party and...," he kissed my neck, "have a little party of our own...," his fingers began to undo the zipper on the back of my dress, "right here."

I laughed and twisted around to face him. "It is very tempting," I said, and he pulled me closer. "But look at me! Do you really want to deprive the rest of the world of this vision?"

I broke away and twirled once so he could see me from all angles.

Tripp shook his head and smiled. "I guess not." He brushed the back of his hand across my cheek. "But we are leaving the party early."

We laughed and sang all the way to the party. My anxiety about the gathering had long since subsided, and I was excited.

We arrived about thirty minutes late due to horrible holiday traffic, so everyone was aware when we made our entrance. I suspected the people attending were also anxious about seeing me for the first time because the looks of surprise and relief washed over many faces. There were hugs and introductions and champagne. Despite not liking parties, Tripp had always been a social person, never meeting a stranger, so he went on his way networking and talking football with other men.

After accepting hugs and numerous compliments on how I looked, I saw Kayleigh. My eyes had to adjust to the dim lighting, but she was simply breathtaking. I had only seen her in a nursing uniform or casual attire, but tonight was different. Her long hair was down but in large, soft curls that framed her face. Her olive-colored skin seemed to glow in the light. She wore a long gold gown that was clinging to her perfect figure. I rushed over to her and pulled her to me.

"You look wonderful," I whispered in her ear. She blushed and returned multiple compliments.

"So, where is the gracious host this evening?" I peered into the enormous living room to find Dr. Ricardo and thank him for the invitation. A beautiful stone fireplace was surrounded by modern Christmas décor. Glass ornaments of rose and seafoam green covered the tree, not the traditional green and red. Large matching bows seemed to be in every corner. A fire was glowing, flickering off the decorations on the Christmas tree. The home was absolutely breathtaking.

When Kayleigh spotted Dr. Ricardo amid the crowd, he raised his hand in a wave, and his face became soft and relaxed. Kayleigh stepped up to him and casually slipped her hand into his, and he kissed her cheek.

Javier noticed me then, and he reached out his hand. "Layla, my dear girl! You look absolutely lovely!"

I was shocked at how he and Kayleigh interacted with one another. I had not seen them out in a social setting, but they seemed like a true couple. His hand rested on the curve of her lower back. He would, often kiss her affectionately, and his eyes never stopped surveying the exquisite gold package standing next to him. Kayleigh had confided to me that they had not been intimate yet, but if they made it through tonight without that changing, I would be shocked.

The night was wonderful with laughter, silly party games, and too much drinking. Stories were told of crazy patients and hospital in-jokes. Tripp seemed to have a great time and made fast friends with most of the men. Being so close to Charlotte, football was the topic of their conversation. The Panthers were going to the playoffs and were favored to go to the Super Bowl.

"Hey, you and Layla should come to our Super Bowl party," one of the men said a little too loudly, slurring the words "Super Bowl" into "Sewer Bowl."

"Oh, you should," someone else chimed in. "It's always a blast."

Tripp was nodding a little uncertainly. "Sure, yeah. Okay. Sounds fun."

"It's always a blast," the second man repeated. "And the Panthers are going all the way, baby!"

I took this opportunity to excuse myself to visit the ladies' room. As I walked down the long hallways, I took my time and appreciated the beauty of the home. The smell of pine trees and Christmas still filled the air. Music played overhead from speakers hidden in the walls. I could hear laughter coming from everywhere within the house.

I got to the end of a hall and realized I was at the library. I love books, so I decided to be nosy and explore. One wall was dedicated to medicine and what appeared to be Dr. Ricardo's books from med school. The next wall was a collection of volumes about wildlife, and then classic novels and even some first editions on the upper shelves. Elaborate furnishings filled the room with the finest leather chairs and sofas. Multiple glass cases around the room strategically displayed precious artifacts encased inside.

I knew the doctor was an avid sports fan and was not surprised to see a small glass display with a baseball in it. I could not help but smile. I went closer to see what was so special about the ball. It looked like a normal baseball to me: white with red stitching and the word Rawlings printed on it. It was signed, but I could not read to whom the signature belonged. There was a gold plaque in the case that read "Mark McGwire's Seventieth Home Run Baseball." Once again, the man's decision to place a single baseball in a glass case to protect it from dust and damage made me giggle.

The artwork in the room was astounding. I am poorly educated in fine art but am familiar with some of the more famous paintings and current artists. The one piece I really admired I recognized as *The Madonna and Child Being Crowned by Two Angels* by Alesso Gozzoli. I was aware this most likely was a print because the original is hanging in a museum somewhere in Italy. The walls were lined with what had to be prints of great masters. I admit, his taste in art was impeccable. I was somewhat shocked as I knew the salary of hospitalist physicians, and this seemed like quite an expensive collection.

When I saw that the library had a small restroom, I decided to take advantage of my situation. I went in and closed the door, and I was touching up my lipstick when I heard someone enter the library. Embarrassed that I had been snooping around, I decided to be quiet and wait until they left before exiting the bathroom.

It only took a moment to realize it was my host and Kayleigh. They were sneaking away from their duties of entertaining and having a sweet kiss. The moment was romantic and touching. I remembered how tender and loving Tripp had been earlier that afternoon, and a warm feeling rose within me. I prayed that this upcoming year would be full of love and new beginnings.

After the ball drop, the traditional kiss, and New Year toast, Tripp and I decided to head out to get a few hours' sleep before our travel the next day. It was over an hour drive back to our house, and it started in comfortable silence. We both had enjoyed our night, and the kiss we had shared at the stroke of midnight had been long and full of the passion I had resolved to rekindle in our marriage.

As I reached over to hold Tripp's hand in the dark car, I felt flushed. It wasn't an odd thing for us to hold hands. We still did when we were in the car or walking somewhere together. But tonight, it was different. The touch of his hand sent a surge of heat throughout me.

Any doubts I had ever had about Tripp were in the far reaches of my mind. The night had been so amazing, and tomorrow, our trip would start our New Year off in paradise.

Chapter 19

The next morning was busy with last-minute packing and arrangements that are routine when going out of the country. We were both excited, and the thought of my past and the suspicion of Tripp never crossed my mind. This fact alone was a small miracle. Since my first suspicions had been aroused, I typically had not gone an hour without wondering what my husband was doing and if he was planning to kill me. But the holidays had given me a new perspective. Doubtful that he had anything at all to do with the horrid events, I was determined to live my life and be happy.

The flight was perfect. We were both fatigued from the previous night's events, but the sexual tension was already building. The excitement of a tropical paradise and a much-needed vacation was exhilarating. Just after we landed and were proceeding into the red tape at the airport, I took out my phone and changed it from airplane mode. I immediately saw that I had multiple missed calls from Kayleigh. I couldn't help feeling a little irritated. I had been looking forward to this romantic vacation without interruption from the real world. Kayleigh could wait. I tucked my phone into my purse.

Once Tripp and I were finally through security and our passports were stamped, I walked over to the restroom to call her back while Tripp awaited our luggage.

Kayleigh's voice when she answered sent an instant chill down my spine.

"Where are you? What are you doing?" her tone was sharp and stern. She had never spoken to me in this way. "Why did I not know about this trip?" she demanded. "I am so upset right now!"

"Kayleigh what in the world is wrong?" I couldn't figure out why she was so offended that I hadn't told her about our last-minute vacation. "I must have forgotten to tell you. Tripp got us tickets to a resort for Christmas, and with the holidays I must have forgotten to mention it. I mean, we both have been busy." I started to feel defensive, and my words came fast. "I am not sure why you are behaving this way. It's not like we don't go weeks without talking when you are out on assignment."

"Layla," she interrupted, "listen to me."

"We just landed in the Dominican Republic. We are staying at an all-inclusive resort. It's going to be so much fun." I tried to keep my voice from shaking. I wanted her to be excited for me.

"I need to hear from you every day, Layla. I mean it. I don't want just a text. I want a snap or a call so I can see you or hear your voice."

"Why?" I demanded.

"This is not negotiable. Twice a day I need to hear from you."

I sighed, confused and angry. "Fine. A snap or call twice a day. I promise. But you are scaring me," I said. "What is wrong? I am with Tripp, so why would you need to see or hear me? Please explain, Kayleigh."

But she was done talking. The conversation ended abruptly, and I hung up puzzled at the conversation that had just taken place.

My heart was racing by the end of our conversation. She must suspect Tripp of something. But why? They had found nothing to link him to the auction, and I had moved past this. I knew I could not go on living in fear. As I stood in the hot, humid airport, watching excited tourists with floral pattern shirts and obnoxiously large floppy hats, I felt deflated. Why would she bring this up and stir up the suspicion like this?

I had agreed to her demands to Snapchat or call twice a day, but now I was regretting it. My heart was overflowing with love for Tripp, and I refused to believe he was the bad guy or to let my irritation with Kayleigh infect my feelings for him. We would have a glorious vacation and put this nightmare of a year far behind us. I stepped into the bathroom, splashed some water on my face, and went to find my husband.

Outside the airport awaited the limousine Tripp had arranged. Even the ride to paradise was simply luxurious! We sipped expensive champagne, laughed, and kissed like teenagers on prom night. The resort was simply breathtaking, with elaborate décor and beautiful artwork along the walls throughout the courtyard and vestibule. Lovely boutiques lined the corridors so visitors could admire the products while walking in the courtyard and to the suites. Quickly, the conversation with Kayleigh left my mind, and I had the thrill of a new adventure running through my veins.

Entering our suite just accelerated my excitement. The room was something out of a movie. The enormous mahogany doors opened into a lavish foyer. The butler placed our luggage in the large walk-in closets and led us into the main room. The beautiful canopy bed was a Victorian-style piece that was surrounded by the same type of furniture. The bathroom had a double shower into which I could have fit our entire bathroom from home. Out on the balcony, which was at least one thousand square feet, there was another cabana bed and an outside hot tub. The view of the Caribbean Sea simply took my breath away. Aqua, blue, and green all mixed with the sunlight shining off the waves. It looked so beautiful that it appeared artificial, resembling a painting.

After Tripp tipped the butler, we just stood there and stared at the beauty. I was so thankful to be here, to be alive, and, yes, to be with Tripp.

It only took a few moments and a few soft kisses on the neck before Tripp took me in his arms and gently lay me on the outdoor cabana bed. We laughed and joked and peered out at the gorgeous scene in front of us.

The vacation was exactly what we had needed to rekindle our romance and put the past behind us. We enjoyed wonderful dancing and gourmet meals. Wearing dresses and heels instead of lab coats and sneakers made me feel young and sexy again. We lay on the beach in the white sands during the day, and our nights were full of shows, cocktails, laughter, and lovemaking. Only occasionally a leak of suspicion or doubt drip into my thoughts. As soon as it did, I commanded it away. For this week I wanted to forget what had happened and remember the past we once had.

Chapter 20

It wasn't until the fourth afternoon of our trip that things took a turn. I had called Kayleigh daily, just as she had insisted, and still, she sounded very odd. She seemed suspicious of why Tripp had planned this vacation. I was getting quite upset with her. I refused to let her suspicions bring me down, but there was an incident that made me question my own instincts.

There was a weekly adults-only "foam party" at the pool. The waiters and butlers would spray white clouds of foam all over very intoxicated adults. The pools and the grounds were perfect; then there was a pool filled with adults of all ages jumping around and screaming. Most of them were drunk and acting like teenagers as the foam covered them.

I had had nothing to drink, but I had to admit, it was so much fun. So silly, messy, but still fun, making us feel young again, different from the life we had to lead outside of this paradise, like a temporary reprieve from reality. I looked around in wonder at the different people. Some old, some young, various sizes and ethnicities. I laughed to myself as I saw a group of typical rednecks, very country men, hug and fist-bump with other men who looked to be wealthy businessmen. They laughed, joked, and acted like best friends. I knew that if they had met on a city street, either one would have ignored the other. They were from totally different lifestyles and economic statuses, but today, here at this moment, covered in foam with their senses dulled by alcohol, everyone was a brother.

As I stood and laughed, observed, and got covered in the white, fluffy clouds of foam, the loud music roared all around me. I noticed a beautiful couple coming to join in. It was one of those couples that people notice because they seem so perfect. He was dark-haired and looked to be of Arab descent. He wore a small, manicured beard and mustache that accented his sharp jawline. Since he was wearing only his swim trunks, I could see his sculpted shoulders and arms and a six-pack of abdominal muscles that let everyone know he worked hard on his flawless physique. Beside him was an exquisite, dark-haired lady. She wore a very small bikini that made me jealous of her youth and beauty. She was adorned with large, gold earrings, gold diamond bracelets, and a diamond ring piercing just above her navel. The diamond on her left hand looked to be at least a four-karat if not more. He was all smiles as he led her down the narrow path in front of the cabana beds, weaving in and out of the palm trees. The crowd peered up at them. I think everyone noticed their arrival. I wondered if they came in late just to make the entrance. If this was their plan, it worked. All eyes were on them. The women screamed and cheered like at a strip club, and the men let out some type of low, growling cheer. Quite primitive, really, but the man loved it. He waved and did a fist pump in the air.

I wondered if I was the only one to notice that his partner never looked up. Her eyes were cast down the whole time, I thought initially to try to keep her balance and maneuver without falling into the pool. But it seemed like when he finally chose a cabana bed for them, she remained melancholy. He was joking and laughing with every other man he passed, still pulling her along like a child. Not a single smile crossed her perfect face. Her full, pouty lips, painted a pale pink that perfectly matched her designer swimsuit, never moved in the slightest.

He let go of her hand, quickly threw his towel down onto the cabana bed, and plunged into the pool. Men and women were naturally drawn to him, just like in the real world, I assumed. But she just sat on the end of the chair. She carefully placed her bag on the table and sat there with perfect posture, not even offering to get involved in the action taking place. He never spoke to her, never addressed her, and he was quickly engulfed in the sea of foam and never looked back at her.

I was so intrigued by her. Not just her beauty, but the oddity of the situation. I was aware that some cultures treated women differently, and I was only assuming he was of Arab descent at first. After hearing him speak, I was positive.

I glanced around to see where Tripp had disappeared to and discovered he was having a blast playing a game at the other end of the pool with the good ole country boys from Texas.

I decided I'd had enough of hot, sweaty, drunk bodies bumping up against me. Most of them smelled of body odor and booze mixed with the sweet aroma of the foam. I was ready to move away from it.

I got out of the pool, walked over to the cabana bed we had placed our bag on, and decided to bake my winter-white skin in the sun. The bed I was stretched out upon was perpendicular to the mystery lady's bed, and my eyes were drawn to her. I knew I shouldn't stare, but I just couldn't help myself. Her perfect olive skin seemed to glow in the sunlight. She eventually decided to lie back and recline on the cabana bed, I assumed to soak up some sun. I felt like a weirdo staring at her, so I decided to read my book. This was a good thought but short-lived because the blaring music made it hard to focus, and I found myself reading the same sentence over and over. Feeling like I was going to self-combust in the midday heat, I wrapped my sarong around my waist and went to the bar. As I strolled by the bed, I could not help but look down at the beautiful young lady.

Immediately, I felt my heart stop, but my pulse pounded in my head louder than the music playing around me. Despite sweating, a cold feeling ran throughout my veins, and nausea quickly followed. For a moment, I wondered if I were having a heat stroke. Was I just too hot? Then I remembered this feeling—it was a panic attack. It had been so long since I'd had one that I had forgotten how horrible it was.

My brain took longer to catch up to my body, it seemed, because it was a few moments before I could register why this one had started from nowhere. I had completely frozen, like a sick, voyeuristic woman just staring down at the mystery lady. I could not move. I was screaming in my head to move and stop looking like a freak, but I could not. Since I was blocking her sunlight, she eventually opened her eyes and sat up. She slowly pulled off her sunglasses and made eye contact with me. We stared at each other. She looked at me at first with irritation, but as she evaluated me with her eyes, surveying me up and down, her expression changed. Her eyes rested on my abdomen, right above my sarong, and her expression changed from hardness to fear and pity. Then I knew. I saw her incision on her right upper abdomen, and I knew what had caused my body to once again betray me without warning.

Chapter 21

Women have an uncanny way of communicating without saying a word. Sometimes it's a nod, a look, or a gesture, and in this situation, all it took was the movement of her eyes toward the pool. I knew quickly to act like I had dropped something, pick it up, and move away. As I turned from her, trying not to look suspicious, my heart was racing so fast I feared I would pass out. The feeling that the men in the pool were all staring at us, that they had noticed me, was making the panic worsen with each stride toward the bar.

When I arrived and found a stool, I tried to nonchalantly look over my shoulder at the activity in the pool. Of course, no one cared about what I was doing. The foam was pouring out, the booze continued to flow, and drunk bodies jumped and screamed in the pool. All eyes were not on me, and I sighed in relief as I tried to see where the mystery lady had gotten to. I knew she had also gotten up but was not behind me when I made it to the bar.

I asked for the Orange Delight, the resort's signature drink, which was like an orange dream popsicle with tequila in it. As I waited for the bartender to finish blending the tropical concoction, another butler approached me and handed me a small note, tightly folded. He discreetly placed it in my hand and quickly disappeared. I knew not to open it right there, so I acted like it never happened. Quickly surveying my surroundings, it seemed that no one was even paying attention to me. When my Orange Delight arrived, I took a long, hard drink and slowly made my way back to our cabana bed. I tried to locate Tripp among the writhing bodies in the pool, but really everyone by this point was covered in foam, and I could not tell my husband from the other twenty-five or so men acting like drunken maniacs.

Finally, the lady arrived back at her bed, never even letting her eyes drift toward me. She kept her eyes down, adjusted her towel and sunglasses, and resumed her previous position. Briefly, her companion walked over to her and whispered something in her ear. His hand caressed at first her thigh and abdomen, but very quickly, in one fast motion, he grabbed her chin as he spoke, a tight smile on his face. He placed a forceful kiss on her full lips and walked away. The whole exchange was fast, and no one would have noticed that it was awkward, but I was watching, and I knew.

After a lengthy stay in the pool, my intoxicated spouse emerged from his sea of foam, laughing and singing off-key to the latest Justin Bieber hit playing too loudly from the speakers. This had become his favorite song, not only because it was number one on the charts right now but also because they played it constantly, so he knew all the words.

I hurriedly got him back to the penthouse suite, knowing he would be snoring as soon as his head hit the bed. An afternoon nap was common, and he would take a good two-hour siesta before dinner. When I had gotten him back to the room and he was snoring like a grizzly during hibernation, I ran my bubble bath. While he napped, my afternoon ritual was to have a bath and read. But today I would not be enjoying my typical suspense thriller. I would be reading the note the mystery lady had relayed to me.

I wanted to do nothing to draw suspicion to myself because the very ugly monster in my head was running crazy with thoughts of deception. How could it be a coincidence that we were at the same resort as another victim of human trafficking?

The large jacuzzi tub filled, and I poured in the bath salts in the resort provided. Soon, the room was filled with the aroma of tropical flowers. I could hear the rhythmic cadence of Tripp's snoring, but I still placed the note within the open pages of my book. I was not sure why I was so overly cautious. Tripp was clearly in an alcohol-induced sleep and would probably not regain consciousness within the next hour. But deep within me, I felt the horrible feeling of fear and mistrust that I had suppressed for so long, and I went into defense mode. With the warm water surrounding my sunburned body, I opened the note. Quickly, chills covered me as I read the tiny words in perfect penmanship.

I know you, and you know me. We are sisters in a very special family. I would love to meet you and talk. Discretion is imperative. I have a spa appointment at 2:00 p.m. tomorrow. Please join me. The spa is women only.

She was smart in not saying too much but saying just enough to let me know I was right, and we had been in the same situation. My mind raced. I needed to figure out if she had been with me or if she was from a different auction. I adjusted my bath pillow, lay back into the warm water, took slow, deep breaths, and tried to relax. The strong smell of the perfumed salts floated in the air, and I felt my tense muscles relax. The memories of those terrible events had been pushed deeply into my mind, and I hated to allow them back. But I needed to. I needed to remember those women, the faces. The problem was that I did not see a lot of the faces, only the bodies of some of the victims.

I pressed on, pushing my subconscious to the limit. I went back to the time in the auction, the smell of the roses and feel of the sheets, sounds of soft music filling the air. I tried to recall each face, but I did not remember seeing the lady I had seen at the pool. She had such distinct features, and from my memory, I did not recall her at all.

More time must have past than it seemed because I was snapped out of my trance by Tripp touching my arm. My loud scream made him jump, and he looked quite shocked by my state of anxiety.

"Are you all right?" he asked. He reached to pick up my book where it had fallen on the floor.

"What? Oh, yes," I said, forcing a laugh. "I'm fine." I rose quickly from the tub and wrapped a large, thick towel around me. "What time is it?"

"Almost four," he said. "Are you sure you're all right? You look really shaky."

I took the book from him, trying to sound nonchalant. "Too many suspense novels, I guess. I'm finished now, so you can go ahead and get your shower." I clutched the book tightly to my chest and left the bathroom. I felt sure he had not seen the little piece of paper tucked inside.

While he showered, I sat on the edge of the bed trying to gather my thoughts. I wasn't sure if I should just go meet her or if I should talk to Kayleigh first. I knew how she would react. She would immediately start again with accusations that Tripp was involved again in my abduction. I wasn't sure if he was or was not, but I did not want to jump to that assumption yet. I was not ready to fall back into that life of suspicion again. I thought that was over, that we had moved past it. Tears streamed down my cheeks, and I began to weep before I had even realized it.

My heart broke for the normal life I used to have, the simple life of going to work and coming home. The weekends of cleaning the house and lying by the pool. Aubrey in college and Tripp at work, cookouts and family gatherings. Nothing would ever be the same. These men had taken my life from me. But the lingering question was creeping back into my mind: Was my own husband involved in this?

I could not help but to think how odd it was that he had arranged this trip a thousand miles from home, and I saw a woman who had been at an auction like myself. It seemed too much of a coincidence to me. Maybe Kayleigh knew more about this than she had revealed. I had known something was not right since her call at the very beginning of our trip.

Trying to decide how to handle this was almost overwhelming. I wanted to crawl into a shell like a turtle and hide from this whole nightmare. I needed to get myself pulled together and get a plan. I dried myself off and chose an outfit to wear to dinner.

Tripp emerged from the shower and was dressing for dinner, so I slipped into the bathroom to retrieve my makeup bag and flushed the note down the toilet to made sure he would never see it just in case he was involved. As I dried my long hair and applied a light coat of makeup, I decided not to make Kayleigh aware yet of what was going on. At dinner, I started to formulate a plan of action.

The Italian restaurant was our choice that night. It was a beautiful restaurant, decorated with lavish couches and paintings covering the walls. A huge mural surrounded the entire back wall where we were seated.

Tripp looked handsome in his tuxedo, and I felt a tug of sadness and despair, not knowing if he was secretly involved. But I had to pull out the actress in me once again and behave like nothing was wrong. We laughed and flirted and discussed the wonderful time we were having on this trip.

"I can already feel the tension leaving me," I lied to my husband. "In fact, do you mind if I book myself some spa time? It has amazing reviews, and you know how I love a good massage!"

"Of course, baby! Go have fun," he said. "As a matter of fact, I wanted to hit the casino anyway and try my luck at Texas Hold'em."

"Oh, no!" I jokingly said. "There goes our retirement!"

He laughed and said, "I'll try not to lose too much cash!" He seemed excited for the opportunity.

The rest of the night ended like all the others, sitting on the balcony, drinking a glass of wine. I was able to fake some stomach issues and excused myself early.

My night was not a restful one. I had dreams of tight boxes and being buried alive. My mind traveled back in my sleep to the dark, tight spaces in the hospital, and the fear I had suppressed for months came back that night. Like a dark enemy, the terror crept its way into my dreams and in my mind. When I woke up, the sweat was beaded all over my sunburned skin, and the Egyptian sheets were damp. I did not feel refreshed like I had the previous mornings. My insides felt nervous and jumpy.

Restful nights were a luxury of my past, I would soon come to realize.

Chapter 22

The spa was located at the sister resort next door, and it was three stories of pampering fit for a queen. The weather was gorgeous, and the walk along the perfectly manicured paths made me feel better and less on edge. After the horrible night, I needed to relax and calm down. I had spent the morning out on the beach sipping a variety of mixed drinks, and that took the edge off, but this was what I needed. A great massage and getting some answers would put my mind at ease.

The waiting area was full of women, all excited and ready for their various treatments. This was a five-star spa and offered multiple services and packages. I did not see the mystery lady immediately, but as I signed in at the desk, I could see into the hot springs room. This was a huge, heated indoor pool that was made to look like an outdoor paradise of hot springs. Large rocks lined the walls with a beautiful waterfall in the middle. The resort claimed the water had minerals and Dead Sea salt to rejuvenate and replenish the skin. The flowers and tropical plants grew in every open space possible, and I could not help but be utterly shocked by this breathtaking beauty.

Women were lying in various areas of the rocked oasis, some in swimsuits, many naked. This spa was strictly for female use only, so clothing was optional. Then I saw her—just as I signed my name on my credit card receipt, my eye was drawn to a far corner. The light was dim in this area, and I knew why she had chosen it. If I had not really been looking, I would not have noticed the area at all.

Upon seeing her, I did not act any differently and reviewed my spa schedule. I had an hour in the hot springs before the massage, then sauna time. Going to the dressing room, I found the locker assigned to me and changed my clothes. Being naked was not in my comfort zone, so, putting on my bathing suit and robe, I headed toward the secluded area where I had seen the woman. I walked slowly, sipping the expensive champagne an attendant had handed me at check-in. I pretended to admire the flowers and acted like I had no reason or urgency to talk to the woman I was headed toward.

As I walked toward her, I had once again admired her beauty. She was simply astounding, with flawless skin and hair. The steam from the springs had caused some small droplets of condensation to gather on her upper lip.

Finally arriving by her side, I sat, not speaking a word. After a few moments had passed, she spoke in a low, throaty voice. “I am glad you decided to join me.” I didn’t respond verbally but with a subtle nod, so she continued. “We have much to discuss, and I know time is of the essence, for we cannot communicate outside of the safety of this spa, and even here, I am hesitant.”

I noted an undertone of anxiety in her voice. She was clearly very nervous to be here with me.

Not knowing exactly where to start, I introduced myself. "My name is Layla Matthews. I am from the United States, and I live in North Carolina."

Her eyes remained fixed ahead, looking out into the oasis full of women. The picture resembled a classical artist's depiction of women bathing at a medieval volcano in ancient times. I could not help but be amused.

She nodded at my introduction. "My name is Somaya Ahseed. *Now.*"

The way she said it instantly let me know that this was not her given name. She did not have the same Arabic accent her spouse had. Hers was definitely American, and I could detect a northern undertone.

"I've lived in Dubai for the past two years." She kept her voice low and even, and I could tell she had put a lot of thought into what she needed to say during our short amount of time together.

"Before living in Dubai, I was from Philadelphia. I am twenty-four years old. At the age of twenty-two, I had graduated from Temple University with a degree in broadcast journalism. I'm not sure how it had happened, but one day I awoke and found myself in the United Arab Emirates. I had become the property of a wealthy man who lived there." Her voice caught, and her dark eyes flitted to every corner of the room before she continued. "For the first few months, I was kept captive and isolated from everyone else, and he told me over and over that I was his property now and could never leave." She chuckled joylessly. "I was once a strong-willed, independent young woman, starting my career in journalism, so the task of brainwashing me was not easy for him. But I finally realized that I would not ever be able to leave, so I resigned to my new life, a new identity, and knowing that I would never be free, I began to play the part." Somaya allowed a sidelong glance to where I sat stunned, trying not to let my face betray that I was listening to a horrific story of abduction and slavery.

Somaya shifted in her seat and casually arranged the hem of her robe to cover her legs. "My new husband and his staff monitored me constantly. This," she gestured to the beauty around them, "is ironically the first trip we have taken where his staff has not been with me and the first time I have been truly alone in the past two years."

At one point, she paused cautiously when the waitress approached and inquired if we needed more refreshments. Somaya smiled sweetly and shook her head.

"No, thank you," I answered, handing over my empty glass.

Acting very casual, Somaya gracefully changed the conversation to the latest fashion trends and never lost her tempo. If the waitress had been sent to check up on her, she would never suspect a thing. Sensing the woman's nervous tension, I stretched as to appear bored with the conversation and stood up. I stepped off the small rock perch we had been sitting on and dipped down into the water. The hot, salty water felt amazing, and the tension that had slowly crept into my back and neck released. Waiting for a few moments, making sure no one was watching us, Somaya lay down, rolled over to face me and continued on with her story.

"I was scared at first and had no way of knowing what had happened to me. I had no access to the internet or phones, so I could not contact anyone at all. Eventually, my husband showed me my obituary from a newspaper back home in Philadelphia, and he informed that everyone I had known in the US thought I was dead, and if I ever tried to contact them, they would all die."

I shuddered even in the warm water, and I marveled at how casually Somaya told her story. "I knew my captor was a dangerous and powerful man, and I knew he would keep his promise. I had no other option but to become the submissive wife and slave he desired."

The woman leaned back and closed her eyes.

I said, "Do you remember anything about your abduction? Did you see or hear anything?"

Without opening her eyes, Somaya said, "I have no idea what has happened to me, Layla, or why I ended up there, but I do know that the scars on my body were not there before. Until I saw you and saw the same scars on your body, I thought I was the only one." She smiled a little, a sad smile. "When I saw those scars, I wanted to grab you, scream, and run, but over the past two years, I had learned how to control any emotions I felt. I am not allowed to speak without being spoken to. My opinion does not matter. I am to keep my appearance flawless and be available to fulfill his every desire at all times. If I do not submit to these demands, I am punished."

"Punished?" I asked, my heart pounding. "Punished how?"

Somaya shrugged as if it were nothing. "Never scarred but beaten, starved for days, and—" She shook her head a little. "You don't want to know." She looked at me, daring to hold eye contact. "I was hoping you could provide answers to what had happened to me and how I had been declared dead when I knew I had not died."

I sighed. Knowing that my massage time was quickly approaching, I knew I could not even touch the surface of what had happened to her. I did not know how she'd gotten to the auction, but she obviously had been purchased at an event much like the one I was taken to.

I could see her chest rapidly rise and fall as the clock ran down on our time together. Knowing that typical spas are on a very tight schedule, we would both be done in exactly ninety minutes.

"We're almost out of time here," I said. "Meet me in the sauna, and we can talk some more."

She nodded to me, and I got out of the warm, soothing liquid just as an attendant called my name. I was practically in a fog as I went up the marble staircase to the rooms designated for massages. Unable to really enjoy the experience, I used this time to get my thoughts together. I knew the time I would have in the sauna would be short, and I would not be able to tell her all the details. I knew she had rehearsed the information relayed to me, giving me important pieces about who she was. I needed to do the same for her in what little time I had. When my massage was finished and I was dressing, I grabbed my cell and quickly messaged Kayleigh. I knew I needed to update her ASAP.

Need to talk as soon as possible! Urgent but don't panic. I am fine, but something has happened. Text me the best time to call!

Hurrying to the sauna, I looked for my new acquaintance. This was not the typical small box with steam. It was a huge room with bamboo benches lining the walls. A large pit of hot lava rocks filled the room with a steady fog of steam. Glistening bodies lay on the benches, and in here, no one was dressed. So, I thought, *What the heck?* and disrobed.

Somewhat self-consciously, I tried to adjust my eyes and find Somaya. Hearing her clear her throat, I was able to locate her and swiftly went to her side. I lay the opposite way on the bench, and we were essentially face-to-face. The steam was so thick we did not have to act like we weren't talking, and the room was loud with the constant sound of sizzling steam and the low hum of music.

Quickly, I told my story, that there was a group of physicians and businessmen who had made a sick franchise of selling women, some for organs and others into sexual slavery, a "body auction." I explained how I had been given the medication to paralyze me, and due to a malfunction, I was able to escape. She listened and never changed her expression. She was lying perfectly motionless on the bench, her long, black hair billowed to the side, and her eyes remained closed the entire time I spoke. My words were quick and deliberate.

"The FBI has always felt that this was a much larger operation. The investigation is ongoing, but it has been almost impossible to track down the victims because they are all presumed to be dead."

She shook her head, a barely perceptible movement. Knowing this would most likely be the last time we could talk, I wanted Somaya's real name. Planning to give Kayleigh the information, I wanted to find out all I could in what little time we had left.

"Somaya," I said, "who are you? Really? What was your name...before...?"

That was the first time I saw a small tear escape the side of her eye. Her mouth quivered with emotion that was smoldering underneath, being held tightly inside of her. Like a quiet volcano, her core must have felt like lava waiting to escape its shell. I could not imagine how she felt hearing the things I had just relayed to her. It literally took me months to be able to deal with what happened, and I had just let it flow from my mouth like it was a casual happening. Not rushing her, I waited for her to respond.

She repeatedly swallowed like you do when trying to hold in a sob, then finally, in a small, meek voice, she said, "My name was Rhonda Asad." She swallowed again. "I think he chose me because of my Arab heritage. He has mentioned that he would never marry a woman who was not Muslim. I was born in America, but my mother and father are both Egyptian. He could not find a suitable wife, so he has told me many times I was 'handpicked by ALLAH' to be his wife." Her brow furrowed as painful thoughts came to her mind, thoughts she had pushed down for too long. "He knows many details about my family, and I think he had researched me."

My mind raced, wondering about how she'd been chosen for the auction, but there was no time for details at this moment. She rapidly fired off the names of her father and mother and was getting into more details when a tall, slender woman came up to us. Startled by her appearance out of the fog, she spoke to Rhonda in a somewhat condescending tone.

"Mrs. Ahseed, I am sorry to interrupt you, but your sauna time is complete and your husband requests for you to meet him out front shortly."

I immediately felt a hot rage well up inside me, and I sat up and started to object when Somaya softly touched my hand and shook her head. Her dark eyes met mine, and even though she didn't say a word, her expression spoke volumes to me.

Grateful for the steam and the sweat that was constantly running down my face, I knew the messenger would not notice the tears that had begun to pour from my eyes. Pain surged through me. How could I let her leave? I had to help her. I had to save her! I had been saved, and I had left those other women behind to be taken. So many times, I had blamed myself and wondered what had become of them, and now I knew somewhere they were just like Rhonda, scared and not knowing what had happened to them.

Watching her walk away, I was shocked by her poise. She stood, tall and proud, and seemed to literally remove the sorrow from moments ago, like taking off a cloak. With all the elegance of any of the wealthy women surrounding us, she sauntered out of the sauna, never looking back.

As I looked down in awe, I saw something glimmer like a light breaking through the fog. A small diamond earring was lying in the place where her head had just been. I jumped up just as the door shut but stopped her in time.

"Excuse me," I called after her. "I think this is your earring." I approached her and placed the jewelry in her hand, holding her hand just a moment longer.

"Oh thank you, ma'am!" she said, her eyes moist. "It is one of my favorites."

She hugged me, and quickly I whispered in her ear, "I will find you. I promise. I will save you!"

Without a word or even a sign that I had spoken, she was gone.

Chapter 23

The plan for the next few days of our trip was to spend the time relaxing. I felt like my head was in the clouds most of the time. Everywhere we went, I looked nonstop for Rhonda. I wanted to see her so badly. I knew I could not talk to her, but just seeing her would give me some semblance of comfort. But this did not happen. I never saw her again after leaving the sauna.

I had called Kayleigh that night after dinner when Tripp had gone to get a drink at the bar. Knowing I had plenty of time because the football game was on, I was able to give her details of the encounter.

"I have met a woman who was sold at an auction!" I practically yelled into the phone.

"Wait a minute, *what*?"

"Yes, at the pool I noticed a lady who has the same type scars I have. We met up and talked, and she told me who she was and what has been happening since her old life ended. She is being held by a crazy man who purchased her! It is so sad. Kayleigh, we have to try to help her."

She listened intently, and I could tell she was taking mental notes like she always did.

"Okay," she finally said, "give me her name that she goes by now and her birth name. I will try to find out who she was and who she is now. But this is going to get hard since this reaches out of the United

States." Reassuring me, Kayleigh said she would start investigating ASAP. When we hung up, I called Aubrey. I relayed to her the same information I had shared with Kayleigh, but one part I added.

"I haven't told Dad yet," I impressed on her. "He is having a great time, and I do not want to ruin his trip."

"But Mom, this is important. He needs to know."

"I agree. But let me tell him when I know the time is right. Please, Aubrey. Don't say anything to him about this. Not just yet."

Reluctantly, she agreed not to say anything, and relief flooded me.

I was so proud of my daughter. Who would have ever thought she would be training to be an FBI agent? Both she and Kayleigh had agreed to start a full probe into Rhonda's story, and I felt somewhat better about the situation.

The next thing on my mind was getting home. It was amazing that, a few short days ago, this horrible event had been far behind me. Now rearing its ugly head, I was staring it in the face once again. Not knowing who to trust and being on guard all the time made me miserable and exhausted, and I was relieved when the day finally came to head back to North Carolina.

The flight and ride home were uneventful, but Tripp sensed my distance. With a look of concern, he asked, "Did you have a good time? You seem sad." He squeezed my hand. "I hope you did. I had a great time!"

"Oh yes, baby! It was amazing. I am just so tired, and I am sad to leave." My smile, I hoped, did not look as fake as it felt.

We arrived home late in the evening, and Aubrey was there waiting. I was anxious to see what, if anything, she had heard about Rhonda. It got late as we told her about our trip and showed her a few pictures, and she decided to spend the night. I had very little in the house to eat, but we put some things together.

I found some frozen steaks and Aubrey and I cooked side by side, laughing and talking more about the trip over the sizzling of the meat in the skillet. In the back of my mind, I wondered if I could ever tell her of my suspicions about her dad. It felt like it was right in the back of my throat, but I could not get it out. She looked so sweet and innocent, a grown woman, but she was still my little girl. I knew my suspicions, if true, would make her hate either me or him. I could not risk breaking her heart without proof that my doubts about her dad were right. Probably due to severe fatigue, I felt a tear fall and quickly had to wipe it away.

We had a nice late dinner. I had taken the next day off, as I typically did after a vacation, to recover, but Tripp had to work in the morning, so we decided to turn in right after we cleaned up the dishes.

Aubrey bounced into the living room where Tripp sat in the recliner looking over the mail that had accumulated during our absence.

"Good night, Daddy," she said, and he looked up at her with tired eyes.

"Goodnight, baby."

"I love you and am so glad you guys are home safe," she said, reaching down to hug Tripp. He returned the tight hug, and she squealed and giggled when he pulled her onto the recliner with him. Laughing and joking, they looked adorable. *I could never tell her*, I thought. *How could I ever hurt her*?

Hoping to catch up more with Aubrey in the morning, I finally was able to sleep more peacefully with her in the house. Being able to sleep in my own bed and shower in my own bathroom left me feeling refreshed and renewed the next morning. I was tackling the laundry and unpacking, starting my second cup of coffee, when the doorbell rang. Taking one gulp, I sat the cup on the kitchen counter and went to the door, careful to peek out the window before opening it.

Kayleigh was a sight for sore eyes, as the saying goes. Her hug, filled with emotions, startled me, and out of nowhere, I started to tear up a little. It drove me crazy how my emotions had a tendency to give me no warning anymore. One moment I was fine, and then the next, waterfalls. We just stood there, embraced tightly, and I had no intention of letting go until I heard Aubrey walk into the foyer. Embarrassed by my show of emotion, I let Kayleigh out of the death grip.

"Hey, Aubrey!"

Aubrey greeted Kayleigh with a loving embrace.

"How are classes going?" Kayleigh said, quickly trying to cover the emotional moment.

"Great! I am so happy and loving every minute!"

We all went into the kitchen and started opening the bag of bagels Kayleigh had brought with her.

"So," I said, tentatively getting to the point. "Any new information about Rhonda?"

Kayleigh gratefully accepted the cup of coffee I handed her and nodded. "Rhonda lived in Philadelphia and was a student at Temple. Her father was a well-known physician who had come to the US from Egypt to finish his medical training when he was in his early twenties." She spread a generous slather of cream cheese on her bagel and licked it from her fingers. "This was when he had met Rhonda's mother, also Egyptian but born in the US. Rhonda had a younger brother who was still in college at Temple."

"They did this to a physician's family?" I gasped. "Are you serious?" I was unthinkable to me that a doctor would betray one of his own.

"Yes, it's insane, isn't it?" Kayleigh said, chewing and swallowing a mouthful of bagel. She picked up a paper napkin and wiped the corners of her lips. "We have no idea yet about the details of her being in the auction. This is just the preliminary information."

"Well, I think you guys have done an amazing job in such a short time," I said. "At least we have a start."

"There are some glaring similarities," Kayleigh said, reaching into her oversized purse for a file folder. "Rhonda was just listed as deceased, and the details of her supposed death were more difficult to find out."

She handed the folder to me. In it were copies of articles from online newspapers and pictures of Rhonda, and seeing them made my stomach churn with anger. She'd been a promising student in the journalism program, had an internship at CBS, and was ultimately working for CNN when she died. The articles talked about how energetic and talented she was, with multiple references to her young life cut too short by tragedy.

"We need to know all the details of her death," Kayleigh said, "where and how this had happened. Your meeting Rhonda has sparked a fire under the FBI. We knew this was a much larger crime ring, but not being able to get any leads for months had made the investigation somewhat stale."

"Good job, Mom," Aubrey said with a wide grin.

"This is very exciting," agreed Kayleigh.

I did not feel excited for the same reason. Don't get me wrong—I wanted everyone on earth who was involved in this to be put in jail, but I only wanted to rescue Rhonda. I needed her to be safe. I was sitting there in my cozy kitchen and eating a bagel with my daughter and friend. I could come and go as I pleased, but she was being held captive. Focusing on anything else was impossible for me at this point.

"So, here's the thing," Kayleigh said, her glance flickering to my daughter. "Aubrey and I are going to Philadelphia to meet with Rhonda's brother to get some details about her death."

I looked at Aubrey. "You too?" Aubrey was not finished with her FBI training yet, and she nodded excitedly. With the help of Kayleigh, my daughter was getting a lot of "on the job" experience.

Now I felt a surge of excitement. "I'm going too."

Aubrey winced a little, and Kayleigh shook her head firmly.

"You need to go back to work tomorrow, be normal, and let us do the investigation." Kayleigh was leaving no options open. After all, the last time I was allowed to assist I, once again, almost died, and I was not ready to take that kind of risk again. I could not put myself or my family through that. Knowing I needed to work the next day, I did not put up a big fight, but I knew I would be distracted the whole day wondering what was going on.

"Well," Aubrey said, gathering her plate and empty coffee cup, "I'm hitting the shower. I have a lot to get ready before our trip."

Finally alone in the kitchen with Kayleigh, I immediately wanted to know what else she knew; it was clear she was hiding something because she had not yet mentioned anything about Tripp. And I still wanted to know why she acted so bizarrely when I was away.

"Okay," I said, "tell me what else you know because I can tell you are about to self-combust!"

"Well," she said, dropping her eyes, her cheeks pinking up, "after the New Year's party, I ended up spending the night at Javier's." I wanted to beg her for details, to giggle and whisper with her about it like two schoolgirls. But her expression was serious and stern as she talked, so I let the detail pass and just listened.

"The next morning when he ran out to get breakfast, I was bored so I went down to the library to find something to read. Looking on the shelves, I came across a photo album. Out of curiosity, I flipped through it. The album was full of pictures of fishing trips and groups of men in various locations. Some hunting boar on a huge plantation in what looked like Georgia, others on a yacht trophy fishing."

"Okay," I said. "What does this have to do with you calling me on vacation and acting so crazy?" I glanced over her shoulder toward the stairway. "You need to speed up too. Aubrey is fast in the shower."

"I am getting to that, hold on." She also looked toward the stairs and then leaned in closer and dropped her voice. "In one of the sections, there were pictures of a group of men at a resort, a five-star resort in the Dominican Republic."

She paused, staring at me strangely, probably because my face had gone white.

"The place in the picture was gorgeous," Kayleigh said. "Of course, I stood there and imagined going on a trip there with Javy someday. So, when Javy returned, I asked him about the resort. He told me the name and explained that it had been a group of physicians he had worked with and a few drug reps."

"What is the big deal about that?" I asked, feeling impatient and disappointed that she had no smoking gun. "None of this is surprising," I explained. "Drug companies used to pay for trips and host physicians all the time and, in some cases, their entire families.

The laws have changed now, and this is no longer allowed, but sometimes drug reps will still play favors."

"Yes," she said tolerantly, "but I recognized a few of the men in the picture from working at the hospital. Later that morning, I spoke to Aubrey. This is how I learned of the vacation Tripp had surprised you with. When I heard the location and the name of the resort, I got suspicious, thinking that was an odd coincidence. So I went back to the library, took the photo album out, and hid it in my car. After I left Javy's, I went to headquarters to really study the pictures."

"What did you find?" My voice sounded flat in my own ears, and I wasn't sure I wanted to hear her answer.

"I was able to look at all the pictures and start a log of the men, their names, the different locations, and dates. Discovering that the resort Tripp had taken you to was the exact one in the photo just did not sit well with me at all. What made things worse was the men in the photo. One of them looked familiar to me. Remember, at the initial auction, some of the men did not return for the sale, so we hadn't been able to arrest them. We caught up with most of the buyers due to the logs and financial information we recovered at the scene, but not all of the physicians were found. You know how I can remember a face," she said with a bit of pride.

"Yes." I forced a smile.

"Well, I remembered a dark-haired man. He had been one of the men we had seen in the OR that night helping with the testing they were doing on Sara."

When she told me this, I felt dizzy remembering that night, huddled in that dark space watching them do those horrible things to my friend. I closed my eyes while Kayleigh spoke and forced myself back to that night. I looked at the faces in my memory one by one, and I did recall one man who was in that OR, but I did not remember seeing him again. There had been so many faces and so much drowsiness from medications, I had not even given that another thought.

"Layla?"

Kayleigh was asking me a question, and I shook my head to focus on what she was saying. "What?"

"I asked if you have any idea how Tripp picked that resort? Did he say if he booked it himself or used a travel agent?"

I tried to remember what he had said on Christmas morning, the eagerness in his face as he presented the gift he knew would thrill me. "I have no idea," I said, feeling the weariness return. "He always takes care of our vacation arrangements. I assumed he googled it and did research. I mean, it was a gift. I did not ask questions."

Kayleigh was not deterred. She gathered the papers about Rhonda from the counter and slid them into the file folder. "I had to research this guy from a nationwide physician's database. It was hard without a name, but I finally was able to find a photo of him with a surgical mask on, and I remembered he had a very distinctive scar above his right eye. This is most likely why I remember him so well. So even with the mask on, I could positively ID him."

A scar above his right eye. Of course Kayleigh had noticed that. "Did you bring a picture of him?" I asked.

"No, sorry," she said. "But we know he is an orthopedic surgeon from Miami. He had gotten into some trouble with the medical board for doing excessive and unnecessary surgical procedures. He also had been accused of sexual misconduct with a few patients." Her eyebrows went up and she tipped her head derisively. "No shock there. Ultimately, the board suspended his license to practice. It is still inactive, and his location is currently unknown."

I was trying to piece things together and decide how Tripp could have possibly picked the same resort these men had been to.

"How can we find out if this is a coincidence?" I asked, my words coming quickly. "What can I do to help?"

"Just slow down, I found out..."

Suddenly Aubrey was standing in the kitchen doorway. "Found out what?" she said, her eyes as eager as a young FBI agent's should be. "Slow down doing what, Mom?" Aubrey wasted no time asking about what she had just overheard.

I stood awkwardly with my mouth open, but Kayleigh quickly recovered. "I was just updating your mom about our trip, and you know how she is, she wants every single detail."

Aubrey had no trouble believing it since they were planning on leaving in the late afternoon for Philadelphia.

"Yes, honey." I played along. "You know how I worry about you!"

Later that afternoon, as I hugged my sweet, beautiful daughter goodbye, an eerie feeling came over me, like something bad was about to happen. I did not want to let her go. I had the same feeling as I said goodbye to Kayleigh.

A quite whisper from Kayleigh, "Try to look at his computer about the resort."

I watched as they pulled away from the curb in Kayleigh's car, watched until they turned the corner out of sight. Why did I feel like this was a last goodbye? I shook this off. I mean, they were just going to talk to Rhonda's brother—how dangerous was that?

So, I made myself busy washing clothes and trying to put my crazy suspicions out of my mind. I also had the assignment from Kayleigh to look through Tripp's computer and search his browser history to try to find some clues.

As the day went on and I finished the work around the house, I finally sat down to look at Tripp's laptop. This was an office day for him, so he wasn't traveling and had left his computer behind. His password was easy. It had always been my first name and the year we were married.

I started at his search history, and, just as I thought, he had googled multiple resorts. Then I went into his emails and scrolled back to around October, when I assumed he'd booked the trip. What was odd was that he had multiple emails to and from Dr. Ricardo. I didn't even know they knew each other that well, let alone communicated with each other. I went back as far as I could until I found when their correspondence started. It was right after I had come home from my last admission to the hospital.

To: Tripp Matthews

From: Dr. Javier Ricardo, MD

Subject: Layla

Hey Tripp, just checking on our girl, how are things going? Does she need meds, pain or anxiety? Please let me know what I can do. You know how to reach me anytime.

Javier

He had emailed Tripp to see how I was doing, and they had communicated sporadically throughout the months. Nothing worrisome or suspicious. In fact, I found it heartwarming. Then I found what I was looking for.

To: Dr. Javier Ricardo, MD

From: Tripp Matthews

Subject: Vacay ideas

I hope you are well. Thank you for all you have done for Layla and myself over the past months. I am thinking about a surprise trip for a Christmas gift for Layla. I think a tropical paradise is the best medication at this point for us both. Any destinations or resorts you can recommend would be appreciated.

Warmest regards,

Tripp

Of course, this was the resort Dr. Ricardo suggested. *That's innocent enough*, I thought. He had been there, and it was probably a coincidence that they had been there on a drug rep trip with one of the psychos. Dr. Ricardo would have had no idea what was going on, I reasoned, and his trip had been a few years ago anyway. Finding this made me feel much better because I could reassure Kayleigh that Tripp was not involved and that there was nothing sinister about our vacation. But in the back of my mind, I knew it was too much of a coincidence that Rhonda was there also. So, in my typical way of dealing, I shoved it in the back of my mind and prepared dinner.

The afternoon was normal. Tripp got home from work. We had dinner and watched TV. I could tell the distance between Tripp and me that had disappeared during our vacation was already back. There was no kiss when he entered the house, no "How was your day." Just eyes looking down at the mail, scrolling on his phone during dinner, and body language that spoke volumes. The fact is, I knew all too well it was my fault. I just could not face him. I could not shake the feeling that he was involved or shrug off the evidence as coincidence. So I went to bed with my mind wandering once again.

Chapter 24

I had missed so much work and had not been as productive as I had in the past, but I was glad to be back into a normal routine. The office decided to hire a physician's assistant named Krissy. She was much younger than I was, blond and perky. She talked nonstop about her upcoming wedding.

"I am just so excited! A new job, getting married! I can hardly wait, but I am stressed, ya know?" She seemed to talk to herself incessantly.

I barely responded as my mind was on other things. Since I had been there so long and had the experience, the administration expected me to train her. Typically, this would have been fine, but I was so distracted with not knowing how Kayleigh and Aubrey were doing that I could barely stand to talk to her. She was engaged to be married and was just starting her new, young career and life. I was envious of her—I couldn't help it. I wanted to start my life over. Take out all the ugly pieces that had made the once-beautiful puzzle of my life so sad and messed up. I needed to focus and teach her the hospital's routine for making rounds and charting the patients. Graduating from PA school with honors had made Krissy the top choice for the position, but nothing is like experience, and there's so much they don't even teach in college.

Walking into the hospital during flu season always made me nervous. It was packed with sick patients of all ages. Most of my patients were elderly, but during this season, age didn't matter. Influenza does not discriminate and is a killer of all ages. This year, the season had been particularly bad with the flu shot being less than 10 percent effective. Deaths were reported every morning on the news, and I never knew what I might encounter during my day in the CCU.

I decided to take the wide-eyed, new PA to the basement level first. This is where the critical care unit held the sickest patients, some already on life support, some getting ready to be placed on ventilators, and others on the way to death.

"Basement," I told her as we stepped into the elevator.

Her long, pale fingers shook when she pushed the elevator button. I smiled to myself, reminiscing about when I'd felt that way. I tried so hard to shake the heavy feeling I was having and remain positive and enthusiastic to teach her. I didn't want to ruin this experience for her, but in the back of my mind was my daughter and friend out on a mission to get intel on one of the evilest things one could imagine. Of course, as a mom, this weighed heavily upon me. A dark, heavy cloud loomed above me even though I was sure Aubrey's was a perfectly safe assignment.

The large metal doors opened, and then the smell of fresh feces greeted us like a foul, tropical breeze. When there is a fresh bed of diarrhea close by, there is no mistaking or masking the smell. This odor is often mixed with the aroma of death. A human body is meant to be upright and mobile, but when someone is terminally ill and lying in bed, often dependent on machines, the flesh starts to break down. I have seen a person's entire buttock literally rot off and fall into the bed.

The pink hue of Krissy's cheeks turned to a mix of green and white.

"There are a lot of people who are on the ventilator, life support machines," I explained. "They just lie here, day after day, practically rotting. I think it is cruel."

"Then why do we do it?" Her voice now shaky and unsure.

"Well, people may not have a living will, and their families refuse to take them off life support. They may be brain-dead, and the family will not let go. I have never understood how they can see their loved one just lie in the bed, completely sustained by machines. I can honestly say I love my family way too much to do that because I know I will see them again in heaven." Her eyes were wide as she listened, nodding imperceptibly. "There is a lot we can do in medicine to keep a person alive," I said, pulling a pair of disposable gloves from a box on the counter at the nurses' station, "but sometimes you must love someone enough to let them go."

I could tell by the look on the face of the young novice that she was quite overwhelmed. I was not sure if it was because of me or the smell, to be honest.

"That is just my opinion," I added, handing her some gloves. "Just always be honest to the families, and some do make what I think is the right decision."

I spent the morning going over policies, reviewing procedures, and introducing Krissy to various physicians and nurses. She remained nervous throughout the day, but I knew her sweet personality and loving heart would make her amazing in this field. By the end of the day, I was feeling good about her, and I looked forward to helping mold her young career.

As I watched Krissy walking out of the building at the end of her shift, one of the older, more skeptical nurses pushed herself into my personal space.

"Well how'd she do? She looks green to me," the nurse asked without a shred of optimism in her tone.

"Actually, I think she's going to do great."

Her thick, ungroomed eyebrows raised in shock.

"Yeah," I confirmed. "She is smarter than most and willing to learn." I turned to face the nurse. "You ladies take it easy on her! I am looking forward to working with her." I smiled, but she knew I was also serious.

"Okay, Okay," she said, holding up her hands in surrender. "I will give the young thing a chance, whatever you say."

A smile crossed her lips as I walked away.

By the time I got home, Tripp had made my favorite chicken fajitas, and they tasted great as always. The dinner conversation was normal, and after casual talk of our day's activities, I quickly helped with the dishes and excused myself to the bedroom to make a phone call, anxious to get the update from Kayleigh and Aubrey.

Aubrey picked up immediately, barely giving the phone time to ring. "Hey, Mom!" Her voice sounded electric with excitement. "Kayleigh's here too. I'm gonna put you on speaker, okay?"

"Sure!" I pushed off my shoes and pulled my feet up onto the bed to get comfortable.

Without my having to prompt her, Aubrey launched into a retelling of the day's events.

"So, we got to Rhonda's brother's house this afternoon, and we got *so* much information. We approached him as if we were interns from a local newspaper who wanted to write an article on Rhonda. She had been a great student at Temple, graduated with honors, you know, and died before her amazing career started."

"He was very open with the idea," Kayleigh interjected. "He obviously loved...loves his sister a great deal and wants to keep her story alive."

"His name is Ahmed. He's also a medical student at Temple. He's tall with dark wavy hair and deep brown eyes—"

"Aubrey!" Kayleigh's voice cut her off. "Um, can we stay focused on the facts of the case?"

I felt embarrassed that Kayleigh had scolded her but a little giddy that my daughter might have a crush on this young man.

"Anyway," Kayleigh continued, "it all started when his mother became ill. When Ahmed was young, his father had moved away to North Carolina to practice medicine. His mother had essentially raised Ahmed and Rhonda. She had been their best friend, a tough disciplinarian who pushed them to excel in school. At the same time, according to Ahmed, she was loving and understanding. They both felt like she was their best friend as well as the best mother in the world. They were devastated to learn she had terminal cancer and did not survive more than two years after her diagnosis."

"That's tragic!" I said.

Aubrey picked up the story. "During their mother's last stay in the hospital, Rhonda stayed by her side almost non-stop. There was one night toward the end that Rhonda had been extremely fatigued—she had not eaten or slept in days and almost passed out. This was when she met a physician who became friends with her. He was worried about her and took a special interest in her. He made her promise that she would get a checkup and follow up with him after the arrangements were made and their mother had been laid to rest."

I could hardly breathe. "I can see where this is going."

"Right?" Kayleigh said. "Aubrey and I tried to stay calm, but we were already putting the pieces together. Ahmed said that Rhonda seemed depressed and declined physically very quickly. He tried to encourage her and get her to speak to a counselor, but nothing seemed to bring her out of the fog she was in. She had lab work and some testing, and their father came home and tried to help all he could. But their mother had been the love of his life, and he, too, was broken-hearted and provided little comfort for his daughter."

"What was wrong with her?" I asked.

Aubrey said, "It was not just depression, but she was diagnosed with a condition called Takotsubo cardiomyopathy or 'broken heart syndrome.' It's actually pretty common in women and can occur after they've had a severe physical or emotional stressor. Typically, the patients will improve over time, and she was given encouragement and some medications."

"So, what happened?"

"She did not improve," said Kayleigh. "Ahmed was on a trip with some college friends, when he got the call that she had gone into the ER after passing out again and ultimately went into cardiac arrest."

I gasped.

"Doctors told Ahmed that her weakened heart could not recover and that she died," Kayleigh said. "He, of course, was devastated and never had any reason to question things."

"He cried," Aubrey said softly.

"Oh!" I couldn't help feeling compassion for this boy, knowing what my own family had gone through.

"Yes," Aubrey said. "He is still quite torn up about losing her. And their father had completely lost his will to live after this. His wife had been the love of his life, and now, with his daughter's passing, it was too much. He stopped practicing medicine, moved to Florida, and is living as a recluse."

To think Ahmed was all alone and he had no idea the truth. His father, who was a renowned physician and had a reputation for being a brilliant man, had stopped doing what he loved. How many lives had been ruined by this horrible business of death? “This is infuriating,” I said.

“Right?” Aubrey said. “I wanted to vomit the truth right then and there, but I knew I had to hold back. I kept thinking about you, Mom. And Ahmed and I are about the same age, so I felt like we had a kind of connection—"

“So, at that point,” Kayleigh said quickly, “we didn’t want to torture the poor boy any longer, so we finished up our conversation. Tomorrow, we head over to Mother of Mercy Medical Center.”

“Let me guess,” I said. “That’s the hospital where Rhonda’s mother died.”

“And the one where Rhonda allegedly died,” Kayleigh said.

“Mom, this is so cool,” Aubrey said. “We get to go undercover as investigators from the Joint Commission on Accreditation of Healthcare Organizations so we can get access to their—!”

I heard Kayleigh hissing something at my daughter and realized that Aubrey, in her excitement, had probably said too much. But I couldn’t help but laugh to hear about the JCAHO cover, reminiscing about those days when JCAHO agents would arrive, sending the hospital into a frenzy. Undoubtedly, the hospital administration would be upset by the surprise visit.

“We’ll call you tomorrow and fill you in,” Kayleigh quickly added.

"Okay," I said reluctantly. I was excited to hear more details and help go through the records when they arrived back in town.

"Bye, Mom. Love you!" Aubrey's sweet voice called.

"Bye, baby!"

Knowing she was exhausted, I let her off the phone without drilling her for too much information. But the call had ended so abruptly, I was left sitting on the bed feeling somehow disappointed. Quickly, I shot a text to Aubrey.

I love you! I'm so proud of you!

I love you, too, Mama! she replied.

I sat on the bed feeling tired and worried. The house was not quite back in order from our trip, and for one minute I thought about pulling out the vacuum cleaner. It always takes so long to get life back on track after a vacation, and I feel off balance when the house is disorganized. But not tonight. It had been a long day. Figuring Tripp would not be coming up until after the ball game ended, I decided to get ready for bed.

While we were on vacation, Tripp had purchased my early Valentine's Day gift, and it sat wrapped in brown packing paper and bubble wrap on the floor of our bedroom. While I brushed my teeth, I made a mental note to have Tripp hang it this weekend. Kandinsky was one of my favorite artists, and I had always wanted an original, but of course, financially, that was impossible. This knock-off *Beach Baskets in Holland* from his Post-Impressionism era was gorgeous, and finding it was one of the highlights of our trip. The $750 Tripp had paid was mere pennies compared to what the original would have been, but I loved it and could not wait to admire it on my wall daily. I am not sure where my admiration of art had grown from, as I am from a family that had no interest in art and would have found it a waste of money to purchase a piece of artwork that was more than $39.99 at Big Lots.

I wrapped my body up in the soft down comforter and realized I was much more fatigued than I had thought. I would have to readjust to those rigorous days at the hospital. Drifting off to sleep, I let my mind wander back to our trip and the beautiful things we got to see. When we were leaving for the trip to paradise, all was well in my world, but quickly it had come crashing back down the moment I'd met Rhonda. I pushed that back out of my mind and tried to remember good things that had happened recently. Dr. Ricardo's New Year's Eve party that was so fabulous to bring in the new year, the wonderful dresses, drinks, laughter, and the funny but awkward moment when I was trapped in the bathroom of the doctor's library.

Then, suddenly, I sat straight up in the bed. I was shaking so hard the huge sleigh bed began to tremor as if a small earthquake had hit. My suspicion that my husband of twenty-one years played a part in this true-life horror show had just become much stronger. At that moment, I knew who and what was behind this horrible ordeal.

Chapter 25

I knew I had to talk to Kayleigh and barely slept the rest of that night. As soon as Tripp came to bed, I faked back pain and slept on the downstairs couch, as I could not sleep in the same bed with someone I felt I did not even know. I had finally pieced together the clues about who had a large part in this dark business, and there was nothing I could do about it at that moment. The signs had been right there in front of me the entire time, but why did it take me so long to put it together?

I needed to do my job at the hospital, but I also needed to talk to Kayleigh as soon as possible. Once again, I had to put on a fake smile and a white lab coat and go make rounds. That phony smile and cheerfulness had become as much a part of my work uniform as my stethoscope. The young PA was waiting for me with big, anxious eyes when I arrived at the hospital. She had already printed the list of the patients we needed to see and had started taking notes. She was motivated—I had to give her credit.

The morning was uneventful, and we, once again, started in the CCU in the basement. I saw Dr. Ricardo on the way down.

"Hey, how are you?" he said, touching my elbow familiarly, but without giving me a chance to answer, he went on, "How is Kayleigh? I haven't talked to her in a couple of days. Have you?"

His voice seemed to waver, and his conversation was rushed, almost nervous. I didn't know if it was him or me, but something was odd about the conversation. I decided it was my lack of sleep along with paranoia and continued on.

"I haven't talked to her lately," I lied. "But I know she's crazy busy right now."

Around one o'clock, I asked Krissy if she wanted to go to lunch in the doctor's lounge. Using this time to find out more about Krissy, I was hoping to take my mind off the other dark monsters that were lurking in my subconscious, the ones that were trying to get out and torture me.

We went through the cafeteria the line, choosing the lunch special of oily grilled fish and slimy steamed spinach, and found an empty table.

"So," I said, trying to start the conversation as naturally as possible, "where are you from?"

Instead of her face lighting up, triggering a gush of words, she said simply, "I was raised in Mooresville, North Carolina, but went to physician's assistant school in Philadelphia."

I could not help but get a chill up my spine when she informed me of this. Philadelphia? I tried to keep staring down at the pungent fish on my plate and not reveal any of the smoldering emotions inside of me.

"I loved my family," she continued, "and missed them so much, but I wanted to get out of the small town." I noticed she was also picking at her fish. “I wanted to see what it was like living in a big city. Does that make sense?”

Finally, I looked up at her. My eyes met her baby blues, and we just gazed at each other. The episode was long. At first, I don’t think I noticed her tears that were tiny, like minute diamonds slowly trickling down her cheeks. My mind was going in so many different directions. Why was she emotional? Was it that she was homesick, nervous about this new job, fighting with her fiancé? I had learned long ago that young women of this generation seemed to have thin skin and got emotional easier than past generations. But finally, I realized it was none of those things. There was something about the way she looked at me. The gaze was peering into my soul.

I watched her patiently during the long stretch of silence, not wanting to interject and say the wrong thing, and finally, after swallowing back tears, she seemed to want to explain. But her eyes flitted around at the doctors, nurses, and other staff members having lunch all around us. I knew this was not the place to discuss anything private. The doctor’s lounge was a constant revolving door of physicians in and out for the free food, and it was especially busy that day. I was often amazed that physicians who made close to a million dollars a year would eat the disgusting food that the cafeteria served daily for free.

“Hey,” I said before she could speak again. “You want to get out of here? There’s a great Thai restaurant up the block.”

Eagerly, she agreed, and I drove us to the restaurant. She seemed as if she was about to burst to tell me something but held it in. We were quiet on the drive there and waited until we had ordered to start the conversation. It was evident how nervous she was, and once again, she was shaking and having a difficult time hiding her severe anxiety.

"Krissy," I said, leaning toward her, "I know we don't know each other well, but I can tell something is bothering you. Please tell me."

She sighed, smiled sadly, and took a deep breath. "I had a best friend, Whitley. She was like a sister to me. I loved her more than anyone could love a sister. We grew up together. We attended middle school together. All through high school, we promised we would go off to college together, and we did. No two people knew each other better, and our bond was closer than most blood kin."

Between her words, she would take a drink of her tea, wipe a tear at times. I could tell this was very hard for her; each word seemed to take so much effort for her to get out. My heart was hurting for her, and she had barely gotten started on her story.

"We went to PA school together and shared an apartment." She pulled out her phone and started scrolling through her picture gallery. "We both landed our first real internships at a hospital in Philly."

The hairs on my arms started to stand up, and I had that familiar chill start to snake its way down my spine.

"See this picture?" Krissy turned her phone screen to me and showed me the picture she had pulled up. It was Krissy, slightly younger, standing next to another woman I assumed was Whitley. She was shorter than Krissy and had black hair cut in a short bob that stylishly framed her perfectly round face. I felt like her big, dark eyes were staring straight through me. She looked like a modern version of Snow White. She was cute, and her smile looked as if it would be one that would light up even the darkest mood.

Krissy turned the phone and looked at the picture. "We were so excited about the internships and could not wait to start our new careers. She was working on the cardiothoracic service and loved it. Every night, we would go home and discuss our days—talk about what we had learned and procedures we got to do." She placed her phone face down on the table and smiled her sad smile again. "Whitley was lonely for a romantic relationship though. School had been rigorous, and she had not had time to date, but now she wanted to make the time. She quickly fell for a young doctor and was swept off her feet, and the time we spent together got less and less." Swallowing back tears every few moments she continued.

"I tried to be happy for her, I really did. But I guess I was a little jealous. I missed her so much, and I was alone." Now Krissy sat back, folded her hands in her lap, and stared at them as she spoke. "Then one night," her voice was soft and trembling, "Whitley never came home. The last thing she had told me was that she was going out to dinner. No other details. She didn't say who or where or how long. It got later and later, and I called and texted without any response. This was not like her at all." Tears were falling freely down her cheeks now, and she self-consciously brushed them away. "Whitley never ignored me like that," she said. "I had assumed that she was with her new man, but then the next day came and went without a word from her. She would have never gone this long without checking in."

When the waitress came by and delivered the hot plates of pad thai, I noticed that my previously ravenous appetite had been replaced by nausea. I had the sick feeling I knew where Krissy's story was going.

"I kept calling and trying to reach her with no luck," Krissy said, and I could hear the despair in her voice. "I went to the hospital later for my scheduled shift in the afternoon, and that is when I heard the horrible news."

I felt myself growing cold, shivering, as Krissy took a ragged breath and said, "Whitley had become very ill while she was out to dinner with Dr. Garrett." She looked up at me. "That was the physician she had been seeing." Her eyes dropped again to her hands in her lap. "He took her to the ER."

I hated to interrupt her, but I had to know. "What was the name of the hospital where you worked?"

"Mother of Mercy Medical Center. Why? Are you familiar with it?"

I could feel my heart start to race but just shook my head no and asked her to continue.

She picked up a paper napkin and wiped her eyes and nose. "No one would really tell me much at all. I was forced to wait until her family had arrived to hear the details. Once she got to the ER, the doctors suspected Whitley had a severe case of cholecystitis, an infected gallbladder. They took her straight to the OR for emergency surgery, and she died intraoperatively."

At this point, I had no doubt that Krissy had sought me out to help her. I tried to stay composed. But my old companion of panic started creeping into the picture. From shivering with cold, I now felt the perspiration start on my forehead and run down my back. I picked up my glass of water, but the increasing tremors in my hand made the ice rattle against the side of the glass. Krissy noticed and paused to give me a moment to digest what she had said. She really could have stopped here because I already knew how this story ended.

My phone buzzed, and I saw that I had a text from Aubrey. Relief flooded me. I didn't want to be rude to Krissy, but I had been waiting to hear from my daughter all day. I opened the text and read:

On the plane home. Scared the hospital staff to death posing as JCAHO agents! Found some great info in hospital records. Took lots of pics. Same doc treated Rhonda and her mother. Tell you more later. Love you!

A second text from her popped up immediately.

Probably shouldn't have told you all that, haha. Still learning.

I turned my phone face down as Krissy had done, deciding to reply later and give Krissy my attention.

"Should I stop?" she asked as if reading my mind and feeling my panic.

"No," I said, taking another swallow of my cool water. "I need to hear the rest."

She nodded and continued. "I was devastated that my best friend had died so suddenly, but the worst part was the confusion I felt. Cholecystitis can start suddenly, but Whitley would have had plenty of time to contact me. And she would have called me—I am certain of that." She slapped her palm on the table to emphasize her point. "Finally, I got to meet face-to-face the physician Whitley had been dating, but questioning him did not go as I expected. He had a sarcastic answer for everything, but a huge red flag was his arrogance. I explicitly asked why Whitley had not called me, and he responded with, 'I was with her and was taking care of her. She didn't need to call you.'"

I shook my head in disbelief.

"This was when I knew something was fishy with the story," Krissy said. "But life went on. I was empty inside and just went through the motions of finishing school. I was lost without my 'sister' at my side. I had no idea what could have happened…" She looked up at me and met my gaze.

"Until you heard about me," I said finishing her thought.

"Until I heard about you, yes. It was like a fire started burning inside of me." She pressed her fists into her chest. "I read and pieced together what I could and noticed similarities. I researched it day and night and was able to find details that had not been on the news. This was when I concocted the plan to try to talk to you, but I knew just talking to you would not be enough—I needed to get close to you, to know you. That sounds extremely creepy, huh?" She winced, her shoulders rising in embarrassment.

"Yes, it does," I smiled reassuringly. "But I understand what you mean. So you actually applied to work at my hospital so you could, what, pick my brain?"

"I wanted to meet you, and when I was researching you, I saw the link for the job. It was actually easy getting the position, I guess since your hospital has a bad reputation now."

At one time, such a comment might have raised my hackles, but not anymore.

"I am not sure, but I was hired pretty quickly." She picked up her chop sticks and toyed with her food. "My original idea was to not bring the topic up until I knew you better, but I was about to burst on the inside to talk to you about my suspicions. I had tried to reason with Whitley's family about my concerns, but they would not hear of it and kept going back to the fact they had seen her body, seen her buried, and all that. They thought I was crazy, like my grief had pushed me over the edge of sanity. My only hope was..." she looked up at me, "you, Layla."

The FBI had kept many details out of the news when it came to my case. The fear of the public's reaction and the fact that there were likely more auctions in the area kept the story contained as much as possible. Of course the tabloids had the best angle and told the most truth, ironically. However, a woman declared dead and found alive can only be minimalized so much.

Krissy had gotten more information than I would have thought possible. The once-tearful blue eyes that were full of sadness had changed to fearless, bright orbs of determination. Once she heard my story, she was convinced that her friend had succumbed to a similar fate, and she would prove it and find her.

I soon realized I sat there with my mouth gaping open with a cold spring roll in my hand. I knew this was a far reach, but it was very possible this was true. The hospital was in Philly, and the physician's name sounded familiar to me. I was not sure where I had heard it, but I recognized it. Mentally, my brain was firing at 1,000 percent. Flashes of my coffin, of Sara, and of Rhonda played like an old silent movie in my mind.

I desperately wished I could tell Krissy that her friend's family was right. Whitley had suffered a surgical complication, and Krissy was delusional, holding on to a hope that wasn't there. But I could not. I didn't know this for sure and hated to admit that Whitley could have been another victim. Whitley was the perfect age, beautiful, and perfectly healthy. She would have brought a great price at an auction, and I knew this sick fact all too well.

Chapter 26

The fact that I didn't hear from Kayleigh or Aubrey that afternoon disturbed me. I knew their flight had landed, and at the very least, Aubrey would have texted me. On my drive home from work, I tried over and over to reach one of them but with no response. I could feel a strong sense of something having gone wrong. The connection between a mother and a daughter has been described as supernatural in some instances. My daughter and I were incredibly close, and I felt it—I knew it deep in my soul. Something was wrong. I had no proof, and I spoke aloud to myself in the car to calm down.

My mind was going in so many different directions. I knew that even before Kayleigh and Aubrey would make contact with the rest of the investigators on their team, they would contact me to let me know they were safe. But I did not hear a word from either of them. I wasn't sure if the uneasy feeling in the pit of my stomach was due to worry over them or the situation Krissy had just laid in my lap. I knew I had to help her find the truth about Whitley. She had to have closure, and I, of all people, knew what that feeling was like.

I tried to hold myself together to make it home and talk to Tripp. The gulf had continued to widen between us. We played house at times, eating and acting normal, but there was an awkwardness between us, and I am sure he felt it too. However, when it came to our daughter, I knew he loved no one on this earth more than Aubrey. I had no idea how I could tell him as little as possible about what had been going on and at the same time express my concern for our baby girl.

By the time I got home, it was getting dark outside, and no lights were on in the house. I was surprised that Tripp was not there yet. Though in his new position he was now setting his own hours, he typically arrived home at least an hour or two before me, especially if he was not travelling. As I walked the path to the front porch, my anxiety continued to climb as I hit redial over and over on my cell, trying to locate either of the women who had not been answering me.

When I finally unlocked the front door and stepped into the foyer, I could immediately tell that Tripp had not been there all day and, at first, assumed he had a meeting or something that was making him late. But that odd sixth sense of mine made me wonder why he was not home yet on this particular day.

As minutes turned to hours, I paced back and forth from the foyer to the kitchen. My phone was an extension of my hand, hitting redial over and over, alternating between Kayleigh and Aubrey's numbers. With each moment that passed, the anxiety became suffocating. I was scared out of my mind. I can handle a lot of things, but not something happening to Aubrey—not my daughter.

Finally, well after eight, Tripp arrived home, and my welcome was anything but warm.

"Where in the hell have you been?" My tone was between scolding and shrieking. Tears streamed down my face, but he calmly placed his brief case on the floor and took off his coat.

"What is wrong with you?" he said impatiently. "Why are you screaming at me? I had a meeting, and I told you I would be late. You obviously forgot, but that is not my fault!" His irritation equaled my dramatic greeting.

"I can't get in touch with Aubrey," I blurted.

Now he stopped and turned to look at me, waiting for me to explain.

"She's out of town on an assignment with Kayleigh." That's all I could say about it. I could not be totally honest because he didn't know about Rhonda or the reason for the trip Aubrey and Kayleigh had taken. "I can't reach either of them," I said, my voice shaky and hoarse. "I'm so worried. I know something has happened. I can feel it."

"Good grief, Layla!" He placed his coat on a hanger and closed the closet door. "She is a grown woman training in the FBI. She can handle herself." He brushed past me and headed toward the kitchen. "And take into consideration who she is with," he continued over his shoulder. "Kayleigh is a trained agent who is helping her. You worry too much, and this has to stop. You will drive yourself and me crazy if you don't. Our daughter has joined the FBI, so she will be in danger. You know that. She can't answer you all the time or hold your hand when you get worried. You are too controlling, and it's got to stop!"

The volume of his voice climbed as he scolded me, punctuated by his last word.

I fought to keep my voice calm. "Don't try to handle me, Tripp! She's my daughter, and she typically answers me. I'm sorry if I worry too much, but I can't help it! I was almost buried alive after all!" Fresh tears streamed down my hot face, and I suddenly couldn't look at him a minute longer. I turned and stormed up the stairs.

Trying to sleep that night was pretty much impossible. I paced the floor and continued to burn up their phones. Finally, at about three in the morning, knowing that Aubrey's flight from Philadelphia had landed over twenty-four hours before, I decided to call someone I knew could help.

I had not spoken to Agent Johnson in months, but his number was embedded in my mind. He answered on the first ring, and I knew by his tone of voice that he was already awake.

"Hey," I said, as soon as he answered. "I am sorry to bother you, but I am worried. I—"

"I know why you are calling, Layla," he interrupted. "We are already searching for them."

My blood ran cold. With those few words, Agent Johnson had confirmed my fears. Aubrey was missing.

"Agents are required to do standard check-ins," he explained, "and when they missed it, we became concerned. However, this can happen sometimes, especially when travelling, but then they missed the second check-in. Kayleigh, as a seasoned agent, would never do that. So, we are already working on the situation."

I had been hoping he would tell me I was being stupid, no reason to worry, that—like Tripp had said—I was too controlling. But the news was quite the opposite. My worst nightmare was coming true. My daughter was missing, along with my best friend. All of the horrible things I had survived during the past year were nothing compared to the utter terror I felt at that moment. I knew I could be a strong woman—a survivor—and I had proven that. But one thing I knew with 100 percent certainty was that I could not survive losing my daughter.

I froze in terror, the agent's voice in my head as I held the phone to my ear. I did not hear a lot of what he was saying. I was already imagining horrific things that might be happening, not even knowing where to start or what to do next.

Finally, I was able to pull my mind out of the fog. "What can I do?" I gasped. "Where can I meet you?"

"No, Layla." His voice was firm. "You need to stay home, and I will update you if anything changes."

"You know I can't stay home and do nothing! This is my daughter! Please, please let me help."

He sighed heavily into the phone. "If it will make you feel better, you can come to headquarters and wait here."

I hung up, got dressed, and only then decided to wake Tripp.

Shaking him, I urged, "Tripp, you need to wake up."

He shrugged me off and rolled onto his side.

"Baby, I have bad news."

His eyes opened, and he rubbed a hand over them.

"What is it?"

"I was right," I said. "Aubrey is missing. I just spoke to Agent Johnson, and they are trying to locate her and Kayleigh." I straightened and stepped back from the bed. "I am going to the headquarters. They are setting up downtown."

He flung the covers back and was up and out of bed just about as fast as I could finish my last sentence. He glared at me, "You didn't think this was something I needed to know? Why didn't you wake me up sooner!"

Indignation burned in my chest. "Oh, I don't know, Tripp. Maybe because you treated me like an idiot earlier?"

He recoiled, looking guilty, and stomped to the bathroom.

We rode in silence to the FBI's temporary headquarters. I knew there was so much Tripp did not know about the situation, and I wondered how to go about this without utterly destroying my marriage once and for all, especially if Tripp was innocent of all the things my irrational mind suspected he was involved in.

Kayleigh had kept Agent Johnson up to speed on my suspicions about my husband, and the agent quickly directed a cadet to show Tripp to a briefing room so Johnson and I could talk in private.

"Wait—what?" Tripp said, looking back and forth between me and Agent Johnson. "Why are you separating us? Why are you keeping me out of the loop?" The second question was directed at me, and I could tell my husband was furious. I'm sure he thought he was being taken away as some kind of punishment for the way he had brushed off my concerns the night before.

"Standard procedure, Mr. Matthews," Agent Johnson replied. He motioned with his head to the cadet, who placed a wide hand on Tripp's back and guided him firmly to a room across the hall.

"What do you know?" the agent asked me when Tripp was out of earshot.

"I spoke to them on the phone the other day, and they told me very little." I knew the women had shared with me more than they should have, but I had no idea what I could tell him without risking Aubrey and Kayleigh's jobs. "They told me a little about Rhonda's brother, how she died, and how he was doing. Aubrey said they got some information from the hospital, but they didn't share it with me. They seemed fine and were headed home the last time I spoke to them." I choked, wondering if it really would be the last time. "Oh, there's one other thing. I don't know if this will be helpful or not." And I told him all about my conversation with Krissy.

I couldn't read his face, but he pulled a small notebook from his breast pocket, made some notes, and abruptly turned. "Follow me."

Agent Johnson showed me to a room he called the viewing area before leaving me alone. A few minutes later, he and Tripp came in chatting like old friends, Johnson making lame excuses for having to separate us when we first arrived.

"It's standard procedure to get separate statements from all parties involved."

Tripp nodded his head but still looked agitated. He stood next to me but didn't say anything. I longed to reach for his hand, to put my head on his shoulder, or to feel his strong arms around me holding me together. Instead, we stood silently side by side, like strangers at a bus stop.

As we awaited the surveillance videos to come in from the hotel and the airport in Philadelphia, my anxiety levels were at an all-time high. We had no idea how long it would take to retrieve the videos as the agents had to get the local FBI involved for assistance.

I knew I needed to pull myself together, so I excused myself and went to the ladies' room. As I looked at myself in the mirror, I was shocked at what I saw.

The person looking back at me was not a person I recognized. The face before me was pale, stressed, and worn. The signs of stress and lack of sleep had really begun to make their mark. I had aged twenty years overnight. I had always taken pride in how I looked, and I never left the house without making sure my hair was fixed and makeup applied. I was never the kind of person who went out wearing jogging pants and a t-shirt.

Never being the most attractive woman, I often wondered over the last few months why they even picked me to auction. My appearance had not even crossed my mind in the past twenty-four hours, and I did not have the time or the energy to worry about it now. I washed my face, yanked my hair back into a ponytail, and pulled myself together.

Chapter 27

I knew something had happened when I walked out of the rest room and saw multiple FBI agents crowded around a small computer monitor. I could tell this was not a situation they were accustomed to. The scene reminded me of a piece of candy on the playground on a hot summer day with bees and ants swarming around it. The agents were tightly gathered, trying to nudge one another aside and see the tiny monitor. All were trying to get the proverbial lick of the candy. I, however, was the "Queen Bee," and I pushed my way through. That was my daughter, and I had to know what was going on. Tripp was standing at the back of the crowd, eyes set and face in a contorted mask of anger and concern, Agent Johnson beside him with a similar expression.

The first video we looked at was from the restaurant. My heart sank, and I had to steady myself against the table as I watched my beautiful daughter and my friend sitting at the table having dinner. I could tell they were tired. I could see the stress on Aubrey's face, but they laughed and chatted, sometimes with great animation, other times leaning in close to share something confidential. I had forgotten how long Aubrey's hair was. She had turned into such a beautiful young woman. I felt like I had not seen her in years. Tears welled up in my eyes, and I brushed them away before they could fall. How could I ever survive if something happened to her? But I wasn't watching this video to look at my daughter. We were watching to see what had happened. I shook myself back in focus and concentrated on the surroundings at the restaurant.

The agents also scanned the tables around the women, looking for someone alone, someone watching them. We could see from the angle of the security footage the people at the bar. I didn't notice anything out of the ordinary—just typical diners and others enjoying an evening out. There were a few couples with their heads close together, some men with their eyes on the game on the TV above the bar, and a woman sitting by herself.

Then an agent standing next to me pointed to a dark corner on the monitor. Toward the back, near the kitchen, there was a man. He was nursing a drink, pretending to look at a magazine, trying to be incognito. Every so often, his eyes would shift upward, clearly watching the two women. Chills went through my body.

The next video clip was from the Philadelphia International Airport, with footage from multiple views of the airport terminal. We watched for what seemed like an eternity as the two women went from security to the boarding area. I was exhausted, my lower back aching, and I felt like this was useless. I must have looked very fatigued because Agent Johnson pulled a folding chair over and offered it to me. I gladly accepted and glanced at Tripp, who didn't seem to notice my fatigue and anxiety. But right at that moment, several agents at once poked at the screen.

"There!" one said.

"Same guy," another muttered.

In the boarding line, the man from the restaurant was clearly following Aubrey and Kayleigh, and we could see him peering around the crowd to keep them in his view.

He has no bags.

"You're right," Agent Johnson said, and I realized I had said it aloud. I began to hyperventilate.

Quickly, the agents were barking orders.

"Get the manifest for that flight!"

"Who's the facial recognition guy— sorry—person? Get her in here now!"

"Roll that back. Let's get a look at his face!"

"Okay, guys," Agent Johnson said, unceremoniously taking Tripp and me by the elbows. "You need to go now and let us get to work." He escorted us to the door of the room and walked away quickly giving us no time to respond.

Then, for some reason, there was fog in the room. I could see it from the corners of my vision. My eyes were full, and I started to feel dizzy. I looked to my side and saw Tripp still scowling.

I pictured palm trees in a hurricane, each one so strong. Wind could blow more than a hundred miles per hour, but they will not break. They just bend and rebound each time the wind assaults them. The tall, straight trees are so pliable. They always amaze me, how they don't break from all of the stress of the relentless winds. I was like a palm tree. I had been beaten by the wind over and over this past year, almost to a breaking point, and I had rebounded each time.

But not today.

Seeing the man stalking my daughter, following her onto the plane, was the end for me. That was my little girl, and I had no idea how to help her. I could not withstand any more force on my body, so I finally broke.

As I hit the floor, I pictured the tall, strong, palm tree finally ripping apart and blowing away in the storm. Just like I was.

Chapter 28

I didn't remember much after that. I saw a flash of Tripp's face looking down at me, twisted and distraught. I heard someone saying I was dehydrated and needed fluids. A man's voice (was it Johnson?) suggested I was exhausted. My husband was by my side, comforting and consoling, touching my arm, trying to be there for me.

But as soon as I woke up and saw that I was on a gurney in the emergency room, my instincts kicked in, and all I could think about was getting Aubrey back.

"Hush, hush," Tripp said, gently pushing me back to my pillow. "Everything is going to be fine. Just rest. The agents have it all under control, and they are doing all they can to find out who that man was." He kissed my forehead, his own brow still tight with worry, his eyes rimmed red as if he, too, had been crying over our daughter.

Despite the tense words we had exchanged the day before, I felt so much love and compassion for Tripp in that moment, but it was quickly replaced by the feeling that he was involved somehow. But now was not the time to start a war between us. My suspicions had to wait for now. I closed my eyes and surrendered to sleep.

Another twelve hours had passed with no news from the investigation. With an IV in my arm, I was powerless. I knew that protocol said I could not get out of that bed, and the doctor on call was not going to let me leave. They ran tests, took blood, ruled out possible reasons for my syncope, and finally determined I was dehydrated and exhausted. I was furious with the diagnosis. Why was I so weak? Why had I let myself pass out? My daughter needed me!

I was feeling stronger, and the fluids had renewed my energy. When I was finally able to eat, I knew I could be discharged. Once again in this horrible nightmare, I needed to pick myself up, dust myself off, and find a way to fix this. It was my fault that my daughter had been brought into this, and I was going to make sure she survived.

Finally, after multiple bags of IV fluids, I was able to be released from the hospital. I received strict instructions to go home, *not* back to the FBI headquarters. Tripp helped me into the house and tried to take care of me, and I played along. Yes, it's true, I would have liked, for a moment, for someone to take care of me. I felt like all I had ever done was take care of other people. Let me assure you, this was only for a moment. I'll admit I was weak, but I was pulling my stuff together. I knew I had to.

I poured a glass of Diet Mountain Dew, submerged myself in a hot bubble bath, and lay back. There would be no way on God's green earth I could sit idly by and rely solely on the FBI investigation. I wasn't going to be one of those moms who sit there, cry, and wait to hear that my daughter was found dead. I looked comfortable and relaxed in the tub when Tripp came to check on me. But make no mistake, my mind was formulating a plan for how to find out who had Aubrey. I could not be the victim any longer. I had to be strong and find my girl.

Whoever had followed them had most likely started following them at the hospital. I had a suspicion that they had not reviewed footage far back enough to pick that up. Maybe they had missed a clue at the hospital. I wasn't sure, but the FBI suspected Aubrey and Kayleigh's disappearance was related to the fact that they were asking too many questions at Mother of Mercy Medical Center. Aubrey and Kayleigh must have found something they should not have. The trip had started at Ahmed's apartment, so I knew I needed to get there and talk to him. I needed to retrace their steps. How was I going to do this? Knowing Tripp probably would never let me leave, I decided I would have to be upfront with Agent Johnson. Heck, I had done it before, and it had worked out.

After I had soaked away the hellish events of the previous forty-eight hours, I got out of the tub, dried off, and put on fresh clothes and fresh makeup. Then I put on an "armor of courage," so to speak. Come hell or high water, I would find my daughter and my friend. And after all this was over, I would make sure the people who were responsible for this, who had tried to ruin my life, would pay. As I dried my hair, I had a realization: I had a job!

Like getting hit by a ton of bricks, I remembered I had a job. I didn't know how I still had a job, but I did. So once again, I called the hospital to let them know I would not be in. And then I remembered Krissy! I had completely forgotten that she had shared her secret with me. I had been so wrapped up in my current situation that I'd forgotten about hers.

While I pulled on my shoes, my mind went back to the story she had told me. Immediately, excitement started to surge through me. Krissy was from Philadelphia, and she had worked at Mother of Mercy Medical Center. If the mysterious man had followed Aubrey and Kayleigh from the hospital, Krissy may recognize him! I didn't know how I could do it, but Krissy had to help me find him.

Though the night had been a bit of a blur, I remembered I had already told Agent Johnson the story that Krissy had relayed to me, but his focus for the last few hours was to find the two missing agents. The FBI hates to involve civilians, but Krissy could possibly recognize the man following Aubrey and Kayleigh. It could mean a major break in the case and help find my daughter.

I dialed Agent Johnson's number. I pleaded my case with great conviction.

"Look," I said as soon as I sensed his resistance, "you need to think about this logically. Krissy worked there, at that hospital in Philadelphia. She knows a lot of the people there, and she could tell us who belongs and who does not."

"Layla, I wish you would just let us do our jobs."

"I am," I insisted, "but why don't you accept a little help? Especially if it gives you insight into who did this? Letting Krissy review the video could save you hours of precious time."

Of course, he was hesitant, but once I finally got him to agree, I called Krissy. She was on her way to the hospital to see patients, and I quickly explained the events that had transpired. She agreed to meet me right away, so I gave her the address of the small, makeshift FBI headquarters, and she promised to be there shortly. Finally! Finally, a breakthrough. If Krissy could recognize this man, it could mean finding my daughter.

Tripp was in the kitchen making some calls and taking care of work issues, but when I updated him on my plan to put Krissy in touch with Agent Johnson, his focus quickly shifted back to finding Aubrey. He grabbed his car keys, and we set off.

Krissy beat us to the FBI headquarters. I could see anxiety etched across her face. She was trembling, and I wasn't sure if it was excitement, anxiety, or nervousness over what she was about to see. Agent Johnson met us at the door and escorted us to a little room outside the viewing area. The agents had adjusted the video footage for better picture quality. Large TV screens had taken the place of the small monitor we had all tried to look at the day before. Technology truly amazed me. The faces we saw were so much clearer on these screens. The footage from the restaurant wasn't as good as the airport footage. I really could not distinguish the facial features as well. But the technicians had done an amazing job of filtering the video footage from the airport.

Krissy just stood there, arms folded, a solemn look on her face. I could tell she was quite intimidated by the FBI agents around her. She never said anything. I don't even think I saw her blink for the longest time. I stared at her intently, waiting, wanting some semblance of recognition to cross her face. Then finally it happened. When the man handed the airline agent his boarding pass, she could see him clearly. The color drained from Krissy's face. Her lower lip started to tremble, and for just one moment, I thought she, also, might pass out.

"Wait!" she shouted. "Pause it! I know him!" Her trembling finger pointed at the screen.

Although she was terrified at that moment, I was excited! She recognized this man, and we all knew it immediately.

Agent Johnson got her a chair, barked orders at the others to get her a glass of water, and I, of course, went to drill her.

"Who is it?" I demanded, leaning close to her face. "What does he do? Where can we find him?" I nearly grabbed her shoulders and started shaking her.

"Layla." I heard Tripp pleading behind me, but I ignored him.

"Tell us Krissy!"

"Layla!" Agent Johnson's sharp tone startled me. He stepped between me and Krissy and took my arms into his strong hands, pinning them to my sides. "Let her think," he said too calmly, "and you need to stop talking, now. You don't ask the questions. We do. If you cannot sit quietly and let us do our job, I will have you escorted out. Do you understand me?"

I nodded my head, recoiling. He let go of me, and I stepped away, embarrassed, and stood next to Tripp. I knew he was right. We had to let her calm down; we had to let her mind process what she had just seen.

"Krissy," he said, leaning close to her as I had just done, "take your time and tell us what and who you see." His voice was completely different from the voice that had just scolded me.

"His name is Dean Kepler," she said in barely a whisper. "He works for a cardiology group at the hospital. He is also a physician's assistant like me. If I remember, he was best friends with the physician who treated my friend Whitley before she...when she was so sick."

My heart wrenched. She looked so small and young, like a child, and I knew how painful it must have been for her to relive those memories.

"There is a big group of them that hang out socially outside of the hospital." Her voice was almost robotic. She stared at the screen, her eyes set on that face.

Once again, I had to feel sorry for her, but at the same time, the excitement rose inside me. I was so hopeful at that moment. We had a lead! We had a name!

I grasped Tripp's hand spontaneously and could see the glimmer of hope in his eyes too. I wanted to grab that man through the screen and find out what he had done with Aubrey. I didn't want to wait another second.

"Let's go! Let's go get them," I said. I started for the door, pulling Tripp behind me. But Agent Johnson stepped in front of me, took my shoulders in his hands, and forced me to sit down on one of the folding chairs that lined the wall.

"Calm down," he said patiently.

"Every second we waste here is another second that my daughter's life is in danger." I tried to keep from shouting, to keep my voice from shaking. Agent Johnson held my gaze for a long moment, and I felt my breathing slow, my muscles relax.

"Let me do my job," he said softly. He immediately directed one of the cadets to put out an APB, all-points bulletin, for Dean Kepler.

Krissy, coming out of her trance, started opening up about the character we had been peering at on the screen, bringing him to life.

"He is young, not the best looking man but a great personality, so he was popular with the young ladies. He always liked to drive elaborate vehicles, travel to exotic places, and live very lavishly. I know what a PA's salary is," Krissy explained, "and I wondered how he could afford all the things he did on that salary. He hung around a lot with the physician who had dated Whitley, but he wasn't cocky or rude like Whitley's boyfriend. PA Kepler was always friendly and sociable." She winced a little. "I can hardly believe that he would have anything to do with this."

These were details I simply didn't care about. I just wanted to run out the door and find my daughter. The rational side of me knew that I had to be patient until the time was right. Moving too fast could send these men deep into hiding where we would never find them—or the missing women.

After a while, the agents were quietly discussing Mr. Kepler's possible whereabouts, and they started looking for places near the airport where he could've taken Aubrey and Kayleigh. Large GPS maps appeared on the screens with highlights of possible places using geographic profiling. But the area was huge! My heart sank. They could be anywhere.

The women had boarded the plane in Philadelphia that had landed in Charlotte, North Carolina. The video footage from the Charlotte Douglas Airport was taking more time than expected for some reason.

While agents were waiting for it, I could not help but think that Aubrey and Kayleigh may have left Charlotte. Or North Carolina, for that matter. No one really knew the extent of this crime ring. I was doubtful that the headquarters for this nefarious business was in North Carolina. It could be in a completely different state or even another country. They could have boarded a plane, or another vehicle could have been waiting to take them anywhere.

Unable to sit still, Tripp and I moved to a corner of the room and were standing impatiently, watching the agents work.

"I just cannot keep standing here doing nothing," I whispered to Tripp. "I am going crazy."

He took my hand and squeezed it gently. "I agree. This is torture. I feel so helpless."

"What should we do?" I asked, keeping my voice low and remembering how Agent Johnson had reamed me out earlier for taking matters into my own hands.

"I have no idea what to do," said Tripp, "but I feel like doing nothing is the wrong thing."

An agent walked into the room holding some papers.

"Wait here," Tripp said, and he sauntered over trying to be cool, trying to get any information he could. "Hey man, how's it going? Anything new?"

I winced at Tripp's awkward efforts.

The agent did not respond. Tripp tried again and again. I could tell that he was getting irritated and restless. When the agent blew him off for about the third time, Tripp became flushed, kept rubbing his hands over his face, and stomped back to where I was standing. The agents were not easily seduced into talking, and Tripp leaned against the wall, arms folded in sullen embarrassment

By this time, Krissy was tired of talking to the agents, so she asked for a break and walked over to me.

"I want to do more," she said. "I want to do something, anything! Helping you is also helping me. Maybe Whitley is alive, still out there somewhere. I have to help her. I have to find her!" Her voice rising almost to hysteria attracted attention from some agents, who looked our way. Tripp motioned for me to calm her down, and he placed a hand on her shoulder to comfort her as best he could.

Feeling the eyes on us, I put my arm around her and guided her to the door. "Let's go to the ladies' room," I suggested.

In the bathroom, she pressed cool water on her face and dried it with a stiff paper towel. "I just don't know if they would be in North Carolina." She was pacing in the small room. "I really think there are a lot of physicians involved, and any time we waste, we could be finding your daughter and Whitley." She stopped, her eyes wide, and she gasped, grabbing my hands with her still damp ones. "Why don't we just go there and snoop around ourselves?" Her face was wide with excitement. "They don't have to know."

I knew why I liked this girl. She thought just like I did.

We went back to our waiting room and joined Tripp and the agents just in time to hear the alarming news. Agent Johnson's voice seemed strained and different than I had ever heard before, almost with a hint of panic that I did not find comforting.

"Unfortunately," he announced to the room, clearing his throat, "there is no security footage from when the agents exited the aircraft. There was, apparently, a computer glitch, and the footage has all been erased, from the entire terminal to the parking decks. We have no idea how something like this could happen, and we have agents at the airport questioning security personnel now."

I started to shake, and I could feel Krissy stiffen beside me. I knew this was not a coincidence. This business ran so deep, it was like an evil octopus that had tentacles everywhere, from funeral homes to physicians, surgeons, respiratory therapists to businessmen. With so many people involved, who knew? It wouldn't take much to bribe someone at the airport to adjust the cameras.

The lead ended there. Agent Johnson shared with us more information about PA Kepler, referring to a printout one of the cadets had handed him.

"It seems his physician's assistant license is still active, but, by looking at the registries, it is apparent that he has not been prescribing any medications recently. We were able to find out that Mr. Kepler had not been on his job at the hospital for…the last month?" He looked over to the cadet who had handed him to paper. "Is this right?"

"Yes, sir, it seems he'd been fired for some false documentation, and our technical analyst couldn't find any record of his employment elsewhere."

I pulled Krissy aside with Tripp, and in the spur of the moment, I had a plan.

"Okay, we have to do something, anything. This is taking too long. I want to go to Philly and visit this hospital."

"Yes!" Krissy exclaimed. "I'm coming too!"

Tripp was already starting to object.

"Just hear me out," I insisted. "I think retracing the steps Kayleigh and Aubrey took will be helpful."

"Don't you think these guys are already doing that?" Tripp argued.

"Not fast enough!"

"Not like we would!"

Krissy and I answered at once.

"Also," I continued, then I stopped myself. I had been about to tell him we could touch base touch base with Ahmed, Rhonda's brother, forgetting that Tripp did not know about the mysterious woman I had met while we were on vacation. I thought quickly, trying to sound reasonable, "I mean, who knows? At this point, anything would help."

Tripp was looking at the floor shaking his head, his arms crossed.

"I know what you are going to say," I said gently, placing a hand on his chest, "and I love you, but you cannot stop me. I refuse to sit home and do nothing. You know me better than that, baby."

He looked at me and our eyes locked for a long moment.

"And I will be with you!" Krissy finally piped in, as if that would settle the matter.

Chapter 29

Since Krissy and I were going rogue, I tried to think of the way Kayleigh would handle this. No one was looking for me, so I did not need a fake ID. But I did think a disguise would be helpful. I didn't want to be recognized.

My hair had always been long and very dark. The past few years, the gray had started to show up, slowly, like weeds invading a flower garden, but it had not taken over. I was proud of my hair, and it usually looked good. Curly, always styled, and I will admit, it was very pretty. People always complimented me. So, when Krissy suggested I go with a new short haircut, I was a little disturbed, to stay the least. But, I reasoned, it was just hair, and I would have shaved my head if it got my daughter home. As soon as we left the FBI headquarters, we hit the store, and I got a box of hair color.

I did not have the time to waste at a hair salon, so I informed Krissy she would be giving me a new cut. Back at my house, I sat on a stool in the kitchen, and she nervously laughed and chopped away. When I looked in the mirror, I barely recognized who I saw. The cut was actually pretty good, and the lighter, dirty brown made me look pale. Some instant spray tan fixed that, and we were on our way.

Tripp was not on board with our plan. At first, he wanted to go along, but I talked him into staying back and trying to follow any leads at home. Then he pleaded, "Just wait. Give the FBI another day or two. With all their resources, they're bound to come up with something."

Needless to say, he was furious when I left after booking the earliest possible flight to Philadelphia.

On the plane, Krissy was giddy with excitement. She knew the people, and she had a way in. She even still had her ID badge for Mother of Mercy Medical Center. I knew our plan would never be approved by the FBI, so I did not dare breathe a word to anyone about it.

When the plane landed, I sent a quick text to Agent Johnson, relieved that I would not be able to see the look on his face.

Decided to fly to Philly. Must look into things for myself. I'll keep you updated. Be back soon. Tripp is there if you need him for anything.

We got the rental car and headed out.

The first place I wanted to go was to visit Ahmed. I needed to know if he recognized any of the men or if any had connections to ones we had identified as almost certainly being involved in human trafficking. For all we knew, he may be friends with one of them or had been associated with them at some point. Any tiny piece of information would help us.

We had no time to call or make arrangements with Ahmed. Things had moved too fast. It was early morning, and I was hopeful the young man would be home. The excitement surged through me. For some reason, I felt like we would get what we needed soon. Krissy waited in the car while I practically beat down the door to Ahmed's apartment.

I felt like a deflated balloon when, after ten minutes of knocking, no one came to the door. After a few minutes, Krissy got out of the car and joined me, taking turns knocking and calling out, "Hello? Anybody home?" There was no answer.

Tears started to come, and I had to swallow hard to get them in control as we slowly turned and walked back to the street. As we got back into the rental car and closed the doors, I noticed a dark young man walking toward me. Instantly, I was nervous. The tall young man, in dark sunglasses, looked very intense and serious.

The he came closer and closer to the passenger side window. He slowly removed his sunglasses and just stood there and stared intently at me. I made a small crack in the window, and all he said was, "I am Ahmed."

It took a moment for my slow, fatigued brain to process who was looking at me. He turned and walked quickly away before I could even fully open the window or door. Krissy got out of the driver's seat as I was jumping out of the passenger's side. Ahmed was not heading back to his apartment but to one on the lower level of the building.

When we finally caught up, he motioned us to not talk until we had gone into a small door in the back of the building. After I got some semblance of direction, I realized we would be almost directly underneath his apartment. The room we entered was a storage unit. I assumed each apartment had one. The room was poorly lit, but I could see multiple computers were set up. I could see more when my eyes acclimated to the dim light. He had a camera set up and multiple TV screens, all watching the outside of his apartment door and some monitoring what I could only assume was the interior.

Realizing he had seen us knocking, I just stood and looked at him. Intense eyes glared back at me.

"Have a seat," he said, and when he pointed to the canvas camping chairs, I could see his hands were shaking. I could not help but wonder what had happened to make him so defensive when he didn't know us or why we were even here. Silence hung awkwardly in the room.

"Why are you here?" asked Ahmed. "I demand you tell me who you are." His voice trembled and rose in tone, and I couldn't tell if he was anxious or angry. "Why are you here?" he repeated, punctuating each word, and I jumped when he shouted, "Tell me now!"

I was taken back and just stood there for a moment before I spoke. He could see he had startled me, and regret flashed across his face.

"I am Layla Matthews, and I need your help." Before I even finished my sentence, he held up his hand and shook his head.

"Matthews? Related to Aubrey Matthews?" His eyes were narrow with suspicion.

"I'm her mother."

"Now I know who you are. Your daughter was here and lied to me. I will not answer any questions until I know what is going on. Since the visit from your daughter, I have been followed, and my apartment was broken into."

"What?" I gasped.

"I know the story your daughter told me was a lie. She was not a reporter. I knew it even before I was followed. There was something more. Your daughter wanted to reach out to me. Her eyes, they pierced my soul. She stood at my door and stared at me before she and the other lady left. I knew she needed to tell me something but could not." His voice broke as he spoke. His tone was soft now and vulnerable. Tears began to pool in his eyes.

"I am sorry you have had such a difficult time," I said. "I can assure you this was not the intention." I gestured toward Krissy, who sat staring at the mess of electronics haphazardly scattered over the table. "This is my colleague, Krissy. We are here to ask you some questions and ask for your help. Please tell us what's been going on since you spoke with my daughter, Aubrey." I knew that Aubrey and Kayleigh had not shared anything personal with him on their visit, for his safety and Rhonda's, but I was past taking those precautions—I needed his help.

"Well, like I said," he began, "since their visit, I started to notice someone following me. I also could see that someone had been in my apartment multiple times." He leaned forward, seeming to feel more comfortable with us. "The strange thing was they never took anything. A person who was not observant would never have known someone had been there, but I did. So, I placed small cameras around and began to monitor my apartment." He motioned to the monitors around us. "A couple of men would come in and look in my computer, check my emails, review my recent searches, look at my mail, then leave. I'm guessing they wanted to know what research I had been doing about my sister. Of course, they found nothing. But in this area," he looked around the cramped, gloomy room, "my secret area, I had done a lot of work. I had found out who Aubrey was but not the other woman. It was easy to identify Aubrey because of her name and social media. She shared your story on her Facebook page, updates on your health, requests for well-wishers not to send roses."

I winced, remembering my daughter's consideration for my comfort during my recovery.

"My question is," Ahmed continued, leaning back in his chair, "why would she need to come here and speak to me and make up a lame story? What do I and my sister have to do with you, Layla?" His dark eyes were now staring into mine with such conviction, I could feel what he was already suspecting. "Now your turn," he said, folding his arms expectantly across his chest. "What's going on? And how does this involve me?" He pointed a sharp finger at me. "No more lies!"

So I started my story. Ahmed displayed a vast range of emotions as I gave a very abbreviated synopsis and told him what had happened to me. As gently as I could, I described the body auction. He sat on the edge of the chair the entire time, hands folded on his lap, with perfect posture.

I took a long, deep breath and got to the hard part.

"I was on a trip in the Dominican Republic in December, trying to put the nightmare behind me. But I met a woman. A beautiful, special woman. Her name was Rhonda. And this is why—"

He suddenly slumped into the chair. His olive complexion was instantly pale. I don't recall ever seeing color leave someone's face so dramatically before. My heart hurt for him. I could feel tears falling from my eyes, and before I knew it had even happened, I was crying as I talked.

"She had been a victim of the auction also," I explained as quickly as I could, seeing how painful my words were for Ahmed. "We noticed one another and were able to secretly meet. I explained to her what had happened to me, and she was able to briefly tell me her story." I felt Krissy grab my hand for comfort. But I did not stop. I kept talking because I was afraid if I paused, I could not start back up.

"She was sold in the auction to an Arabic man. She has been held captive by him and told she could never return to her family." Taking one last gulp of air, trying to hold in the sob I felt in my throat, I said, "I promised her I would help her."

Ahmed never interrupted, never asked a question, just listened. I went on to explain why Aubrey and Kayleigh had visited him and why they had to deceive him. He nodded his head at this point, which was the first sign that he was still breathing.

Krissy finally interrupted. "Are you okay? I know this is a shock. I can't imagine how you must be feeling. Can I go get you some ice water?"

"No, no. I am fine." His voice was now weak and frail. It seemed as if it was coming from someone entirely different.

"Ahmed," I continued, "Kayleigh and Aubrey did not return home after their visit here, so you see why I came to see you. I was hoping you could possibly give us any information that could help. I am so scared for them."

Ahmed sat up on his chair again. He stood and slowly went to a small mini fridge in the corner of the room and grabbed some bottles of water. My mouth felt like the Sahara, so I gladly accepted the bottle. He stood with his back to us for a few minutes. Awkward silence filled the small space. Krissy opened her mouth to speak, and I had to motion for her to be silent. I knew he needed to think about what he had just heard.

When he finally turned around, his face shocked me. Ahmed had transformed from a stunned, sad brother to a determined, fierce fighter. The angry determination in his eyes and across his face made me shudder. He had absorbed the information, processed it, and was ready to move.

He now gave his attention to Krissy.

"And who are you to Aubrey?" he demanded. "Why are you here and involved with this?"

"Well, I work with Layla. I also lost a dear friend, and I think she was in an auction. I have been searching for her. My friend and I worked at the hospital where your sister also passed away."

"My sister is not dead!" His harsh reaction made Krissy recoil.

"You're right. I am sorry. I misspoke." She pressed her lips together as if holding back her pain. "But I also have someone I want to find," she said simply.

We all had a common bond—we had a loved one who had been taken from us. I had a deep, dark feeling that we didn't have a lot of time left.

Chapter 30

For the most part, I feel okay with my computer skills—well, I should say I *did* until I met Ahmed. He immediately wanted to know the names of the physicians we were looking into so he could find their pictures. Krissy still had her computer log in, and with the help of a few hacking tricks, we were able to review the physician profile database.

Some of the faces Krissy recognized, and others she did not. We had gone through so many pictures by now, and when Krissy or Ahmed noted a familiar face, Ahmed would stop and write down the information. Then I saw him. As Dr. Pierce's face appear on the screen, I froze. But what astounded me was that Krissy knew him.

"I remember him!" Krissy said anxiously, pointing to Pierce's face on the monitor. I was already in a state of shock seeing the face of the demon again, so her shrill voice about made me jump out of my skin.

"You do? How?" My voice did not sound like my own. Both Ahmed and Krissy turned to look at me.

She nodded and said, "He was a physician at the hospital when I first started my clinical rotation in college. He looked younger then, but that's him. His name was Dr. Foulks when he worked with us. He worked in a large hospital group and did some of the education in the clinical rotation for the PA program." She shuddered a little. "He was always...creepy. He gave a lot of us girls a weird feeling, if you know what I mean."

I knew exactly what she meant.

"He was always flattering Whitley," Krissy continued, "telling her how smart and pretty she was. She ate it up, loving the extra attention he gave her. I warned her a few times to stay away from him, but she trusted everyone." Krissy went on to explain that he had stopped working there a few years ago and never crossed her mind until now.

It was at this point when I thought about reaching out to what was probably a very furious Agent Johnson. His response to my text after we landed was a terse *I should have you arrested*, but I knew he needed to know what we had discovered. But I waited, just a little longer.

Ahmed's fingers made quick work of his task at hand. On the other screen, he had already pulled up a nationwide physician directory. I had no idea this database even existed, but he started to type in the names Krissy had mentioned. She could not remember a lot of names. However, she did better than I would expect. But really, a hospital is like any job—there are cliques and groups that migrate toward one another.

The hospitalist groups were always a tight-knit bunch, and then you had the new, younger physicians. They were always the most obnoxious group and drove everyone insane. They swarmed together like a group of tropical fish. They were bright and fresh, lab coats clean and crisp. They were ready to "heal the world." It was always the same. They thought they were smarter than the simple nurses, more up to date than the older physicians, and, of course, always the most attractive. The men were usually arrogant and ready to bed any young nurse who would let them, and the women—well, they were trying to prove they could make it in a man's world. This made them a group of barracudas with a chip on their shoulder and something to prove. It typically took about a year before they were knocked off the perches on which they'd placed themselves. They either killed a patient or came close to it before they realized the best teacher in medicine is experience.

The surgeons also tended to hang together even though they secretly competed with one another and constantly debated who was the best at his or her craft.

The specialty groups like cardiology and pulmonology also had little cliques in which they would band together to get what they wanted. But the constant argument over a patient's cause of shortness of breath could throw a little drama in the mix. Pulmonary would argue it was the lungs, but cardio would guarantee it was the heart. It was an old fight that never ceased.

My favorite group was the older physicians. The ones who walked with a limp because their hips and backs were worn out from years of caring for others. Their lab coats were not fresh and starched; they were yellow with various ink spots and marks of the occasional bodily fluids. They laughed at the new doctors and swooped in to save the day when the newbies screwed up. Their days of torrid affairs with nurses were long gone, and they knew their careers were coming to an end. They were the old-fashioned physicians who still hugged their patients and told them they loved them because they did. Some have the same patients for over thirty years and are emotionally attached to them. When one of those patients dies, it hurts them—they are the true healers in the hospital. I fear as these men and women retire, a great part of medicine will die with them. With hospitals being about money and new government regulations, health care is not what it used to be. Patients are numbers, not people.

My mind wandered back to a time when my life was just about medicine. Now, I could hear the background noise of the others talking, pictures popping up, and the low hum of the computers working hard to meet the demand of Ahmed's assault against their tiny keys.

I thought of my old friends, my coworkers whom I actually spent more time with than my own family. I was jolted out of my trance by Krissy tugging my arm. She sounded like she was in a tunnel. As I cleared my mind out of the fog it was in, my eyes began to focus on the screen in front of me. I sat there looking like a complete idiot, mouth gaping open, and the beautiful face on the screen staring back at me.

I had a flashback of the night in my bedroom, opening my Valentine's Day present, the beautiful Kandinsky print, and the revelation I had at that moment. Being so engulfed with the situation at hand, I had forgotten what I had discovered that night. As Krissy was yelling and trying to snap me out of my stupor, my body was frozen, but my mind was moving at record speed, processing what I was looking at and hearing. The face appeared on the screen, and Ahmed said that this physician was one of the men who had taken care of his sister.

Everyone froze until Krissy came unglued. At that moment, we knew—we all knew—who the leader and mastermind was. The entire time, he was right in front of us. It all made sense now, and we also knew where our girls were!

My hands shook as I dialed Agent Johnson.

Chapter 31

We all had a different agenda. Agent Johnson and I wanted to find Kayleigh and Aubrey. Ahmed, of course, wanted to jump a plane to Dubai to find his sister, and Krissy wanted to get answers as to what had happened to Whitley. We knew more physicians were involved, but at that moment, we had what we needed. Immediately, Krissy and I rushed to the airport. My heart racing and the anticipation of what was about to happened were almost too much to stand. Agent Johnson had already arranged for Tripp to be picked up and taken to the FBI headquarters.

At the airport and on the flight, I had messaged Agent Johnson over and over, and he was not responding. When the plane landed, a car was waiting on us, and two FBI agents took us to the headquarters, where Tripp was waiting, along with many other agents. The large screens and speakers were showing in real time bodycam footage of what was getting ready to happen. Tripp's eyes paused on me, his eyes flitting to my new haircut, as if seeing it for the first time. But he quickly turned away, and I knew he was still upset with me. I wasn't sure for what at this point. For not telling him the truth about Aubrey's mission? For keeping secrets from him? But I could not focus on that. My focus was on finding my daughter.

I could see on the screen in front of me the footage on the body cam of the agent approaching the door. How could I have been so stupid? I should have known who was behind this from the start. Sometimes I just get blinded by loyalty for someone and don't see the facts. The evidence had been right in front of me the entire time. I was sick to my stomach that my own dullness may have cost my daughter severely.

The agents were going in the front door and into a large foyer—one I recognized well. The same décor as I remembered, and the familiar feeling of betrayal crept inside of me. It did not appear that anyone was at home. The armed agents went from room to room looking for Aubrey and Kayleigh and any other women who might be captives there. One agent would enter a room, check it, and clear it with silent hand signals. This went on for what seemed like forever, and no signs of Aubrey or Kayleigh anywhere. I was about to explode from the inside out. The next room was the most familiar to me. My mind went back to a night that seemed like a lifetime ago.

The average salary for a hospitalist is $230,000. This can vary greatly depending on procedures, time worked, patient population, and other factors. Physicians tend to have extravagant tastes, and this means some work extra shifts or locum jobs for extra cash.

As I stood there and watched this nightmare unfold, my mind wandered back to when the first clues should have resonated like beacons in the dark. Mark McGwire's seventieth-home-run baseball is worth three million dollars. *The Madonna and Child Being Crowned by Two Angels* painting is priced at $240,000. How had I not realized that it would have been difficult to afford such a lavish lifestyle on a typical salary? I had realized it the night that I unwrapped my imitation Kandinsky painting. I had just put it out of my mind, thinking I was wrong. Javier Ricardo was such a great guy, my friend. Why would he do such a horrible thing to so many innocent people? Was money that important to him?

My heart was racing, Tripp stood beside me like a statue, stoic, tapping his foot like he always did when nervous. A part of me was relieved that we knew now who was behind this, and it apparently wasn't the man standing next to me. The roller coaster of uncertainty was torture. I looked over at Krissy, who had her hands clapped over her mouth in horror, hope in her eyes, and I wondered if she actually expected that Whitley was also hidden in that house.

As the camera swept the library, there were no indications of anything amiss, no evidence of a crime, and no sign of the man who owned the house. I wondered if Kayleigh and Aubrey were even in the house. Had he taken them somewhere else? Then, when the agents stood motionless in the room, we heard a small sound like a tapping noise. Someone was trying to send a signal. The agents mobilized more urgently, searching to determine where the noise was coming from. Apparently, it was coming from somewhere in the library, but where?

"Safe room," muttered one of the agents who stood staring at the action on the screen.

Safe rooms have become popular among the wealthy. The fear of an intruder and robbery prompted this fad. The rooms are well hidden and not easy to find unless the searcher knows where to look. Libraries are a perfect spot due to the multiple ways to hide the door and the lever to open it. Finally, after over an hour, one agent discovered a trigger among the books. He pressed the small switch, and a panel in the wall opened.

I longed to see Aubrey, touch her, and hold her. But I waited in the musty room at FBI headquarters and watched as the scene unfolded on the screen. The thick metal door, concealed by a large bookshelf, opened, and I sobbed as I saw my daughter walk out. Tripp was the first to move as he grabbed my arm, "Let's go!"

With Tripp driving faster than was safe, we headed straight to the hospital where she was being taken. No words, just silent tears and prayers on the way. As we drove, Tripp reached over for my hand. I held it tighter than I ever had. I took slow, deep breaths, and it was only then that I realized we had left Krissy behind, and I hadn't even noticed.

As I ran into the ER, the FBI presence was evident. A strong arm shot out to stop us from passing into the examining room, but the agent must have recognized us and finally let us through to see Aubrey.

She looked small, like a child, on the gurney, an IV in her arm and a bruise on her cheek. She was pale from hunger, dehydration, and days of confinement.

"Mama," she said weakly.

We embraced and cried for the longest time. The smell of her skin, the feel of her tiny frame in my arms was the best thing I had ever felt next to the day I held her in my arms for the first time. When my mind cleared, I pulled back to get a look at her and realized the expression of devastation on her face.

"It's okay, baby," I said. "You're home. You're safe!" But her eyes filled with tears. "What is it?"

"Kayleigh," she gasped before collapsing into sobs against me.

I was horrified that I hadn't even been aware that Kayleigh had not come out of the secret room.

Kayleigh wasn't with her.

"He took her in the middle of the night and left," she said between sobs. "He had come to take me, but Kayleigh put up a fight and begged for him to take her instead." She wiped at her nose with the palm of her hand. "He didn't hurt us. He just locked us in the safe room."

Once again, I owed Kayleigh my life.

When Agent Johnson stopped by the hospital to check on Aubrey, he took me into the hall. For a moment, he stood there looking at me, shaking his head, his lips tight with anger.

"Layla," he began, but I pointed my finger at his face.

"You have nothing to say to me. I did what had to be done. So unless you're going to thank me..."

His expression softened. "We'll talk about it later," he warned. "But for now, I thought you should know that we have Ricardo's house blocked off, and dozens of FBI and CIA agents have flooded the property. We've confiscated computers, and agents are picking over the entire home from top to bottom."

I nodded. "Thank you. That's good."

"Now, as for the matter of you interfering with an ongoing investigation..."

As the agent was speaking, I noticed Tripp had taken my place sitting on Aubrey's bed and hugging her tightly. When Aubrey was finally out of the bear hug her father held her in, he asked if she was hungry.

"How about a cheeseburger?" he asked enthusiastically.

Aubrey smiled weakly and nodded, not wanting to disappoint her father.

Agent Johnson was still talking, but his voice was just a buzz in my head. As soon as Tripp was out of Aubrey's room, I turned from the agent and went back to my daughter's bedside.

"How did you find me?" Her voice was raspy and tight.

"I went to see Ahmed," I told her, "and with his and Krissy's help, we figured it out."

"Oh." Her eyes looked down. "Did you tell him about Rhonda?"

"Yes, I did. He knows everything now."

A sigh of relief left her chest and a hint of pink returned to her cheeks. "I wanted so much to tell him," she whispered, closing her heavy eyes.

I patted her hand. "I am sure he will be here soon," I said. "He wants to know about the plans for finding her."

When the doctors released Aubrey, we decided, instead of taking her to her own apartment, to go back to our house and wait for more information to come in. Aubrey needed to shower and clean up, and I was also exhausted and needed to refresh. I rode in the back seat with her head on my shoulder. I think I kept my tight grip on Aubrey's hand the entire time.

Chapter 32

Darkness, cold, a hard table on her bare back. Kayleigh tried to clear her mind. What had happened? Where was she? They had just gotten off the flight and an Uber was waiting there to pick them up. The details of what came after were still fuzzy in her mind. She had been given a drug; she had been sedated. There was no other explanation. Now she had no idea how long she had been out or where she had been taken.

She tried to stay calm, get her thoughts together, and assess the situation. Panic would only be another enemy right now, and if she wanted to survive, she did not need another foe. She could tell by the way her body felt, her sore and stiff joints, that she had not moved her extremities in hours. She must have been given a potent medication. When she tried to take a deep breath, the bottom of her lungs ached and burned. She had been shallow breathing for a few hours. She was dirty, hungry, cold, and terrified.

She could hear no outside noises around her. Just darkness and total silence. When she tried to lift her head, she could not, and her arms were restrained beside her. Her heart rate started to speed up, as she could not control the sense of doom she felt. Kayleigh realized this may be the time she did not survive. She replayed the events in her mind, still mad at herself for not knowing what was happening around her.

The past few months had been some of the happiest in her life. She had not really had the luxury of dating or being involved with a man, but with this ongoing case, she was able to relocate near her new friends. She had grown to love Aubrey and her family. Then the extra benefit of meeting Javier Ricardo had made it a perfect storm. They had been attracted to each other from the beginning. It never occurred to her throughout this time that he could have been involved in any sinister plots.

As Kayleigh thought back and remembered the photo album in his library and the trips they documented, she remembered that he was in many of those pictures. Had she suspected then? Why hadn't she? It should have been obvious that he was involved, but by then, her heart was affected, and like it so oftentimes did, it outweighed what her brain was telling her. They had taken romantic trips; he had given her fabulous gifts and expressed that he had fallen in love with her. She felt the sting of her hot tears falling down her face onto the cold table. She had also fallen in love with this man, but how could she not? He was so handsome, sweet, and charming. The perfect man for any woman. She had opened herself up to finally trust and fall in love, and he turned out to be a psychopath.

After the New Year's Eve party, things had really started to heat up for them. The holiday season always brings out the best in people, and romance often sparks. Everyone in their beautiful dresses and tuxedos, the champagne and gifts. It was a fairytale for her. That night at Javier's, when all the guests had left, he told her he was falling in love with her. She had not told anyone, but they had spent the night together for the first time and had made love. She had not been with a man in many years; the nervousness and anxiety made it even more special. They had enjoyed each other's bodies and had not slept the entire night.

They were together many, many times after that, and each time seemed to be more intense. But this had all been a lie! He had known the whole time she was FBI and never let on. She had almost revealed to him one night who she was and what mission she was actually working on but decided not to because she was worried about his safety. How ironic!

When she and Aubrey had landed at the airport that day, she had already discovered something was wrong. On the plane, she had gone to the lavatory and noticed a man that she had seen at the hotel and restaurant the day before. She knew they had been followed, and she had missed it. But they could not do anything while on the plane, so she went back to her seat and informed Aubrey of her concern. Aubrey spoke privately to the flight attendant and flashed her FBI credentials, and when they landed, they quickly had each other's back and exited the plane first.

The two women headed out to the ground transport when they had seen a familiar face. Her knight in shining armor, Dr. Ricardo, was loading his Porsche SUV with his suitcase when they saw him.

"What a pleasant surprise to see you!" she had said, accepting his embrace. "What are you doing here?"

"I'm just returning from a conference in Baltimore," he explained. "How about you?"

Kayleigh shrugged and thought quickly, but Aubrey beat her to it. "I had a training seminar in Pittsburgh, and since Kayleigh has family there, we decided to travel together."

He smiled and nodded. "What a lucky coincidence!"

Of course, he offered them a ride, and, needing to get out of the airport quickly, they accepted.

"I don't know about you," he said as they drove, "but I could use some refreshment. What if we stop by my place for a light lunch, maybe some wine, and then I'll take you home?"

Tired and foggy, the two women had agreed. It was evident to Kayleigh now that the drugs were in the drinks, and it was hours later before they woke up in the safe room.

Kayleigh had never been so shocked. She was angry and heartbroken all at the same time. Aubrey had comforted her and reassured her that no one knew, and Javier had been excellent and brilliant at his part in this. When he had come in to see them, he looked at Kayleigh for a long time. It seemed he had feelings for her; his eyes looked sad and regretful. He tried to talk to her, but after only one word, she had spit in his face.

Kayleigh and Aubrey had no idea what had happened that made him come into the safe room the day she was taken. He was anxious, yelling at someone on the phone, and had decided he had to leave and make a clean break. He had grabbed Aubrey, but Kayleigh could not let him take her. She was so young and had her whole life ahead of her. She had fought and got a few good hits in, and it appeared he was in such a rush, he just gave up and settled for Kayleigh. By the few things Kayleigh heard on the phone call before she passed out, she was a "payment." Ricardo was being taken somewhere and protected, but there was a price. And of course, it would be a woman.

This was when it all came back to her: yes, she was the payment for his safety. He was relocating because there was too much "heat" in the United States, but whomever he was on the phone with needed a payment. Javier was in too big of a rush to fight any longer. One of the other men was to come by the house later and "take care of Aubrey."

Kayleigh felt herself start to panic. Aubrey. She was left locked in the safe room. She had seen many safe rooms, and his was state-of-the-art. She knew that no one suspected Dr. Ricardo, so they probably would not look for Kayleigh and Aubrey at his house. No one would know Aubrey was there, and she would either be killed or left to starve in the hidden room.

But something had to have happened for him to panic. Someone must have figured something out, or he would not have had to run. Kayleigh continued to try to calm herself. As the time passed, she became more and more lucid. Her muscles ached, and she was so thirsty.

She replayed the events of the past year over and over in her mind. Working with the FBI was something she would never have dreamed of doing, but it had been the most amazing experience of her life. She made lasting friendships and loved the people she worked with. She had grown to call them her family.

Then, suddenly, a painful stimulus shot into her brain. It was a blinding light, and when it had been turned on, it felt like a gun to her head. Her eyes were on fire, and it took a few moments to be able to focus. Finally, when she could see who had entered the room, she was shocked. These men were not American; they did not speak English. They were not dressed in clothes that she recognized at all. She tried to talk to them, as she spoke a few languages.

"Where am I? What is this place?" she demanded. Then she tried again in Farsi and in the limited Turkish she knew. But they acted as if she wasn't even speaking, completely ignoring her repeated pleas for release.

They kept talking, but they were speaking a slang form of Arabic, and she couldn't understand anything they were saying.

With the light on, she looked around her and saw she was in a type of basement. She had been restrained to a large metal table in what appeared to be a small, makeshift examining room. Fear gripped her, and she felt like she remembered this scene in a movie she had seen before. This looked a lot like the room where the men had prepared the women for the auction. Not as elaborate but similar. The men looked at her, touched her hair, and started to examine her, still ignoring her screaming at them.

When one of them tried to open her mouth and look at her teeth, she bit him. He slapped her across the face so hard her ears rang loudly for a few minutes. One of the men grabbed a syringe from a table close by and gave her an injcction. Thc instant warmth went through her veins. She was awake but calm and subdued. The men proceeded to examine her. One examined her breasts and the other her genitals. She could tell they had to be physicians and they knew what they were looking for. She was self-conscious because she had not bathed in days and had urinated on herself multiple times since she had not had any other option.

The men yelled out of the door, and some women came in wearing hijabs and carrying basins of warm water and baskets of oils and all types of creams. The men left the room, and the women gave Kayleigh a bath, right there in that cold room. They were methodical, not rough but not gentle. They worked quickly and efficiently. Kayleigh was in and out of sleep but would wake up when they rinsed her hair or when she felt the occasional wild hair plucked by tweezers. When her rational mind was able to break through, she knew what was happening. She knew what this prep meant. They were disposing of her by selling her, trading her. There was nothing she could do about it—absolutely nothing.

Chapter 33

It's amazing what a hot shower can do. It can wake you up, refresh you, and wash away dirt and sadness. Aubrey and I emerged from our showers refreshed and renewed. We all had a new fight in our veins. I was ready to find that demon Javier Ricardo, rescue my friend, and help Ahmed get to Rhonda. Ahmed would have the records we needed and know how to get them both. He had arrived at our house soon after we had returned home.

Agent Johnson had been shocked to discover an elaborate computer system located in Ricardo's safe room. It was unthinkable that it had been left behind, but most likely, Dr. Ricardo did not think the room would ever be found—or if it was, that it would be so far into the future that it would be too late. The computers contained a database of web addresses of multiple sites on the dark web that revealed the way the men advertised the auctions. There were lists of hospitals all over the world that had contacts and the names of physicians who were participants in the human auction.

The amount of information the FBI was able to recover was astounding. Since these computers could be erased from a remote area, the agents worked around the clock to get what they could from them.

This was all encouraging but upsetting to realize that the physicians who had disappeared could be at any of these hospitals around the world being sheltered by their counterparts.

Ahmed went to work quickly on trying to decide the best route to get to his sister. He was rational and knew this had to be handled correctly or the consequences could be devastating. This was a different country, and the man who had purchased his sister was rich and powerful. There could be diplomatic ramifications as well as harm to Rhonda. Ahmed's parents were Egyptian, but he had been born and raised in the US. He only spoke very little Arabic and did not have the contacts needed to help him in that country, but he knew someone who did. He had informed me that he had a guest coming, and when the doorbell rang, I was in shock at the man I welcomed inside.

At my door stood a tall, dark man. His face was weary and worn. Lines of stress and worry crossed it, and his demeanor was harsh and cold. Ahmed quickly introduced him as his father, Ishmael. Ahmed, while on his way to our house, had called Ishmael and spoken to him. Trying not to go into great details over the phone, he explained to his father that Rhonda could be alive, so of course, Ishmael came immediately. Once again, we had to retell the details of the events that had happened over the past year. Each time was like a knife to my chest, and I felt like it took more out of me every time I had to repeat the details. Apparently, it was the same for Ishmael. He sat there and listened in utter shock.

Ishmael had been a physician. From what Ahmed briefly explained, he was actually a world-renowned physician with an extensive medical practice. The thing that made him so extraordinary was his memory. He never forgot anything. A date, a diagnosis, a name. He was absolutely brilliant. People looked up to him and respected him more than any physician in his field. But he changed when his wife died; he could not handle being able to save other people but not the love of his life. But when Rhonda died too, well, that was all it took to make him retire and move to Florida. He lived as a recluse, shutting himself off from everyone and everything.

As Ishmael sat in our living room listening to our story, many emotions crossed his face, but the main one was intense and violent anger.

"I don't believe this! How could this happen? Are you sure? One hundred percent sure?"

"Yes, I am." My voice was low and calm. "As Ahmed and I have explained, the same thing happened to Rhonda that happened to me and many other women. It was a miracle Rhonda and I accidently met one another. She is strong and still fighting to get back to you."

When I started to talk about Rhonda, his fist was so tightly clenched that his olive knuckles looked white as chalk. At one point, he hit my glass table so hard I was certain either his hand was broken or the table.

"I can't imagine how you feel," I said urgently, "but you need to use your anger and focus on what we can do to get Rhonda back to the US."

"Are you sure it was her?" he repeated, rising to his feet and pacing back and forth across the room. "Tell me again *exactly* what she said to you. I need to know again. I just cannot believe this would happen. Allah would never allow this to happen to my family!"

"Baba," said Ahmed, "you have family in Dubai, yes? And you lived many years in Cairo. How is your Arabic?"

Ishmael's face registered that he understood his role in the plan. He said something rapidly in Arabic, and I turned to Ahmed for a translation.

He grinned. "Baba says his Arabic is impeccable, what do you think?" Then Ahmed's eyebrows raised and his eyes widened as his father continued to speak, pacing back and forth. "And now he is saying things he wants to do to the men who took his daughter, and I won't translate that in the presence of ladies."

But it didn't matter. We had a way in.

When Agent Johnson arrived, we knew something was wrong. He did not make eye contact and seemed nervous, which was uncharacteristic for him. But I had a feeling nothing at this point could stop Ishmael from getting to his daughter. He did not care about diplomacy or danger. He was getting his daughter, and he was getting her soon.

Chapter 34

Rhonda looked at her surroundings. The room was elaborate, almost obnoxiously so. The enormous bed filled one wall of the room, and all the furnishings and decor were gold. She could not help but laugh at the ostentatious lifestyle of her capturer.

She was able to walk around more freely now that Ahseed, her husband, felt he could trust her. It felt like he had trained her to be submissive. In the beginning, she had tried to escape and tried to talk the staff into helping her. She was beaten many times, always in a way that no scars were visible, her perfect skin never marked. There were times when he would lock her in the dark for days on end as punishment. Finally, she realized there had to be another way. She would have to play along with this narcissistic maniac if she were to have a chance of escape.

All hope had been lost until she had met Layla on vacation. Layla's passion and the fact that she knew what had happened to her gave Rhonda new hope. She dreamed daily of being rescued from the hell she was in.

She was Egyptian by heritage but had been born in the United States. She had known only equality for women and free speech, and even though American women were not entirely equal to men in some aspects, such as salaries, they were not "slaves" of American men. She had never had to submit to every wish of a man, not even to her father, only speaking when a man allowed and having to obey him. She knew that other countries still treated women this way, and even her mother had spoken of such conditions in her childhood. But Rhonda never experienced it for herself.

Now, to her horror, Ahseed forced her to do sexual things that were repulsive to her. She had to bow her head when her husband entered the room, speak only with his permission, and never express her own opinions. At times, she forgot what her own voice sounded like. With no access to TV, news, or the internet, she was lonelier than she could ever have imagined. She knew that living this way, women from this part of the world would have loved the endless food, beautiful clothes, and the lavish lifestyle Rhonda had. But was it a fair exchange? If she were a "good girl," Ahseed treated her well. Her life improved when she learned how she was to behave.

Rhonda had a personal attendant named Ila, who kept her company. Ila was only a few years older than Rhonda but still wore the Eastern Arabia burqa traditionally worn by older women of United Arab Emirates. Rhonda thought they must have made a funny sight as they walked and talked in the gardens, she in her elegant hairstyles and perfect makeup and Ila with a mask covering her head and face, revealing only her chin and her dark eyes.

Without any technology at her disposal, there really wasn't a lot Rhonda was able to do. Her main contact with the outside world were the parties Ahseed hosted, and when these happened, she could select beautiful gowns. He would have a dozen or so brought in, carefully preselected, and she could choose one. They were unlike anything she had ever seen before, and she couldn't help feeling dazzled by them. Ahseed also had a vast array of jewelry for her to choose from, bracelets, earrings, necklaces thick with gems, which he would snap off her and lock away at evening's end to prevent her from using them to make her escape.

The parties always had great music and food, but she was forbidden to dance and could only nibble whatever bites of food he allowed. Ahseed once again instructed her to stay by his side and not to speak unless spoken to. He had trained her on what she could and could not say. But since their trip to the Dominican Republic, where she found out what had really happened to her, she had become much more observant of the visitors at these parties.

Every month, her husband would host one of these events, and this would be for the businessmen not just associated in Dubai but of many nationalities. Very wealthy men and women would come to eat and drink, and then Ahseed would direct them to the theater room in the basement of the mansion. Only certain people could participate in this part of the event. She was not privy to this, and in the past, it hadn't mattered, but now she was curious and had a feeling it had everything to do with the auction.

She noticed that over the past few months, men from different countries attended the parties. They would come alone one month, then a couple of months later, a woman would accompany them. The women were always like Rhonda, the same nationality as the man they accompanied, submissive, heads down. She never really noticed before, but Ahseed and the other men took extra care to ensure that none of the women got too close to one another. They could exchange polite pleasantries, but the men quickly intervened and separated them if they started to talk too much.

Rhonda was able to speak to an Asian woman one time. The woman, wearing a snug, high-slit qipao of dazzling red with gold and turquoise embroidery, looked scared to death, her hands trembling as she held a glass of champagne, which she did not drink. The thing that shocked Rhonda the most was her accent. The woman's husband was Asian and barely spoke a word of English, and when he did, it was so difficult to understand that he might as well have spoken in his native tongue. But the woman, despite her Asian features, had a thick Southern accent. The kind you hear when you visit Alabama or another state in the deep South.

"Are you having a nice time?" Rhonda tried to make some small talk.

"Yes, yes, I am." A little bow of the head. "Thank you for having me." Her voice was soft and shaky.

"You have an American accent," Rhonda said, unable to hide her surprise and delight. "Where are you—"

The conversation quickly ended when the Asian man, alerted by Rhonda's own American tongue, grabbed his wife's arm and pulled her away. Rhonda stood in shock but quickly remembered herself, dropped her eyes, and moved to stand by her husband.

After a lot of thought and remembering word for word what Layla had told her, Rhonda started to fit the pieces together. She needed to see what the men were doing when they went to the basement. Getting there was the problem. She was kept on a metaphorical tight leash, although it might as well have been a real one attached to a collar around her neck. Guards were everywhere in the house. Surveillance cameras lined every hall and room. Security was so tight she had no idea how she could possibly pull off her escape. Then, one day, she had a revelation. It would be risky, and she could be punished severely or killed if it didn't work, but she had to try something.

Her attendant, Ila, had grown close to her over the past few months. In the beginning, Ila showed compassion when Ahseed punished Rhonda. She bathed Rhonda and helped her soak her sore, beaten body. Once, when Rhonda had disagreed with her husband, he punished her by denying her food for a week. Under her abaya, Ila had smuggled some sliced bread, a bite of cheese, and a handful of olives into Rhonda's room.

Ila had dark skin and eyes. As a trusted servant, she went wherever she wanted around the house, and no one seemed to notice at all. Wearing traditional Muslim garb meant Ila's face and head were always covered. Rhonda had a great idea, but the problem was if Ila would agree to it.

Ahseed had been distracted lately. Rhonda had no idea what was happening, but he had been agitated and irritable. The night before, she had been getting ready for bed when she heard her husband arguing with someone behind closed doors. At one point, she could have sworn she heard an American man yelling loudly. Of course, Ahseed always kept her a safe distance from his business, but this was her chance to act because he was very distracted.

Rhonda waited until late one night when she and Ila were alone. Ila was bathing her. This was another issue that made her extremely uncomfortable, to have another woman bathe her. It was another method her controlling husband used to impress on Rhonda that she belonged to him. She did not even have the freedom or privacy to bathe herself. However, it was in this intimate moment when Rhonda decided to try to talk to Ila.

"How long have you lived here?" Rhonda asked in an innocent voice.

The silence seemed to last forever, broken only by the relaxing flow of water as it trickled from Ila's sponge into the bathtub. Ila finally responded by saying, "I came at the same time you came here to live, Miss Somaya."

"Do you have family?" Rhonda decided to keep pressing on.

"I have a mother, father, and brother. My father had been unable to pay his debt to your husband for a business deal they had made, so I was traded for the payment."

What shocked Rhonda so much was that Ila did not seem angry or sad. Like this was a normal thing to happen. Ila looked down the entire time she spoke, and no emotion crossed her face as she talked. Her voice was low, almost a whisper, and she periodically looked over her shoulder at the door.

"I like it here," she continued. "The house is beautiful, and I am taken care of. I am never hungry, and I like to care for you, Miss Somaya."

Rhonda almost decided to let the conversation end, as she could tell that Ila was content with her life and may not want to risk changing it. But she pressed on and took the chance.

"Do you know how I came to live here?" she ventured.

Ila looked at her for a second and shook her head no.

Rhonda shifted in the tub, taking Ila's hands, sponge and all, into hers. "Please let me explain, but this must be a secret between us, or I will be severely punished. You don't want that, do you?"

Another no, as her eyes remained looking down.

"Help me out of the tub." Ila immediately complied, reaching for a towel and grasping Rhonda's arm in one, practiced motion. She gently helped Rhonda dry off and put on her nightgown. Rhonda sat on the edge of the large bed and motioned for Ila to sit with her. At first, there was a long hesitation, as Ila was not allowed to sit on the bed, but finally, she submitted and sat.

"Let me explain who and what my husband is. But you can never repeat this because I think he would kill us both."

Rhonda told her where she was from and gave her a brief summary of the events that led to her coming to Ahseed's house. Ila never moved, showed no emotion, and never looked at her.

"Ila," Rhonda said, leaning close to the other woman. "Women are being bought and sold, and some are murdered. My husband is part of it."

She thought she felt Ila shudder next to her.

"I want to do something to stop it." Rhonda paused before adding, "And I need your help."

Ila did not move, barely breathed.

"Please, Ila," Rhonda said, trying to keep her voice from shaking. "Please. Will you help me?"

Ila quickly stood and picked up the wet towels and dirty clothes from the floor. She left the room without a word. Rhonda sat in stunned silence, and tears started to stream down her face. Knowing soon she would be beaten, maybe to death, she tried to mentally prepare for what horror was ahead if Ila told Ahseed anything Rhonda had just told her.

It seemed like forever when she heard the bedroom door open. Ila walked in with a clothing bag in her hand. She did not look up but said, "Your husband requests to see you in his room within the hour."

Rhonda knew what this meant. This was his routine. He would summon her like some type of concubine. Ila would bring in whatever lingerie he wanted her to wear; then she would fix Rhonda's hair, add any jewelry Ahseed sent along, and escort Rhonda to his room. Here, Rhonda would have to perform whatever sick sexual fantasy he desired. The things that she had done and endured were depraved, acts no decent man would ever expect a woman to perform. She knew the routine, but it had been a few weeks since Ahseed had called for her. Ila said nothing about what Rhonda had shared with her. She silently helped Rhonda put on the light-pink lace and leather outfit. The Swarovski crystals that adorned the bra made it sparkle and shine in the candlelight. Ila brushed Rhonda's long, black hair over and over until it shone like glass. She twisted it in a soft bun at the nape of Rhonda's neck, holding it in place with one long comb. Ahseed liked Rhonda to wear her hair up in a style that he could easily pull down. Sometimes, though, he pulled hard anyway.

"What a beautiful comb," Rhonda commented, trying to make conversation with Ila. The hair comb tonight was exquisite. Rhonda marveled at the elegant accessory for only his eyes, but he was so ostentatious she should not have been surprised. As she often did, she imagined she was getting ready for a night on the town with a man, a kind man, who would treat her like a precious jewel instead of covering her in them.

"Mr. Ahseed is quite proud of it," Ila said, turning the comb in her hand for Rhonda to admire. "He told me the comb was made from diamonds from Africa, Israel, and Russia." With a gentle tug of Rhonda's hair, the comb was in place. "Its value is one million dollars," Ila added, and Rhonda felt sick to hear her husband's brag to this poor woman.

The walk down the corridor always seemed like the walk of doom to Rhonda. It never got easier, no matter how many times it had happened. Ila walked beside her all the way, and then she was expected to wait outside the door and then escort Rhonda back to her room when he was done with her. Tonight was no different.

Rhonda walked into his room. If possible, it was more obnoxiously ornate than the rest of the house. Only a very few people were allowed in this room—Ahseed's bodyguard, one handpicked housekeeper, and Rhonda. Even his personal assistant had to wait outside the room. Ahseed was a paranoid man and always thought people were trying to steal from him. But he also did not want people to see what a depraved man he really was.

This particular night, he seemed more anxious than previous nights. He typically just told her what he wanted her to do. At times, he was violent, sometimes more brutal than others, but tonight he was almost tender and loving in the beginning. She was instantly more scared than she had ever been. She knew this was not his nature; he was never like this. She dreaded what this change in demeanor could mean.

After her mistress was in the bedroom, Ila, heard heavy footsteps behind her. The security guards were coming down the corridor. They were leading at least ten men, all dressed in very expensive looking suits, with sparkling cuff links and tie clips. Eyes forward, the men did not even seem to notice her. The security guard glared at Ila, so she dropped her head, but she could still see through the thin fabric of her burqa. With a slight pressure on the wall, the guard opened a door that was well hidden in the corner of the corridor, and the men discreetly slipped into the tiny room within. Ila stretched her neck to try to see as much as she could. It was a small viewing room containing a row of heavy, leather chairs facing a mirror that covered the opposite wall. Through the mirror, the men could see right into the bedroom where Miss Somaya and her husband were.

Right as the door was about to close, one of the men summoned Ila.

“You! Woman,” he said.

“Excuse me, sir,” the guard said. “She is nothing. She is the wife’s assistant.”

“She can bring us refreshments, can’t she?” the man argued. “That takes no brains.”

“Yes,” another man called, holding up a glass and rattling the ice cubes in it. “I could use another.”

The guard looked at Ila. “Bring the tray from the front room. Make sure there’s ice in the bucket. And make it quick.”

As fast as she could run in her heavy clothing, Ila retrieved the tray and carried it into the room. Taking her time, she served the men drinks while trying to understand what was happening in the room.

The huge, two-way mirror at the front of the room had an enormous, gold frame, but the men in the room were not interested in the decor. These men were going to watch the sexual act between Miss Somaya and her husband. Ila did not recall this ever happening before, but this could have happened many times and she would have never known. She tried to keep her breathing slow and even to avoid shedding tears.

Through the mirror, Ila could see that Miss Somaya was visibly on edge. Her mistress knew Ahseed was acting different than he ever had, but she clearly had no idea she was being watched. Miss Somaya knew from the past to not be shy, to do whatever he demanded of her. Ila could tell by Miss Somaya's involuntary flinches that Ahseed's new tenderness and affection made her uneasy, but she knew what she had to do to avoid punishment.

He started by kissing her, and slowly, as he sat on the top of the bed, he asked her to undress. He sat like a king, his posture arrogant and smug in between the bedposts. He instructed her what clothing to take off piece by piece. Ila saw that every few minutes, he would glance toward the mirror. He then made her stand before him, nude. She was an exquisite woman. Her body perfect in every way, standing there like a trophy or a piece of livestock being sold. She had no idea what was happening, but Ila did.

The men in the room grunted, whispered, and chuckled, speaking in different languages but with innuendo that was easy to translate. Ila was nauseated by what she saw and heard. Looking away at multiple times due to being utterly repulsed by what she was witnessing, she tried to put this all in the back recess of her mind. Ila knew getting involved could possibly cost her life.

"Woman!" one of the men called, holding up his glass. She moved quickly, trying to refill the man's drink with shaking hands.

You do not disobey, she remembered her father telling her. *You do not go against these powerful men because the penalty will be grave.*

She decided to look one last time, and what she saw this time made her regret the decision. She regretted it because her heart broke for Miss Somaya. Ila knew what she had to do, no matter what. She had to help her mistress escape.

Chapter 35

Rhonda was exhausted. She had no idea what had just happened. This night was so different from any other. Ahseed had been so strange the entire time. He'd had her strip and just stand there while he stared at her. Then he told her to do very odd things. She had to walk around the room and then pleasure him in multiple ways. He restrained her at one point, raping her repeatedly, violating her in every way possible. She always tried not to cry out or scream; she refused to give him the satisfaction. But tonight, he was relentless, and she could not take it any longer. The last time Ahseed sodomized her, she could not help but cry out. She typically kept her eyes closed, but when she felt something rip deep inside her, she saw him looking at himself in the mirror, a sick smile crossing his arrogant face. He was watching himself rape her over and over. When he saw how exhausted she was and that she was bleeding, he ended the assault. Calling for Ila to come collect her, he went into his shower and never even looked back at her.

Ila helped her from the bed, untwisting her from the mess of sheets and blankets. Knowing that they were being watched and seeing her mistress's naked abused body, she picked up a throw from the armchair and covered her. Almost carrying her to the room, she helped Miss Somaya lie on the bed while she ran a hot bath for her. Adding lavender and soothing spices to the water, Ila tried to get a plan together to help her mistress. When she went back into the bedroom and saw the woman's broken and bleeding body curled up on the bed, sympathy welled up within her. She could not help but quietly weep for her behind her veil.

Rhonda did not notice. She was like a robot now, taking off her gown and sliding into the soothing, hot bath. Tears fell over and over, and this was not typical. She had learned to hide her emotions, especially in front of others. But tonight, she was done. She had been pushed to her breaking point. She sat with her eyes closed and seemed to be in a different world. She didn't even seem to notice Ila at all, not until Ila spoke to her, in a whisper so no one else could hear.

"I will help you," she said, gently smoothing the sponge over Rhonda's back. Rhonda did not seem to hear her at first. Ila repeated it again and waited.

Finally, after long hesitation, Rhonda lifted her head and stared at Ila. "What made you change your mind?" Her voice was weak and timid.

"What these men do is wrong and cruel, and I will help you. There have been many American men here the last few weeks, and they seem like something is changing. Security is different, and they are all angry and anxious. I feel something worse is going to happen, and I fear for you. So I will help you."

This was all Ila said. She did not tell her mistress about the viewing room. She could tell that this fact might push Rhonda over the edge.

The women said nothing more that night. After putting Rhonda to bed, Ila went to her room in the servants' area of the house. Over and over, all night long, her mind reviewed the things she had learned and seen with her own eyes. She had to help Miss Somaya. She just did not know how. The nights were always cold and dark, but tonight, the house was darker and colder than she had ever known in her life.

Chapter 36

I was correct when I thought Agent Johnson had unwelcome news.

"We have located footage from the Raleigh airport of a private jet taking off with men who looked like Dr. Ricardo and Dr. Kepler," he said, accepting the steaming cup of coffee Tripp offered. "Many other men boarded with them. The flight plan and destination they filed were fake, and at the airport where they had reported they would be landing, well, of course, they never arrived. They could have gone anywhere." His expression was one of distress.

Ishmael stood up and looked more intense, if that were even possible.

"I understand you want answers," Agent Johnson conceded, holding one hand up as if in surrender. "But you must keep in mind that the relationship between the US and this area of the Middle East is already volatile. The US government does not at this time want to get involved when, let's face it, some details are speculation."

Immediately, I jumped up, raising my voice as I charged at him. "What do you mean *speculation*?" Tripp grabbed me and tried to calm me the best he could.

Defensively, Agent Johnson stood and stepped back. "Layla, in the agency's eyes, this is true. They feel like they cannot confirm with 100 percent certainty that the lady you met was Rhonda. She is dead, by all records, and the administration fears you could be mistaken."

"This is unbelievable," I muttered, breaking away from Tripp.

"I know it seems that way," said Johnson. "The government can't risk political unrest to rescue someone they are not certain is even being held against her wishes. The situation has to be handled correctly," he paused extending his hands in a "calm down" position, "and that will take time." He was trying to calm all the raging emotions in the room, but it seemed to have the opposite effect.

The fury on the faces of Ishmael, Ahmed, and me was quite dramatic. Even Aubrey, trained FBI cadet, had started to cry. The emotional stress of the past few weeks was taking a toll on her young psyche. There were no tears in my eyes. I was not sad or anxious—I was simply furious. I could tell that the agent had no idea what to do or say next. He was as upset as anyone else.

Tripp spoke first, asking, "What do we do now? What comes next?"

Agent Johnson sounded defeated. "We will keep going through Dr. Ricardo's house and the computers around the clock, trying to get more intel. At this time, locating Kayleigh is the main goal, and the US ambassador to Dubai will be briefed in a few weeks."

"A few weeks?" I asked, incredulous.

"Yes, and then they will try to contact the accused man in that country. That's all I can offer at this time. I am so sorry."

Once again, I could not control the volume, rudeness, or threatening tone of my voice. "Are they crazy?" I demanded. "If they let Dr. Ricardo know they're coming, he'll kill Kayleigh! We have no idea where they took her." I stepped toward him, taking back his safe space. "You tell us the US can't help Rhonda, but, I mean, what are we supposed to do? Nothing?"

I simply could not contain myself. After I ranted and cussed and threw some things, I felt better. When I was finished with my tirade, everyone in the room just stood there staring at me. Tripp's face serious and sad, and the agent's eyes locked with mine. Everyone else seemed to be in their own headspace, thinking of what to do next.

In the silence of the room, with Agent Johnson still staring at me, I noticed his hand gripped on the weapon at his hip. I took the hint, exhaled deeply, and sat down.

"Okay," he muttered, dropping his hand to his side. "I am going to head back to the office.

"No!" I said quickly. "I–I am sorry. I don't know what came over me. Please stay."

"I really should go," he insisted. "I'll be in touch if I hear anything."

He turned quickly and left the room, and I dropped my head into my hands. When I looked up again, I noticed that Ishmael and Ahmed were whispering in the corner, their faces tight and determined. I recognized that look because I had it often.

"What's going on?" I asked.

Ahmed looked at me with some embarrassment. "We have a plan," he said. "We are going to try to get Rhonda without the US authorities' help. We all knew the men had most likely left the US, and maybe they took Kayleigh wherever they flew to."

That was my hope, too, because the alternative was unthinkable.

"But that's just what Agent Johnson was saying. Dubai is a long and dangerous way to go for 'most likely' and 'maybe.'"

Ishmael's expression was complete sorrow. He met Tripp's eyes and simply said, "It's all we have, sir."

After a moment, Tripp said, "What's your plan?"

Ishmael, with a low tone, explained. "I have wealthy family members there, and we have visas and can go anytime. As Americans, all you need at the airport in Dubai is to get a temporary visa, which you can get when you arrive. I am going to rent a private jet to get us there."

He planned to get there as soon as possible and rescue his daughter. I knew we needed to all calm down and try to get a plan together. But I also knew exactly how he felt. I had just felt the same way when I needed to get to my daughter. He was determined. He was boiling from the inside out. Ishmael *had* to find his daughter, and waiting even another moment was torture for him and probably her. He took this very personally. Someone from his own country, his faith, and his "brotherhood" had taken his daughter as a slave. This was a shock to him, and the fact that these men were using the sacred field of medicine to torture innocent women—well, it was too much for his brilliant mind to conceive.

He walked over to me and looked me in the eye. The look in his eyes sent a charge down my spine.

"I thank you for what you have done for my daughter. I am going to repay you, but right now, I must get her out of the hell she is in, and," he added calmly, "I am going to kill the man who has taken my daughter as a slave. I swear to Allah, I will kill this man with my bare hands." His tone was deep and sinister, and I knew with every fiber of my being that he was telling the truth. He pulled out his cellphone and walked out of the room.

"I need some air," Aubrey said. "I'll be on the front porch." She hugged me, and I could feel the weariness in her embrace.

Tripp stood across the room staring at me, eyes hard and stern. I walked over to him and hugged him. This hug was hard and long. I embraced my husband because I missed him. The hours he had spent staring at computer screens, pacing the floor with worry, and assisting any way he could with the investigation had dispelled almost all thoughts I had about his involvement in the trafficking scheme, and that filled me with relief. I was ashamed I had even considered that as a possibility. I put my face in the soft part of his neck and took a deep breath. The mix of his body wash and his Polo cologne made me feel safe. This nightmare was far from over, but at that second, in his arms, I was safe and loved. I felt tears fall from his handsome cheeks, and I could not help but get emotional too. But not in an anxious or scared way. A way that felt like peace, like I could feel the end of the nightmare coming.

I stood there and could hear the plans around me going forward. We were all going on this mission. We all needed to get into the country and find Rhonda, and to look for Kayleigh. We had no way of knowing whether Kayleigh was with them, but we had to hope.

Chapter 37

Rhonda was exhausted. Physically and mentally, she'd had all she could stand. She had climbed into the hot bath the night before a broken woman, but when Ila whispered in her ear, it was like electricity surged through her. On that particular morning as the sun rose, she sat on her bed and looked out at the Persian Gulf. It was spectacular here. The water was blue and clear, not a cloud in the sky. Under normal circumstances, she would have loved the culture and exploring the country, but not like this.

In the distance, she could see the iconic Dubai landmark, the Burj Al Arab. This spectacular, sail-shaped building was a tourist attraction and one of the most famous hotels in the world. She could see it billowing high above the sea. Only the most distinguished guests frequented this lavish hotel. She had been allowed to attend only one party there, and she had to admit, it was a wonderful experience. Yes, she had been treated as a trophy and paraded around the dignitaries like a show pony, but she loved the things she got to see on the short visit there. As much as she would enjoy seeing this part of the world, exploring and learning, she knew that if she ever escaped this, she would never return.

Anxiously awaiting Ila, she dressed and sat on the balcony. Rhonda was so excited when Ila finally arrived with the morning's array of fresh fruit and pastries. She invited Ila out on the balcony, and they ate together. It would be safer out there, with less chance that anyone would overhear their conversation.

Ila started in a low secretive tone. "Americans have been coming. They have been staying in various parts of the house. There was a heated argument among some of them, but I am not sure what about." She stopped to take a bite of a mango. Seemed to stare off, thinking carefully about her words, before continuing. "The house staff is making plans for a huge party in two nights. The type of party where the men come and then go to the viewing room."

"Viewing room?"

Ila pressed her lips together as if she had said something wrong. "I mean, they go into a private room to discuss their business." She smacked herself playfully on the head. "My English is still confusing."

Rhonda reached over and placed her hand on Ila's. "Thank you so much for what you are doing. I know this is terrifying." Rhonda took her hand and looked deep into her eyes. "I have a plan."

Ila sat up straighter. "Go on, then, and tell me!"

"We could switch places," she said carefully. "I will put on the traditional attire that you typically wear. In the dim light, it will be difficult for anyone to know it isn't you. At the previous parties, I make a short appearance, and he excuses me. Then I stay alone in my room for the remainder of the night. But this way, I could move freely around the house. I can listen to what they are saying and maybe figure out a way to get out. This could work, Ila. I know it could!"

Ila sat quietly, and Rhonda could tell she was considering it. After a long pause, Ila nodded her head rapidly. "Yes, yes, that could work. I never speak, and no one ever comes to check on you in your room but me, so, yes, I think the plan is good."

"Ila, I know it is very dangerous, but we can do this!" A short embrace sealed the deal for them both.

Rhonda had hope. She was ecstatic that this might be her way out. Knowledge is power, and if she could find out what was going on, it may help her contact someone in the US or even escape altogether. The risks and the chance of death were always in the back of her mind, but she knew she could not live through another night like the past one. She would rather die than remain a slave to the hideous monster she was living with.

Rhonda listened intently as Ila tried to tell her everything she could about the layout of the house. Ila was allowed to move freely in certain areas, but there were other areas where she was always escorted by security.

"The hallway outside of your room goes to the right. When you are pretending to be me, never, ever go left. The guards would know instantly this is wrong. The kitchen is this way, and the main entrance of the house is past the kitchen." Ila continued to explain the layout of the house, and Rhonda closed her eyes and imagined herself moving from room to room. The plan had to be close to perfect so no one would be suspicious of her when she was out of her room.

Ila tried to explain some of the conversations she had overheard.

"One American man arrived with a lady who looked to be American. She had been restrained but appeared to be drugged because she was sleeping. I thought it was odd because the woman was handcuffed but also asleep. It was odd also because she had extra guards. One of the other women attendants had gone and cared for the woman and washed her. She told us about it that night in the servants' quarters."

This concerned Rhonda. She had never seen another female held against her will in the house except for the women who occasionally attended the parties. Why would they bring another American here? Were they going to bring more women to auction? She had to try to save them if this were the case. She felt an overwhelming sense that this was her purpose for being here.

They sat on the balcony for hours and walked in the garden that day until they had the plan as close to perfect as they could get. They decided they would make their move on the night of the party, in two nights, and it could not come soon enough for Rhonda.

Chapter 38

The flight from New York to Dubai was close to fourteen hours. I spent most of it dozing, Tripp by my side. Aubrey was sitting with Ahmed, and they were talking quietly, and it warmed my heart to see her smile. Ishmael and Ahmed needed Rhonda back, and I needed Kayleigh. I had no idea if she was there, but I had to try. Also, if the men responsible for this nightmare had sought refuge in Dubai, I wanted to see them, and, yes, I wanted to see them punished. We were doing this all on our own with no help from the US government.

Agent Johnson had called my phone over forty-five times during the flight. His messages warned over and over not to do anything stupid. They were useless warnings. We all knew this was crazy and extremely risky. Being US citizens in the United Arab Emirates without the permission of the government, we were asking for trouble, but we had to take the risk.

Ishmael never spoke during the flight. Occasionally, he closed his eyes and lifted his hands, as if praying. Mostly, he just sat with a stern look on his face, staring out the window. He appeared as volatile as anyone I had ever seen in my life. Seeing him sitting with his fists clenched, lines of stress and fury etched across his face, I could not help but wonder what was going on in his mind. What was his plan? We could not just walk up to the door and ask to come in.

Tripp was dozing in the seat next to me. I knew we would land soon, so I let him rest a moment longer. I got up to stretch my legs and decided to talk to Ishmael. I did not like the thought of being unprepared and not knowing what was ahead of us.

I went over and looked down at him. I stood there awkwardly and asked if I could be seated. Not speaking, he nodded, and I sat. The silence lasted for quite a few moments, and then I finally asked, “Do we have any idea what we are going to do when we land?”

After another long pause, he said, “One of my cousins is meeting us at the airport, and we are going to his house to decide what our next step should be. We have to go about this carefully, or we could all be in danger, especially Rhonda.”

That was all he said; then he turned to peer out of the window, and I knew the conversation was over. That was all he felt I needed to know and all he was willing to share.

After what seemed like the longest flight possible, we landed. As Ishmael promised, a man greeted him and Ahmed with a familial embrace. Without introductions, we were hurried into a black SUV, where two other men about Ahmed’s age waited. The air was dry and hot and felt like a slap as we stepped out of the airport. Luckily the SUV was cool.

During the ride, the men conversed in clipped Arabic, so I was able to look at the unfamiliar, exotic land around me. On one side of the street there was desert, but on the other, a beautiful, very lavish city. I was shocked at how very clean and pristine the streets where. No trash, no vandalism, no homeless people. All of the buildings where modern and clean. Grass and landscaping were perfectly manicured. I had read about this city, City of Gold. And now I could see where this name came from.

Finally, we stopped on the outskirts of town. Ishmael hurried us out of the vehicle and into the small house as if eyes were all around and he did not want them to see us. The house was warm and stuffy but clean and modern. A woman in a heavy burqa served us fruit, bread, and tea. I expressed my gratitude as best as I could.

Ishmael had already updated the men who picked us up—I assumed they were the family he had spoken of—about what had happened. He had told them to start asking questions around town, looking and trying to locate who could have Rhonda. Ishmael and his relatives mainly spoke in Arabic, so I understood nothing except what Ahmed translated.

"We have been blessed by Allah," the oldest of the men said. "A rich man's servant saw Rhonda's picture, and she recognized Rhonda. The servant delivers food to the rich man's house for great events and had briefly seen Rhonda a few times. She remembered her because she could see the woman was very fearful and anxious. The man's name is Ahseed. He lives in a large mansion, and he is well known for his vast wealth. He also has a reputation for being extremely powerful and cruel."

At this Ishmael made a little gasping noise, and Ahmed placed a comforting hand on his father's shoulder.

As luck would have it, there was some type of party at Ahseed's house the next night. The servant who had recognized Rhonda had been brutally beaten by a guard in the past, so she had no feelings of loyalty and was willing to give information and help. Ahseed apparently had many gatherings, and she had served at the house often.

We now needed to find a way in. There was no doubt that security would be quite impressive for a man of Ahseed's wealth, and it would not be an easy task getting in.

Ahmed turned to us, "Determining what type of party would be of great value. These wealthy men were always having benefit dinners and fundraisers. Maybe this will help us find a way in."

I knew he was right, but I was very out of my element here. I had no idea what to do next. I decided to walk outside for just a moment to get some air. I had been closed in that plane for so long, and now in this tiny house, I just needed air.

It was hot and dry. No breeze at all, and the temperature was at ninety-six degrees. The neighborhood where Ishmael's family lived was small but neat and clean. The "workers" lived in small communities like this one that skirted the elaborate high-rise buildings. I could see them off in the distance. The massive buildings looked like scary giants looming over a miniature city. The ocean glimmered in the distance on the other side. I would have loved to go and spread a towel on the sand and lie in the sun, but this was no vacation; rather, it was a life and death mission.

I felt Tripp's arms wrap around me.

“The men have concluded that there is no way to get in to Ahseed’s,” he reported.

I felt my spirit deflate, and I turned to face him. “There has to be a way!”

He shook his head sorrowfully. “This party was by invitation only, and we have no way to get invited. It is very secretive, and no one has any idea what’s taking place. Ahmed’s cousins asked around town, and no one even knew the event was taking place except the caterers, who were ordered to maintain strict confidentiality.”

I frowned. “This seems odd for someone who is known to flaunt any event that could put his wealth on display.”

Discouraged, we turned to go inside. As we walked back into the small living area, I had an idea. With everyone looking defeated, I spoke up.

“Okay, hear me out.”

Ishmael immediately began translating my words for his family. “With the help of your contact, couldn’t we go in as kitchen staff? We could pay off the regular workers and then take their places.” I was becoming more excited about my idea. “That could work!”

I watched the expressions of the others as Ahmed translated. Tripp’s face had that look, the one I had grown to dislike because it meant he was going to argue.

Still sounding upbeat and positive I carried on. “If we put on the traditional attire and do not speak, I could go in, and so could Aubrey.”

One of the men interrupted, and Ahmed relayed his words to me. "My cousin wants to know how you will understand what the staff orders you to do while serving."

This hadn't occurred to me, but it seemed like a minor detail. "It's a risk we can take." I turned to my husband. "I know you can't go in, Tripp. There's no way to disguise you. But we need to do something. This is our only way in." I walked over and hugged him.

"I don't like this," he said feebly.

"We have come so far, baby. You just wait right here for us, and when we come back, this will all be over. I love you!"

He shrugged and reluctantly agreed, probably not because he wanted to but because he knew it was our only recourse.

Aubrey, Ahmed, Ishmael, and I planned to go disguised and work in the kitchen. At some point, we would break away and look for Rhonda. Ishmael's family agreed to find a way to smuggle weapons into the house by hiding them in with supplies and food for the party. I felt nauseated, but I knew in my heart this is what it would come to. Ishmael had sworn to kill the man who did this, and I had no doubt that's just what he would do.

Chapter 39

Rhonda had a wonderful dream while she slept. She dreamed that her father, a man whom she admired and loved, had come to rescue her. When she awoke, she lay for a long time thinking about the dream. She knew in her heart this was impossible, and she wasn't even certain her father was still alive. But the dream had felt so real. She could see his dark eyes with the crows feet at the corners that only appeared when he truly laughed. He had not laughed often since the death of her mother. In her dream, his strong hands grasped hers, smooth, the hands of a healer. He had pulled her into his arms and hugged her, and in that moment, she was safe. She could smell his earthy aroma, and this made her even more nostalgic. The dream had refreshed her and renewed her hope.

Ila was already in her room, busy with morning preparations. Rhonda could tell by her demeanor she was nervous.

"Are you okay?" Rhonda's voice was small in the large room.

"Yes, I want to help," Ila said, her voice uncharacteristically sharp and short. "I know I must help you, as it is the right and honorable thing to do, but I fear for both of us." She twisted her hands together. "No matter what happens, Miss Somaya, I know that Allah has blessed me in this."

She was nervous but her voice had an undertone of resolve. She knew she had no choice but to carry on with the plan even if it cost her life.

The staff spent the day decorating the house with massive bouquets of flowers, preparing the rich foods, and adding the final touches for the party.

"I have never seen the master of the house go to such extravagant lengths for any other parties," Ila nervously talked as she straightened the room. "He has spared no expense with the most expensive champagnes and foods flown in from all over the globe."

The dress Ahseed had chosen for Rhonda to wear that night was the most gorgeous one yet—simply breathtaking. The dress was couture from a famous designer in Dubai named Rami Al Ali. A pale blush, floor-length gown with a plunging neckline. The tight fit revealed her perfect figure. The fabric was exquisite, and she had never felt anything like it. It was satiny but soft like a polished cotton. Attached to the shoulders was a beaded cape that was longer than the dress itself, creating a train. The belt was covered in beautiful crystals. Rhonda knew he was trying to impress someone to go to this expense. She could not help but feel beautiful and desirable in the magnificent dress, a reality that caused her stomach to cramp. The last thing she wanted was to be *desired* again, not now, not ever.

As Ila was assisting, she continued to update Rhonda. "The master's assistant directed me to make sure you looked most beautiful tonight. I ask questions as to why all of the fuss, but she would not answer me. I ask who the guests were being entertained, but she also did not answer. I did not feel safe asking any further questions."

Rhonda could almost feel the electricity in the room. Getting ready in the gorgeous gown and the excitement of the mission they were about to undertake had Rhonda's adrenaline running high. She replayed the plan over and over in her mind. She would go to the dinner as always; she would be the obedient wife, smile, and keep her eyes down and lips closed. When Ahseed dismissed her, she would come back to her room with Ila, and she would put on one of Ila's niqab and abaya. This would allow her to move more freely in the house, and Ila would lie in Rhonda's bed and appear to be sleeping in case someone decided to check on her.

The ballroom was decorated unlike anything Rhonda had ever seen. The food and champagne were in unlimited supply. Uniformed servers carried fancy pastries and cocktails on silver trays, offering them to the guests, and what a gathering it was. Trays of beluga caviar and beautiful oysters were only a few of the delicious offerings. For dinner, they were served lobster and spider king crab. Her master had spared no expense.

Rhonda had never seen such intimidating men in her entire life. They were wealthy, powerful men of all ethnicities. The way they carried themselves, their attire, and demeanor made her feel small and invisible. She also noticed some guests had translators and some did not. But what was the most interesting was the American men who had joined them. This was not normally the case, so she was shocked. At one point, she peered at an American man a little too long, and her husband's twist of her wrist quickly reminded her to put her eyes down. She was not to make direct eye contact with any male, ever. This offense had been the cause of many beatings when she first arrived.

It seemed as if everyone were on edge. She could not tell if it was excitement due to the party or if it was just her own mindset of high alert. The dinner and socializing portion of the party lasted longer than usual, and once again, Rhonda could not help but to notice how over-the-top her husband seemed tonight. He always demanded to be in control of the room, but tonight he was louder and more flamboyant than normal. Constantly calling attention to his house, his money, and to her.

"Look at my gorgeous wife, Somaya, gentlemen. Look how perfect she is in every way!" He laughed and paraded Rhonda around like a show horse. Finally, he dismissed her, making a show of kissing her hand and then her neck. *I love you. I own you*, the gestures seemed to say.

But even without this display, Rhonda had felt that she was being watched all night. Was she paranoid? At one point, she even felt like the kitchen staff had been staring at her, brushing too close to her, lingering in front of her. She was about to panic, thinking that her husband was on to her and was having everyone keep an eye on her, when Ahseed signaled for a guard to escort her to her room. Ila followed, and once the two women were alone behind the closed door of Rhonda's bedroom, the true excitement started.

Rhonda peeled off the beautiful gown. It was a symbol of wealth and power to most people looking in from the outside. But to Rhonda it was a prison, a jeweled, diamond prison. Pulling it off felt like releasing herself from the bonds that had held her captive. Then as she placed the niqab over her face, she started to feel free. She smiled at the irony. Most American women felt this was a demeaning attire, that it represented oppression. But this meant freedom for Rhonda. She had come full circle as a woman and as a Muslim, going back to her heritage would be her salvation.

Rhonda was able to walk freely. It felt amazing to her since, in the past, she had been privy to very little of the house. Her heart was pounding in her chest and head. She was terrified but excited all at the same time as she closed her bedroom door behind her, remembering Ila's instructions to turn right only, and walked back down the stairs to the party. She would be invisible, a simple servant, and would be able to listen and spy practically unnoticed.

Rhonda passed many people in the hallways, all servants rushing in and out, attending to the needs of the guests. She passed the ballroom just as the other women were excused. Security guards or personal attendants escorted them to their cars and, she assumed, back to hotels. Just like before, the men followed Rhonda's husband down a long hallway to—what had Ila called it?—a viewing room. Ila's instructions were perfect, and Rhonda was able to get ahead of the group of men while they were refilling their drinks. She slipped into the tiny room and hid herself up in the loft. She was able to slide in and lay flat, looking into the room through a small vent in the floor. The theater room had rows of leather chairs that faced a huge movie screen. The ornate, stained-glass windows lined the top edge of the room.

Rhonda counted twenty men entering the room, laughing and talking, holding glasses of expensive scotch or other after-dinner cocktails. Finally, after a lot of banter, an Arabic man stood to speak. He was joined by an American man who stood beside him. Rhonda did not know either man and was puzzled that her husband was not taking the lead. He was sitting in the front row and appeared to be unhinged with excitement. A huge toothy smile covered his face. She could not help but feel utter hatred for this human. Silently she prayed for forgiveness.

"Welcome! Welcome!" the man said. "We are so honored to have you all here tonight. I want to thank our generous host for inviting us into his gorgeous home and for the wonderful food and drink." The men collectively gave a short cheer toward the host who smiled even bigger.

"Let's get straight to why we are all here," the man continued. "Let me introduce our American visitor, Dr. Javier Ricardo. He has graciously joined us from the USA to discuss what he has to offer us tonight. Let us give him a warm welcome and our undivided attention."

Intoxicated cheers once again filled the room. The Arabic man sat, and the American surveyed the room.

"Thank you all for inviting me here," he said, speaking slowly for those whose English was not fluent. "I am so excited to meet some of you in person. As you know, our auction has been hugely successful across the globe."

Several of the men applauded politely.

"Since so many different women come to the US, it is the proverbial melting pot, making it easy for men like you to request whatever type of women they desire. So many different nationalities come to the US and are born there. No matter where you are from, we can match you with the perfect woman."

Rhonda could feel the bile rising in her throat.

"Here is the basic method of operation. We painstakingly arrange the circumstances so that the woman is declared dead, so there is no way to trace her—no one comes to look for her. Any family or friends have no reason to believe she is not buried in the ground or even cremated. The method is discreet and virtually foolproof."

He was describing what had happened to Rhonda. She watched the men's faces and how happy and excited they looked. She silently prayed again but this time not for forgiveness. This was a prayer of vengeance. She prayed for Allah to strike these men down.

"Of course," the American doctor droned on, "any and all of you are welcome to attend the next body auction, but there is no guarantee your specific needs will be met. If you are looking for a particular product, all you have to do is explain what you desire, pay the initial fee, and we *will* find you a match."

There were nods and murmurs among the men, and at this point in the presentation, Rhonda's husband stood.

"I can't say enough about this," he said sincerely. "You have all seen my wife, yes?"

The men grunted and chuckled, and Rhonda felt a fire of rage in her chest.

Ahseed continued, emboldened by the appreciation of the other men. "I explained to my American friend here that I wanted a pure woman of Egyptian descent. Beautiful, intelligent, and with no ties. I did not want to deal with family issues or other baggage, so this option was perfect for me. I was relieved that she was not able to be traced, and I did not have to worry about her ever being located. Yes," he conceded with a little shrug, "she was challenging to train at first, but she has been trained now, and as you all witnessed the other night, she will do whatever I tell her to do. I have broken her to my will like a trained stallion."

The room erupted in cheers and primal noises from the men, whistles and clapping seeming to go on and on.

Rhonda had no idea what he meant, but a sick feeling consumed her as she remembered the night he'd been so strange, especially his bizarre and insatiable demands in the bedroom. Tears stung as they streamed from her eyes. Putting her hands tight against her lips, she forbid the sob to escape. She could not allow herself to get emotional now. She had to remember the task at hand and focus.

The lights in the room went dim, and a film flickered on the large screen. It started by showing the flag of the United States blowing gently in the breeze, and for a moment, Rhonda felt like crying. She missed America—not just her family and her home but also the freedom and the culture. She had taken for granted that not all countries allow women to be free and independent.

Then the faces of powerful women appeared across the screen, multiple rich women in business, entertainment, and politics. A male voiceover with a thick accent Rhonda could not place said, "Women in the United States do not know their place. Some even think they can be president! Women have no right ruling over men, and this is a way for you men to put the American woman back where she belongs."

The images now switched to elegantly dressed women standing close to their husbands, eyes down, hands open in servitude, other women standing behind their husbands, serving them dinner, sitting on the floor beside their chairs.

"You can purchase almost any American woman you choose," the narrator continued, "and in secrecy, she will belong to you—be a slave to you in every way."

As the images continued to show all types of women of different ethnicities, the voiceover went on to explain how the women learned that if they ever tried to escape, the families and people they loved would die. "Women are so protective and ignorant," he said matter-offactly, "that they don't try to escape, and they submit to their new lives easily. You see, women are lower than men. They were created to serve man, not be equal. They are ignorant and easily broken. But if you aren't happy with your product, you can sell her back for resale or dispose of her yourself."

Rhonda once again swallowed back the bile that had gathered in her throat. They were discussing American woman like they were cattle at a sale. Individual men stood and gave personal testimonials of the wives they had purchased and how well it had gone for them. These were the men Rhonda had seen with women at previous parties. They also explained that they could purchase more than one woman, and once again, they could always attend an auction. Some of the men wanted a woman of their ethnic background to bear children but wanted the true, typical American woman to have as a concubine. Rhonda squeezed her eyes shut and pressed her hands to her ears as the men casually discussed this option.

When she looked again, the presentation seemed to have shifted to a question-and-answer session. One man stood and asked Dr. Ricardo, "How can I trust you? After all, you are American."

Dr. Ricardo stood slowly, a smug smile on his face as he tugged disinterestedly at the cuff of his tuxedo coat. "I feel like a woman's place is by her husband's side," he said. "And in the United States, this relationship is out of control. The women have no respect for men, and when one woman almost became president, well, that was enough for me."

The man who asked the question seemed to soften as the men around him murmured their approval.

Ricardo continued, “This auction will not change the course of women in that country, but it makes some men feel better and more powerful, and I make money doing it!” With that, he raised his glass, and the men laughed and cheered.

They discussed that no women were ever taken from their country of origin, and none would ever be. If a woman was taken from outside the US, she was an American who had moved there from her home country or was visiting. The operation had contacts all over the globe, so the possibilities were endless.

At that moment, Rhonda almost started to cry as she realized the overwhelming reach of this business. She knew she could not beat these men and save herself, let alone anyone else. These psychopaths were out of control, and she was not sure how she ever thought she could save herself. Quietly, she crawled out of her little hiding spot and started to make her way back to her room. She had her head and eyes down and was hoping the tears that were streaming could not be seen. She was so distraught that she did not notice she was being followed and didn’t see the man who grabbed her from behind.

Chapter 40

Ila lay still in the bed, frozen, paranoid that someone would come in. She could hardly breathe when the door slowly opened. It was dark; they would think she was asleep and leave. But when she heard footsteps coming toward her, she was about to panic when she heard a low male voice. "Miss Somaya? Is that you?" Ila turned to look and saw a man who appeared to be a kitchen servant looking at her over the side of the bed. The man looked shocked when he saw Ila instead of Rhonda.

"Please don't kill me!" Ila begged, sitting up in the bed and pulling the coverlet up to her chin. "Please let me explain! Please mercy, mercy..."

He held his hands up in front of himself as a sign of peace. "I am not here to hurt you. I came to help Miss Somaya. Rhonda."

Relief overcame Ila as she realized by his voice that he was American.

"I am Rhonda's brother," he explained, "and I am here to rescue her. Do you know where she is?

"Yes, yes, I know," the woman said, jumping excitedly from the bed. "We switched places. Miss Somaya, Miss Rhonda, is dressed in my clothing and went out into the house to try to find a way to escape. I have been helping her."

Ahmed was overwhelmed that Rhonda was trying to escape on her own, but this worried him. This would make her rescue much more difficult.

"I have people with me to help. How long has she been gone?"

"She has been gone for a while now, over an hour, but I do not know where she is. I had told her where to go, and she was going to come back here when she had gotten any information."

"Okay, you stay here. I am going back to the kitchen to update my people. There are many security guards here, but when the party ends this should decrease. Then it will be safer. I promise I will return for you soon."

He turned and was gone.

Ila, overcome with joy for her mistress' escape, paced slowly around the room, her palms lifted in silent prayer. When the door opened only a few moments later, Ila thought the American man had come back early. She was shocked to see it was Rhonda returning.

"Miss Somaya! You will not believe—"

Rhonda shushed her, quickly pulling the heavy garment from her face and head. "A man grabbed me in the hallway," she whispered fiercely. "He thought I was you, Ila. He told me to go straight here and tell 'Rhonda' how she was going to be rescued."

"I do not know who that was, but there are many saviors here for you, my sister." She took a dramatic pause. "Your brother came here and found me."

As Rhonda was taking off her garments, she stopped, frozen with shock.

"My brother?"

"He said he was. He is in this house to save you!"

Tears of joy filled Rhonda's eyes and she embraced Ila, spinning her around and laughing with abandon. Then fear gripped her.

"No, no! If they catch him, they will kill him. He is my brother. I can't let him die!"

Ila saw her fear and tried to comfort her. "Listen, miss, listen. He promised he had help and that he would be back. All we can do is wait."

Time seemed to move at the pace of a turtle. Rhonda paced the floor for ages. She and Ila had seen most of the men and the security leave a few hours ago and could not understand why nothing had happened yet. Finally, when a light knock came on the door, Rhonda could not get to it fast enough. When she opened it, she could not believe what she saw.

A woman was standing there in a burqa, and when she pulled the face cloth down, Rhonda looked confused. Then recognition spread over her face.

"Layla!" she breathed. "You found me!"

Chapter 41

Rhonda pulled me into the room and embraced me hard and long. "What are you doing here?" she gasped. "Ila," she gestured to the other woman in the room, "said my brother was here. Where is he? What is going on?"

I motioned for her to keep her voice low. "We are here disguised as kitchen staff, and as we were being dismissed for the night, I was able to get away. Rhonda, your brother is not the only one here for you. Your father is here."

Like a water faucet, the tears poured down Rhonda's face.

"Ahmed and Ishmael, along with the other men, have gone to look for your captor."

Rhonda was crying, smiling, and shaking with a flood of emotions. It seemed her body and mind could not agree on which one to exhibit.

"Get dressed," I urged. "We are going to leave with the other servants, but we need to hurry."

"No, no, this will not work," Ila pleaded. "They will know me and that I would not be leaving. This will not work!"

"It's our best shot, Ila," Rhonda said, covering her face with Ila's veil. "Come on. I won't leave you behind."

"There is a supply truck parked out back, the one that brought in the crates of food. It will take us off the property. My daughter, Aubrey, is already there waiting for us."

As Rhonda packed a few necessities, Ila went to check the hallways for security. When she returned and let us know it was safe, we quietly stepped down the long corridor.

Suddenly, there were popping sounds all around. In shock at first, we didn't realize it was gunfire. Two of Ahseed's security men, dressed in white caftans, came running toward us with guns drawn, and they shoved us back into Rhonda's room. Yells in Arabic surrounded us. The events were like something out of a movie. A movie—yes, it felt like we were in a movie, the never-ending horror film. The security men wore earpieces, and this seemed to be where their orders were coming from. Following instructions we could not hear, one man tied Rhonda and Ila with their hands behind their backs, and when the man came to me and pulled down my face covering, he was clearly shocked.

"American?" he coughed. Yelling loudly into his mouthpiece while he restrained me, I caught a glimpse of Ila's expression. I had no idea what he said, but by the look on her face, it wasn't good.

Soon, Rhonda's husband and a few more security men arrived. Ahseed walked straight over to Rhonda and backhanded her so hard she fell to the floor. With her hands still bound, she quickly struggled to sit up straight, proud, and ready for more. This infuriated him even more, and he drew his hand back for another strike when the door opened again. To my great surprise, in walked my old friend, Javier Ricardo. He looked around the room at the chaos, and our eyes met. I just stood there, my mouth hanging open, wanting to say so much but, at this moment, lost for words.

He walked calmly over to me and laughed with fake cordiality. "Layla, my dear, it sure took you long enough to figure this out, didn't it? Bless your heart, as you Southerners say!" He was laughing almost hysterically in my face.

I held up my hands. "Why don't you tie me up too?" I dared.

He grinned. "You fight like a tiger. It turns me on."

Before I could think about it, I spat in his face. I received the same punishment as Rhonda, with a sharp backhand to the face. I had not even noticed one of the security guards until he walked over to us. He pulled out a small gun, and before Rhonda could do anything, he shot Ila in the head. Not a word, not a warning—he just shot her. Rhonda screamed in agony. Tears started to pour, and I was once again in such shock that I just stood there.

He then walked over to me, gun ready, pointed at my head. Dr. Ricardo stood back with a sickening smile. I knew I needed to stall them. I breathed slowly. *Help is on the way*, I reminded myself. They were here in the house. We just needed to give them time to find us. Surely the gunshots would lead them here.

"Wait, wait," I gasped, leaning toward Dr. Ricardo. "Can I just ask you something before I die?" I held my hands up as if in surrender.

He smiled and motioned for the man to wait on my execution.

"I just want to know why you, as a healer, a physician, would do this? Why would you do this to Kayleigh? She loved you, did you know that? You are a loved man and a great doctor. Why would you do these insane things you have done?"

He tilted his head sympathetically. "You, my dear, of all people should know how I like to live. You saw my home. I love beautiful things. I must have a certain lifestyle to be fulfilled and happy. I also like to collect things. Fine art, artifacts, and, of course, women." His eyebrows flicked upward. "But I am a businessman. Medicine only takes from us. You know this, Layla. We get paid to kill ourselves taking care of rude patients. They are ungrateful, mean, and they never appreciate what we do for them. They yell at us, cuss us, and never consider what we do for them."

I nodded to show I understood and agreed with him.

"People have become so ungrateful," said Ricardo, "and now with the government, we make less and get sued more often."

"Are we really expected to work countless hours, not sleep, and have horrible conditions to get such pitiful pay?" I interjected.

Ricardo snorted. "I stopped caring about the patients years ago. I need to take care of myself. To do that, I joined in the business of the auction, and it has been quite amazing for me." He shook his head sadly. "I know Kayleigh loved me, and you have no business bringing her up, so unless you have anything else to say, it is time for you to die. You have caused me nothing but trouble since the beginning."

I could tell I struck a sore spot with the mention of Kayleigh. I think he cared for her. The tone of his voice and the emotion he had on his face with just the mention of her name showed me as much. He actually flushed with emotion, anger or regret? So I dug in.

"She had never felt that way about anyone. She would have done anything for you, but you betrayed her. What did you do? Kill her? Sell her? Let someone harvest her organs? You are an animal, and I hope you meet the same fate as those women you have tortured!"

Another nice blow to the face sent me to my knees, my ears ringing. Ricardo started to talk again. He was furious, red-faced, and volatile. "I told you to shut your mouth about Kayleigh, or I swear, I will kill you myself, and it will not be as painless as a bullet to the head."

"What about Whitley?" I gasped, tasting blood in my mouth. "Do you remember her? She was a beautiful light, and you snuffed her out in her youth?" I knew I needed to try to keep my word to Krissy, so I decided to keep digging.

A smiled played at the corners of his mouth. "I do remember Whitley," he mused. "She was in one of the first groups. So beautiful, I felt some lucky client would choose her as a wife. Her youth and many years of childbearing would have made her a great choice. She made me a fortune, with her rare blood type. When the emperor of an Asian country called—his daughter needed a heart-lung transplant—well, she was perfect. That wasn't what I had planned for her, but it worked out perfectly. The process of harvesting her taught me a lot about how to use my product to its fullest potential. She made me more than an entire auction with that harvest," he mused, clearly proud of himself.

The vomit spewed from me before I even felt it coming. They took her organs while she was alive. I was in hell! I just sat there on the floor, vomit dripping from my chin, sweat pouring down my forehead, defeated. I could see Rhonda. Her head was down. She was weeping, with blood splatter all over her and brain matter from her friend, Ila, covering her clothing.

The gun barrel felt cool to my hot forehead. I exhaled and surrendered. I was waiting to hear the pop and wondered if I would hear it and feel it at the same time. When I heard the loud pop, I thought, *Hey, that wasn't too bad. I mean, it was loud, but I didn't have any pain.* I felt blood pouring down my face, but I didn't fall over yet.

Then I heard Rhonda scream and opened my eyes. With relief, I realized I was not the one who had been shot, and the blood I felt was not mine.

Shouting and guns, blood splattered all over. Ishmael and Ahmed had come in with guns blazing. They shot whoever they thought was to blame and had no mercy. I was still sitting on the floor, staring at the carnage, with Rhonda beside me. I could determine by the shock on her face that she could not believe what she was seeing. She had not seen her family in what seemed like a lifetime to her. They were here; they were saving her. At that moment, relief came as I knew

Tripp was back at the house safe and that Aubrey was already out of the house waiting for us in the delivery truck.

Time seemed to stop when Ishmael had Ahseed up against the wall. Ahseed had been shot, but it was only a flesh wound. His silk shirt was ripped open, and I could see the wound. But Ahseed was so full of rage he did not seem to know he was injured. Instead, he violently fought against Ishmael, who had Ahseed by the neck, his feet off the ground, and in front of us all, Ishmael wrapped his hands around the other man's neck and squeezed. Ahseed struggled at first but soon he could not any longer. I watched in horror and, on some level, elation, as the life flickered out of him.

Ahmed was wrestling Dr. Ricardo in the corner, and when the doctor broke free and tried to run, Ahmed shot him before he even got to the door. I realized I was sitting in a sea of dead bodies.

We needed to get out of the house before others came. Ahmed explained we needed to be fast and quiet as security would be coming soon. Standing and looking at the room was overwhelming. Blood was all over the walls, and bodies slumped like rag dolls did not even look real at this point. Shaking myself out of the morbid trance, we exited the room.

The food truck was a perfect decoy, and no one suspected its use. Aubrey was leaning out the back, still wearing her burqa, and she waved frantically when she saw us coming. We climbed into the truck, and Ahmed's cousin in the driver's seat quickly took us out of the city.

As we bounced along the roads, Ishmael and Ahmed clung to Rhonda, and Aubrey and I leaned against each other.

For some reason, I did not feel closure. I knew that there were more women out there. I had not found Kayleigh. I knew I had to go home and tell Krissy that Whitley was dead, sold for her organs. My heart ached at the thought of that conversation. The inside of the truck smelled like sweat and blood, and it made my stomach turn. At this point, all I wanted to do was to wash the blood and gore off me and go home to Tripp. I needed to be home. I desperately needed for this to be over, really over. But I knew it wasn't—not yet.

Chapter 42

We had to wait a few hours before we could board the plane, so I took a walk. I was amazed at the ease with which Americans can travel in and out of Dubai. The airport was very lavish, matching the extravagant lifestyles of many who lived in the country.

I walked to the edge of a beautifully manicured courtyard, only a block or so from the airport. The gulf was the most beautiful blue I had ever seen and crystal clear. The water was calm, no choppy waves, no storms on the horizon. I walked down to the shore and let the water swirl around my feet and legs. As I looked out over the gulf, I remembered back to the start of this story. I thought when I woke up in that coffin that I had survived. I had cheated death and was going to live. But I was wrong—I did die that night. The old Layla was dead. The person I was now, standing up to my ankles in the waters of the Persian Gulf, was not the same woman placed in that coffin. The person I was walking out of that ocean was different in many ways. I was not timid. I did not fear death. I was braver, stronger, and no longer naïve. Evil was rampant in this world. I had always known that, but it had not touched my life in my little Southern town.

As I stared into the water, I thought of the wonders of nature. How God in his infinite wisdom created this earth and the creatures on it so brilliantly. He had answered my prayers, and my family was safe.

I remembered reading about the mimic octopus, a very special animal found in the waters of Indonesia. It not only can change colors to adapt to its surroundings, but it also can entirely change its appearance if needed. It can look like various animals in the sea, such as a sea snake, jellyfish, even a stingray. Mimic octopuses burrow themselves on the sea floor to not be seen, and they blend in. This was what those physicians had done. They had infiltrated the medical field, and their poison tentacles had reached around the globe. They blended in, and no one suspected what they were doing. There would be no way to find all the women they had sold. No way to know the number of women harvested for their organs.

I could not go back to practicing medicine as a nurse practitioner. I had to help and make a difference. If Kayleigh was able to be an RN and an FBI agent, I could help even more being a provider turned FBI. I could go places and do things she could not. I may be able to find more of these crazy men. Even if I could save only one woman, I had to try.

I would discuss my plan with Aubrey, and she would understand. Tripp, however, was a different story. But he knew he had lost his previous wife, and this was what was left of her. Changes would be made as soon as we got back to the US. I was nervous, excited, and anxious about my choice. But oddly, not scared. I think that emotion was one I had put in the back of my subconscious, and I intended to keep it there. My first mission was to find Kayleigh. I knew she was out there, somewhere.

Epilogue

Darkness, hunger, cold, so cold. Kayleigh had no idea how many days it had been since she had eaten or heard a voice from outside. Her new owner had promised he would return but had not, and she had no idea where she was. She felt like time marched slowly. The fear of the unknown was the worst; not knowing what they planned to do with her was going to kill her faster than starvation. Something had happened many nights ago; she had heard gunfire over and over. She awaited rescue, daring to hope, but no one came.

Right when she was about to fall asleep again, the door of the small room opened. Taking a few moments for her eyes to adjust wasn't long enough. Because the person standing in front of her was not at all who she expected and reminded her that her torture was just beginning.

Acknowledgments

First of all, I want to thank my Lord and Savior Jesus Christ for without him I am nothing. I give him all of the honor for all he has done for me in my life.

I want to thank my family. Todd and Amber have, from the beginning, been the biggest cheerleaders and encouraged me all the times I wanted to give up. I am truly blessed with the best husband and daughter anyone could ask for.

To my brother, David Bryan Key, thank you for always being so positive and when I needed to vent, you were always there at 7 am!

To my "BFF" Paula Farmer, no words can express how blessed I am to have you and thank you for all you have done for me through this process. You are the best!

A huge thank you to my wonderful publisher Vertu Publishing and Tylie Eaves. Working with you has been wonderful. Thank you for being patient with me when I had no idea what to do or where to go. Your words of encouragement meant more to me than you will ever know. To my editor, Caroline Rock, no words are available to thank you for your help and expertise during this process. You are truly the best! A HUGE thank you to the nurses and physicians of Iredell Health Systems. My biggest fans, my inspiration, and my dear friends. You have been so encouraging and always kept me laughing and entertained so I could write a book about you.

Special thanks to Dr. Ricardo Deleon, Kaleigh Hendren, Sara Mathis, Kristin Himes, Dr. Ahmed Elnaggar, Rhonda Elnaggar, and Sherif Elnaggar who were my inspiration for the characters in this book.

Thank you to Dr. Bruce Harris, Dr. Michael Schlesinger, Dr. Willie Whitaker, Dr. Ray Georgeson, Dr. Mark Hrko who gave me constant feedback, encouragement and new book ideas in the doctors' lounge. I love you all!

Made in USA - Kendallville, IN
18700_9798987067406
10.15.2023 1337